Sisters in Law

SISTERS IN LAW

SYLVIA MULHOLLAND

Sisters in Law
SYLVIA MULHOLLAND

Chapter 1

From a corner of the boardroom, a hulking grandfather clock bonged the half-hour as Kali Miller, Gillian Lawrence and Jada Tyler arrived for the meeting that had been called on very short notice. The clock hearkened back to the days when the law firm of Biltmore, Durham & Spears was created: the bad old days when all lawyers were men and the law was a jealous mistress.

Stylish bags and briefcases thumped onto the carpet and cell phones clunked onto the granite-topped table. On a sideboard, a continental-style breakfast had been laid out. Gillian made herself a cup of herbal tea as Jada and Kali poured coffee for themselves. No one was interested in the muffins, bagels or pastries. Then, since none of the other partners had arrived, the women settled in to check their cell phones for text messages, the morning news and tweets.

Jada, always stunning, was in a yellow suit that contrasted lusciously with her dark skin. The skirt had a zipper running up one side that practically begged to be pulled open, and the drama of the suit was enhanced by patent leather heels as glossy black as her African-American twist-out hairstyle.

Gillian, with her long, pale blonde hair, was in one of her *'I'm really a writer, not a lawyer'* outfits: a hippie-style blouse and longish print skirt, with an intricate woven shawl draped over one shoulder. She'd had most of her tattoos removed when she made partner—and taken out her nose ring as well. There was only one visible tattoo—on her left wrist, in memory of her late husband, Larry. That one she would never remove, not for anyone or any reason.

In her conservative linen pantsuit, with her brown, Sassoon-chiseled hair, Kali wondered if she were the only adult in the room, or if she just lacked a sense of style—as a couple of wardrobe consultants had told her over the years.

"Why are the three of us always so damned early?" Jada complained.

"Because we're women, and our mothers taught us it's rude to be late," Kali said.

"But it looks like we're not busy, right? If we had a lot going on, we'd be late for this meeting, or not show up at all."

"Maybe the real meeting is going on someplace else," Gillian mused, "and this is just a dummy meeting to throw us off the scent."

"They'll be here soon," Kali said. "Rick called it, so he has to show." She didn't feel like getting into one of her partners' *suits versus skirts* paranoid debates this early on a Monday.

As if on cue, the other partners trickled in, starting with Pete Johnson and Dan Chatwell. Moments later, Sandy Krupnik and Alexander Spears arrived, followed by the firm's Managing Partner, Rick Durham. As the men helped themselves to coffee, bagels, and muffins, the last partner, Ross Owen, hurried in, apologizing for his lateness and smiling sheepishly. Jada caught his glance then looked quickly away.

While she waited for the room to settle and for the meeting to start, Kali's mind drifted to her mom responsibilities. Was it snack or juice she was supposed to take to Molly's play-school the next day? She opened her phone and typed the word 'snack?' in the notes section. When she looked up again, she was startled to see Alexander Spears, the partner who'd hired her five years earlier, staring at her with a mournful look, as if his dog had just died.

Tall, handsome, with a commanding presence, Alex was a big-time corporate lawyer with a stable of BlueChip clients. Nobody knew what he did, exactly, since Big Corporate was a mysterious world to most other lawyers. All the Executive Committee cared about was that he was the firm's top biller, so was not to be bothered, since he had the connections, and the willpower, to move to any other firm he liked, taking his clients—and their money—with him. Kali, Jada and Gillian had all tried to set him up with one or another of their single girlfriends over the years, but Alex remained, at fifty-five, resolutely (maddeningly) single. An attractive woman was always on his arm at any social function the firm put on, only to be replaced by a different woman by the time the next event rolled around. Though she was well-qualified, Kali had sensed that Alexander's personal interest in her was what got her hired at Biltmore, Durham & Spears. He was making her uncomfortable now, staring at her. Would the man never give up? Especially as Kali was now happily married with two little kids?

Meanwhile, Gillian was trudging through some small talk about home renovations with Sandy. Though Gillian was weird (and proud of it) Sandy was even weirder—but not in a good or cool way. He had some muddled Eastern European background and his clothes were always musty-smelling, his footwear clumpy. White socks with sandals had even been spotted, on occasion. He was a true geek, doing boring securities work, and though Gillian normally loved geeks (counting herself and her clients among that number) there was something off-putting about Sandy. He had a wife named Natalie who was hardly ever seen because she had some sort of ailment, like Crohn's Disease or Plaque Psoriasis.

Pete was busy boring Jada with details of a trout fishing tournament he'd been to on the weekend. He did bankruptcy and insolvency work—way down the food chain of desirable legal practice areas—but never complained about the "ew" factor of his work. He was single, like Alex, but his excuse, whenever anyone tried to set him up on a date with a woman friend, was that marriage would only get in the way of his fishing.

Jada wasn't really listening to Pete's trout fishing blather, since she was distracted by Dan's biceps that were practically bursting through his Brooks Brothers shirt. He had to be working out or taking steroids or something to be bulking up like that. And didn't he look so wholesomely white boy cute, with his chubby pink cheeks, blue eyes and his little boy crew cut? *Good enough to munch on!* But Jada's interest in Dan was quickly shadowed by a cloud of self-doubt. Didn't she have enough trouble with Ross? She could feel his eyes on her now: longing, caring, lusting. How many workplace romances, she wondered glumly, did it take to sabotage a career? Especially the career of a divorce attorney, as Jada had the utter misery of being.

She glanced at Ross, reading the questions in his eyes: *What did you do last night, after I left? What are you doing tonight?* All questions that he, still very much encumbered with a wife and five kids (whom he had recently left for Jada—*not her idea!*) had no right to ask. Whenever she was in a room with all of her law partners, Jada wondered how many of them knew about her liaison with Ross, how many suspected, and how many were totally clueless. She was hoping most were in the 'clueless' category, the men anyway. But not Kali and Gillian. Women always knew, without a whisper being exchanged, or an office wink or kiss observed.

"We'll get started here as soon as everyone's got their caffeine," Rick announced. He was a litigator, one of the 'real' lawyers, the pure breed, who knew how to get down and dirty in the courts. A little Napoleon, with a look that was called 'preppy' back in the 'eighties, where he was sartorially stuck, he came in extra early every day, and put ice cubes in his coffee mug to speed up the Keurig shots to his system. He was also famous in the L.A. Bar for his cute suspenders and colorful, witty socks—today's selection had propeller planes on them—both of which had drawn judicial ire, on occasion, at both State and Federal court levels.

Seated around that granite-topped table, the lawyers of Biltmore, Durham & Spears represented a basic cross-section of the legal profession—the men taking on the hard-core stuff, the women the 'softer' side of the law. Kali practiced marketing and advertising law; Gillian was a patent lawyer and Jada was down in the trenches, slogging it out in matrimonial.

Rick tapped his coffee mug with his pen to get everyone's attention. "As you should all remember, this is the time of year we need to start planning our annual tie-swap."

Kali, Jada and Gillian rolled their eyes. Was *this* all the meeting was going to be about? The tie-swap was an affront to the women professionals of Biltmore, Durham & Spears. Dozens of ugly or out-of-style neckties were dug out of closets and piled onto the boardroom table, along with copious quantities of alcohol. Then a lot of drunken fun ensued as prizes were awarded for the ugliest, the one with the least natural fibers, the most boring, etc., and the owners roasted for their bad taste in having acquired them in the first place. The luckless ties were then tried on and traded, the goal being that even the worst losers found a home by the end of the night, only to surface the next year for another round of juvenile male hilarity.

"This year, we're going to go big." Rick's eyes shone with excitement. "We've chartered a private plane at a very attractive rate from our good client, Bert King. We're taking the tie party to Catalina Island!"

"Oh, wow. Great idea, Richard!" Pete laughed, dribbling muffin crumbs down his shirt.

"Super plan!" Ross agreed, his eyes still, longingly, on Jada.

"Sweet!" Sandy clapped his meaty, Eastern European paws together.

"Bonus points for the Rick-Meister!" Dan was the last but loudest to shout out praise, since, as junior partner, sucking up was a big part of his job description.

"Thank you, thank you." Rick took an exaggerated little bow. "I've booked it for the long weekend in August, and we'll invite other clients to join us. It's an excellent business development tool."

The women exchanged looks of annoyance. As partners, they would be expected to fork over big money to one of the firm's clients, to take their partners on a silly junket to Catalina to play with neckties and get drunk?

"But on a more serious note," Rick continued, "we all need to examine our business-development tools and keep them sharp and ready in our toolkits. Also, Exec thinks the women partners should do something similar to the tie party, for the firm's female clients."

This statement was met with blank stares from Kali, Jada and Gillian. "What do you have in mind, Richard?" Jada finally said, "an old Spanx-swap?"

"Pantyhose might be another idea," Kali suggested.

"I would *love* the opportunity to acquire another woman's used pantyhose," Gillian nodded.

"Hashtag me too," Jada said.

"You know," Rick reddened, "that's the kind of negative attitude that keeps us from becoming first-rate. This firm is over fifty years old, and I'm sorry to say, it looks it."

"Speak for yourself." Jada patted her elaborate thick curl up-do and was rewarded by a laugh from some of her partners.

But Rick was not amused. "Biltmore, Durham & Spears is stagnating. We've got to do more. Promote like hell, get out there, beat the bushes for work and sell ourselves and our services." *Like hookers*, Kali thought. The world's two oldest professions certainly had a lot in common.

"Yo Rick? What about my breast cancer fund-raiser? Bowling for Boobies?" Jada demanded. "It was a big hit, raised a ton of cash."

Rick's face turned a deeper shade of red. Words like 'breast' were known to thrill and embarrass him, even when followed by downers like 'cancer.' He cleared his throat. "Okay, except for Jada—kudos to her—who has done some great work for women's … ah … health causes lately, we just aren't doing enough. Boutique firms are being swallowed up. The competition's strangling us."

"With old neckties and pantyhose?" Gillian asked, getting a big laugh from the room.

"Richard, hold on a minute," Alex frowned. "You're leaving out the most important part of the Catalina trip."

Rick's face traveled through the brief range of expressions of which it was capable. "Ah, yes. Sorry, my friend." He tapped his coffee mug again. "Everyone? The Catalina Tie Party will also serve as a forum for another, very special, celebration." He paused to heighten the suspense. "It will also be a stag."

"A what?" Kali frowned.

"For who?" Gillian demanded.

"I'll let Alex tell you." Rick sat down as all eyes turned to Alexander.

"Believe it or not," he said, glumly, "I've decided to tie the knot."

"What?" Kali said.

"Damn!" Jada rocked back in her chair.

"Who's the lucky lady?" Dan grinned.

"Do we know her?" Sandy asked.

"Have you asked her?" Gillian asked.

"You know her, you know her." Alex looked defensively around the table, his long fingers caressing the expensive silk of his elegant tie. "And, of course, I've asked her. What kind of moron would make a wedding announcement if he hadn't? And some of you may find this hard to believe, but she's actually said yes." He paused, for dramatic effect. "I'm going to marry Ana."

"Wait. What?"

"*Our* Ana?"

"Ana Velazquez?"

"The *summer student?*"

"When?"

"September seventeenth. Alex Ovechkin's birthday. I figured it was an auspicious day."

"Ovechkin?" Jada said. "Who's *that* dude?"

"Washington Capitals? Stanley Cup?" Alex scowled at her.

"Say—what?"

"Hockey," Kali whispered. "I'll tell you later." She turned back to beam at Alex. "Well, this is great news, Alex! And we'll have a party, too—us girls. You boys have your tie party and we'll have a tea party—at my place. A lingerie shower—we'll have a lingerie tea!" She avoided looking at Gillian and Jada, knowing their eyebrows would be raised up into their hairlines.

"Hey, can I come to that?" Rick laughed. "Lingerie sounds a lot more interesting than old neckties!"

Alexander was fixing Kali with another of his smoldering looks. "We—Ana and I—appreciate this, Kali. It's very generous of you."

"Oh, please! It's my pleasure. So, is she here? Ask her to come in. I'm sure everyone would like to congratulate her in person."

"She took the day off," Alex said, "some woman's thing."

"Oh, what a shame. I hope she's okay."

"She'll be fine."

"Well, I believe we have some bubbly over here!" Rick hustled over to a small bar fridge. "Champagne and orange juice. Let's all have a drink to toast this outstanding news—just nobody tell HR, okay? Helen would have my ass. And Kali? Think about some female clients to invite to your tea party. Hit me up with a list. We'll talk tomorrow."

Female clients? Kali exchanged looks with Gillian and Jada as the conversation dissolved into a chorus of congratulations. Backs were slapped, a cork popped, glasses clinked. Alexander announced that it was never too early for a real drink, and a bottle of single malt appeared, along with a bucket of ice and tongs.

"A *lingerie tea?*" Jada yanked Kali's sleeve. "Are you insane? You expect us to go out and buy fancy underwear for Ana's dirty weekend with Alex?"

"It's not a dirty weekend, it's a dirty life. They're getting married, remember?"

"I'll believe *that* when I see it."

"You won't see it," Gillian said, "since they likely won't invite you."

"But this tea idea," Jada complained, "it's so last century! Come on, Girl, get with the program."

"You're setting the women's movement back at least four decades," Gillian nodded.

"So, what do you radical feminists think would be appropriate?" Kali asked, irritably. "A law book shower?"

"I can think of a hundred things that would be way more fun, and way less embarrassing than buying split-crotch panties for Ana Velazquez," Jada said.

"Why don't we just take her out drinking? Or chip in for a nice wedding gift?" Gillian said.

"But more to the point," Jada said, "Ana doesn't need a bridal shower. She needs an intervention! We partners might even get sued for sexual harassment, after she wakes up to reality. I think we should call our insurers right after this meeting. And you're in a state of shock, Kali, which explains your dumb-ass idea. You've always had a thing for Alex and you can't have been ready for this. Well, none of us were, it's so out there. But you need to think this through. Ana? Racy underwear? A bunch of middle-aged women, including our *clients*—nibbling sandwiches and sipping tea while she unwraps and tries on all sorts of embarrassing stuff? It's so cringe-making."

"But there's time to back out," Gillian said. "Just go up to Alex and quietly explain that you don't know what you were thinking because you're a working mom with two little kids. You get on these hormonal roller-coasters and can't seem to get off." She was studying Kali as if assessing whether she should be put into a four-point restraint and carted off for a psychiatric assessment.

"Yeah, it's just part of your general confusion," Jada nodded. "He'll get it, even though he has no experience with a woman anywhere near his age."

"I just thought we should do something nice for Ana," Kali sulked.

"But what you suggested is not *nice*," Gillian said.

"Not nice at all," Jada agreed. "It's weird. Inappropriate, and unprofessional—especially as it now includes our clients, most of whom hate each other, and us too."

"Well look," Kali said, "Ana will never go for it anyway. I mean, she's young, she's got her own friends. She's not going to want an old-fashioned tea party!" She faked a laugh. "Get serious."

"You better hope not," Jada said.

"She does seem like a smart young woman. Stanford Law Review and all that," Gillian said, thoughtfully.

"Except that she's going to marry Alexander," Jada said. "Figure that one out, if she's so damned smart."

"Gold digger, possibly," Gillian mused. "But she could write her own ticket. Any firm would want her, especially to meet its diversity quota. Besides, we don't really know her. She's only been here a couple of months."

"Alex sure got to know her fast," Jada said.

"By the way, Jada," Kali said, still sulking, "I have never had a thing for Alexander. He's always been after me, if you want the truth."

"Yeah, we know. And now you're pissed that he's lost interest. It's kind of sadly obvious, Kali."

"You're one to comment about office romances," Kali said.

"Zero idea what you're talking about." Jada noted, with irritation that Ross was staring at her, his eyebrows forming question marks. *Are you mad at me? Can we talk later?* He'd arrived late because he'd probably had to drive his million kids around to some lesson, practice or school.

"Ladies?" Rick held up the champagne and single malt. "What can I pour you?"

"Perhaps a sour grape might be appropriate." Jada rolled her eyes in Kali's direction.

"Or at least something *fume*," Gillian smirked.

Then the two of them got up to go have a drink with the men. Just look at them, Kali thought, so smug and full of themselves! They wouldn't even be speaking to each other if it weren't for her, forcing them to put aside their differences, so many times over the past few years. She would never speak to either of them again!

Rick was filling coffee mugs with champagne and orange juice. "Get it while you can, people. It's going fast."

Alex looked around the room, satisfied. When his dark eyes met Kali's again, his lips curled into a thin smile of triumph. With an even bigger smirk, he downed a shot of single malt, his eyes still fixed on her.

For months and years later, Kali would remember that meeting, in the boardroom overlooking the Pacific, and marvel at how casually she had sat there, thinking about cookies and juice and Molly's play-school, only half listening to the details of the Catalina Tie Party, then tumbling down the rabbit hole of wounded sexual pride before absurdly offering to throw a lingerie shower for a law student she hardly knew. She should have known, right then, that it was going to be a bad summer for lawyers. And, over time, she would imagine that she had.

Chapter 2

J*EALOUS? ME? SERIOUSLY?* KALI CONTINUED THE ARGUMENT IN HER head as she drove home to Manhattan Beach that evening. And, given the five-car pile-up on the 405, she had plenty of time to do so. It was pathetic, really, what that horny old goat was up to. After so many women in so many years, did Alex seriously expected to find lasting happiness with a woman—a girl, actually—who was what? Half his age? If that. In truth, Kali felt sorry for Alex and Ana. What would they have to say to each other, once the sex was over?

The marriage—if it ever happened—was sure to be a disaster, and Alex would get what he deserved: dumped by a hot Latina, having to pay alimony—no, child support—for Ana. How funny would that be? Hilarious. In her car, Kali laughed out loud. It would serve him right!

Over the years, he hadn't always been a very nice person. In fact, he'd been a total shit. Although Kali had expected to find herself in some awkward situations with him—given his obvious sexual interest in her— no such awkwardness ever arose. Rather, Alex seemed, abruptly, to wheel around and point his smoking barrel at other, more attainable targets: assistants, paralegals—all single and fair game before the #MeToo movement came along and ruined everything for predators like him. Only the occasional smoldering look from him indicated any residual interest in Kali. No, it was Gillian and Jada who'd come head-to-head with Alex. And those encounters had nothing to do with sex.

"It's a little poem in a little magazine." Alexander had barely glanced at the magazine Gillian pushed into his face. "Are you seriously going to make a big deal about it?"

"It may be little, but it's mine." She'd been in a state of shock since opening *Toadhole Quarterly*, a few minutes earlier, behind her desk. She had long admired the independent literary quarterly and ached to see one of her stories or poems published in it. Instead, what had she found but her poem, *The Granary Floor*, attributed to Alexander Spears?

"What's in there isn't yours," Alexander had continued. "It's totally different from what you wrote."

"You changed a few words!"

"In poetry, as you should know, a few words are enough to make it mine."

"You infringed my copyright! How can you sit there and deny it? I showed it to you, in confidence, and you then ripped it off!"

"I threw out that garbage about the threshing machine and the bits and pieces of your mind scattered all over the floor. That stuff was jejune."

"So, you did steal it! You just admitted it."

Safe behind the polished sweep of his desk, Alexander had started cleaning his nails with a silver letter opener. "You're up for partnership next year, aren't you?"

"Oh, you're threatening me now?"

"I'm simply pointing out that what's published in that literary quarterly—which nobody reads except people who are in it and their mothers—is not the scribblings you showed me. Toadhole never would have published that crap you wrote."

"They would so! The last rejection I got from them said they would be pleased to read more of my work."

"A form-letter. My girlfriend's *dog* could get one of those. You had a thought, a theme—an open source concept, that's all. And besides, there are those in this firm who won't think poetry-writing does a lot for our bottom line, when I get around to sharing this information about you. Why aren't you spending your free time promoting the firm? Giving speeches and seminars, writing papers for law journals? What are you doing with free time anyway? You're an associate. We partners are supposed to be living off your backs. And don't bother repeating that because I'll deny I ever said it." Satisfied with the condition of his nails, Alex had taken a fountain pen from his drawer and began making notes on a legal pad, ignoring Gillian. For a few moments, her heavy breathing and the scratching of his pen had been the only sounds in the room. "Go do something billable," Alex finally said, "and I'll try and forget we ever had this absurd conversation."

"I'm not going anywhere until you admit you stole my poem," Gillian insisted.

Alex had looked up and pointed his pen at her. "People who write are desperate to have their stuff read. I've done you a favor by showing you where that pathetic neediness gets you, though it might be a while before you get around to thanking me. Now, let me get some work done—and I highly recommend you do likewise."

Suppressing an urge to lunge for his pen and plunge it deep into his neck, Gillian had stomped out of his office and down the carpeted hall, to fling herself into a chair in Jada's office, where she'd burst into tears.

"What a total piece of shit," Jada had commiserated, handing her a tissue. "The man's topsoil. Worse. He's that stuff underneath the topsoil."

"I'll sue that fucker," Gillian said. "All those wonderful poems and short stories he's supposed to have written? Ripped off, I bet, from other women who trusted him."

"You *trusted* Alexander Spears?" Jada had hurriedly closed her office door. "Didn't anyone ever tell you never to trust a lawyer? Or a man? And you can't sue him. What are your damages? How much would this magazine have paid for your poem?"

"A free copy."

"One free copy? Give me that." Jada had snatched the magazine from Gillian. "*Toadhole Quarterly*? What is it? Some kind of witchcraft shit?"

"It's a well-respected literary review." Gillian had snatched it back.

"Look, Gilly. You have a perfect right to want to twist his balls off, but let's be practical. Who actually reads this shit?"

"Smart, educated people, creative people. People with soul, Jada. Remember soul?"

"And what's a toad *hole*, anyway? I've heard of a toad*stool*—"

"I'll get punitive damages, if not actual damages, and I'll file a complaint with the State Bar, too!"

"Whoa, now where would all that get you? Say he settles for a thousand bucks, just to shut you up, and you get some erratum notice in this Toadstool thing. Then what? You feel vindicated for about a day, and you're free to be a starving writer for the rest of your life. What firm's going to hire you after that? You'll be black-balled as the poetry-writing dumb ass associate who took a senior partner to court and blew the whistle with the State Bar over some poem in a magazine nobody reads."

"I just told you, it's well-respected! Weren't you listening?"

"Whatever. After the dust settles, you might get a job in a free clinic doing copyright work for starving artists, and that's if you're lucky. You've almost got your partnership here, woman. Think about how hard you've worked, how you've struggled to claw your way up. What's one stupid little poem?"

"If it was so stupid, why would he steal it?"

"Oh, my bad. It's a great poem, practically the *Iliad*. You can write more. And if you can't, you weren't meant to be a writer. Spears might have done you a favor. And who's going to support Isadora, if you get axed and lose out on a potential partnership? Have you thrown a single thought her way? I can't get behind this at all. Sorry, Girlfriend."

"I thought Alex was a kindred spirit," Gillian had sulked.

"Kindred spirit? You shittin' me?" Jada had held out a fresh tissue. "You've got to forget about this and get on with your life. Focus on revenge fantasies. That's what keeps me sane."

Jada had reason to recall her own advice, a few months later, as she found herself in a similar situation: trying to defend her turf and keep what was rightfully hers.

"It's a little file for a little client," Alex had said. "Are you going to make a big deal out of it?" He'd leaned back in one of Jada's client chairs and put his size 13 foot up on her desk.

"Yes, I am, for your information. I've been babysitting this client for over two years."

"You did his divorce and were well compensated for your work."

"It was a very ugly divorce."

"Well, that's your expertise—ugly divorces. You had no business wading into corporate with one of my clients as your personal guinea pig."

"Hey, hold on. I went out to his damned meat-packing plant, put on a hard hat and watched his hams being boned, for your information."

"How you spend your free time is your business."

"Free time?! I put together his prospectus and wrote down two-thirds of my account to give him a break on fees because he was boohooing about how he was just starting up."

"Then you should be glad to get rid of him. He's a leech."

"He's planning a leveraged buy-out, Alex This is not a little file. His company's about to take off."

"You don't know that. Nobody's got a crystal ball."

"I do know it, and so do you. Otherwise, you wouldn't be out to steal my file." Jada had leaned back in her desk chair, arms crossed protectively over the legal folder. "There's a sale sticker on the bottom your shoe. Thought you'd want to know. DSW purple sticker. Wow. That's like eighty percent off, right?"

Slowly, Alex had taken his foot down off Jada's desk. "I brought this client into the firm and I'm taking him back. I didn't want to have to tell you this, but he thinks you're inappropriately friendly. You've been making him uncomfortable." His eyes had flickered over her low-cut top. "He's a married man, Jada."

"What are you talking about? We had a couple of *business* lunches. I have zero personal interest in him. Come on, Alex, that's bullshit, and you know it."

"He says you made suggestive comments."

"What? Like what comments?"

"I didn't ask. The guy was embarrassed enough. I'm only interested in damage control. You're not allowed further contact. We don't need the State Bar on our ass for sexual harassment of clients. So, you can either hand over that paperwork now, or I'll have Rick fire off a directive to you and Helen Sharpe can write up this incident in your HR file. Your choice."

"That bastard!" Kali had sympathized, after motioning to the bartender for drink refills, later that afternoon in the bar downstairs from the firm.

"You believe him, don't you?" Sullenly, Jada had poked at the lime slice in her drink.

"Of course not! At least, I know you didn't *intend* any sort of come-on to your client. It's just your way of being friendly."

"So, you *do* believe him!"

"That's not what I said. I only meant that, well, it's tough for us women. We want to be friendly and try some jock talk, but we really aren't comfortable with it. And sometimes, we might cross some bright line in a man's primitive brain, without knowing it, right?"

"Try being black on top of it."

"Some men are threatened by attractive and assertive women. And you are a very sexy and powerful black woman."

"I'm not changing the way I dress if that's what you're getting at."

"I wasn't. You always look amazing."

"For a while, I did tone it down, you know? Like my mama said, I didn't need to satisfy every white guy's fantasy of an exotic black woman. But now that she's gone, I don't give a shit. I wear what I want."

"I wish I had your style," Kali said. "The way I dress is so boring."

"The Hillary Clinton pantsuits? Nah, you rock that look. Work it."

"Thanks." Kali had nodded, looking down into her drink and wondering what time it was and thinking that the Millers' nanny, Emilie, would already be waiting at the front door, impatient to get out of there.

"Anyway, you don't need to flatter me." Jada had rattled the ice cubes in her glass and taken a hearty swallow. "There's been no client complaint. There's nothing going on here but Alex taking over a file he knows is going to put him over the top with fees this year."

"He is a senior partner, though." *How contemptible I am*, Kali thought. "Not that that makes it right."

"Thanks for your kick-ass support, Sis. You must have been a cheerleader in high school. I feel so much better now."

"Come on, Jada. We've all known that Alex was a shit from day one. Look at what he did to Gillian over that Toad-hole thing."

"Yeah, well, he likes you." Jada had looked at Kali with hurt, accusing eyes.

"I honestly don't know why, if that's even true. We hardly speak to each other." Kali had been checking the time on her cell, in the dim light of the bar.

"You have to go, don't you? Home to Manhattan Beach and your perfect family?"

"No, I can stay as long as you want. I just have to call our nanny—make sure she's okay with me being late."

"Go on home to doctor Matt and your kids. I'll just sit here and get tore up by myself. I don't need an audience."

"If you're sure?"

"Yeah, I'm sure."

"I don't feel like I've done you much good."

"No comment." Jada finished her drink and signaled the bartender for a refill.

"But there is one thing I've got to know," Kali said.

"What's that?"

"Was there really a sale sticker on his shoe?"

"Nah, I was just messing with him."

"Oh, good one! I bet he ran straight to the men's room to look!"

They'd laughed together for a minute. Then Kali had squeezed Jada's hand, and, murmuring apologies, hurried outside, anxiously checking her cell as she rushed towards the parking garage.

Though they'd shared that laugh, Kali had feared that Jada would interpret her comments as a female betrayal. And, as predicted, Jada didn't speak to her for several days: hurrying past Kali's office without sticking her head in to say hi, pretending to check her cell whenever she passed Kali in the corridor, using the Handicapped restroom to avoid coming face to face with Kali in the Ladies. Kali knew how she felt. As women, they had to stick together. Still, Kali didn't know what else she could have said. Or done. They all had to play the game.

Miraculously, the unpleasant incidents with Alex had not hurt the careers of either Gillian or Jada. Both had been fast-tracked—offered partnership in Biltmore, Durham & Spears within a few months of their run-ins with Alex. And though Kali had fully expected to be the next to go head to head with Alex and somehow 'pay' for the partnership offer she also got, it hadn't happened. So far.

Now, as the Millers' ridiculously large house loomed in front of her, Cannon, the family's German Shepherd, came barreling across the lawn, all flashing teeth and hackles, alerting the neighborhood that an intruder was in its midst.

Kali parked in the driveway and rolled down her window. "Cannon, it's me! Down! OFF! Release!"

Stupid dog. Weren't they supposed to become attuned to their master's scent? From even ten miles away, he should recognize her car and come bounding out with tongue-lolling, carpet-wetting joy. Instead, every morning and evening, Kali feared for her life, wondering if Cannon would realize, in time, that she actually *lived* in that house, and resist the urge to tear her to pieces. Was her own dog trying to tell her she was spending too much time at the office?

Chapter 3

ROSS WOULD HAVE THE KIDS FROM FRIDAY NIGHT UNTIL SUNDAY morning, leaving most of the weekend for Jada to spend on her own. Ross's wife, Marcia, was throwing a fortieth birthday party for herself on Saturday night, complete with a marquee and dance band. Gone was the frustrated housewife who kicked in kitchen cupboards at the mention of her husband's name and called him at two a.m. every night to scream abuse until four.

She was blossoming, Marcia was. In the three months since Ross had moved out, she'd dropped twenty pounds, finally gotten her driver's license, begun her master's degree in community planning, and started an affair with her therapist. Ross Owen, it seemed, was the last person she wanted—or needed—back in her life. So Ross was now the sole responsibility of Jada Tyler. They were miserably yoked together, like a pair of villagers in the stocks in the public square, with Jada wearing the scarlet letter—victim of her own lustful desires.

She had awoken early on Sunday, happy about having the day off, until she remembered there was nothing to be happy about. In fact, there was every indication the day would be a total shit-show. She had agreed, reluctantly (having no plausible excuse ready) to have dinner with Ross and his parents at their country home in Simi Valley—a hot, horrible drive up the dreaded 405 Freeway, with weekend beach traffic to compound the misery.

She'd never met Ross's parents and never had any desire to. But she had (*had* being the operative word) wanted to meet his kids, back when things were going good between them. It hardly mattered now, three months to the day since Ross had knocked Jada out of her chair with his text message informing her that he'd left his family and was hiding out in a Best Western in Marina Del Rey. That's where an office affair got a girl, Jada thought: saddled with a half-married man who was broke from bills and child support and emotionally beat up by his rightfully pissed off wife.

Their relationship was now rattling on towards a grim and grisly death. Even the sex between them had deteriorated into a silly sadomasochism due to Ross's guilt. Jada was sick and tired of playing the disciplinarian school teacher to his naughty schoolboy or having him follow her around her condo on all fours, wearing a spiked collar and leash.

Jada had worked out a number of creative excuses—some crazy enough to be almost believable—to avoid going up to Simi, but in the end decided that Ross's hurt feelings would take too much out of her and that he would only reschedule the dinner for another night anyway. And she wasn't yet mentally braced for the big end-of-the-affair-heart-to-heart-talk they needed to have.

And it wouldn't kill her to have a good meal with a kindly old couple, even if they were way up in white trash country, would it? It might even be a pleasant summer outing—unlikely, but anything was *possible*. And why disappoint poor old Mrs. Owen, who rarely got to see Ross and was probably excited about meeting Jada? On the other hand, was it fair? Jada was pretty sure the senior Owens—being lower class English and most likely racists—had no idea about the *guess who's coming to dinner* event that was about to happen.

The shock of meeting Jada might well do in Ross's dear old mum, who was still trying to accept what her son had done—walking out on his wife, and of course, the poor kids. Audrey Owen was terrified she might never see them again, now that Marcia had run off with her therapist, and Ross with some husband-snatching tart that worked in his office.

When he first showed her pictures of his kids, Jada had assumed Ross had a dozen. He'd scrolled through hundreds of photos on his phone, as Jada watched, more interested in his hands—the elegant fingers and perfectly-shaped nails—than his kids. Ross had only five, he'd confessed, sounding embarrassed. *Only?* What kind of married white guy had five kids? Hadn't he and Marcia ever heard of birth control?

As it turned out, Ross might as well have been a hundred kids, for all the money and energy he had left over for Jada. It was either a surprise gift or flowers for Jada or a new retainer for Kaitlyn; a nice dinner out with Jada, or orthopedic shoes for little Obie. Of course, Jada always smiled, she 'got it.' Of course, the kids would always come first. And she made a good buck, with no one to support but herself now that her mama had passed. But she never wanted Ross to leave his family for her! An office fling was all it was ever meant to be. She'd never fantasized about snatching him away from Marcia; she never wanted to marry him, get saddled with five kids and never-ending fights over custody, support, and visitation that she'd be expected to join in, especially since that kind of misery was her bread and butter. It would be all they ever talked about! And she didn't want *any* kids, let alone five ready-made white ones that belonged to some other woman.

It was hard to imagine a man less right for her than Ross, but picking the wrong man was Jada's specialty, and Biltmore, Durham & Spears was certainly the place to do it.

She mentally flipped through the attorneys of the firm as if they were playing cards. In terms of racial or ethnic diversity for professionals in the firm, Jada was about it. There was Dan: single (gay?) and boyishly cute, a ruddy-cheeked, over-pumped kiss-ass junior partner. There was Alex Spears, unpleasantly aggressive and an infamous womanizer, now (hilariously) about to marry the firm's summer student. Rick Durham was one of the good old boys, not Jada's type at all and 'happily married' to Leighton, as he constantly reminded everyone, signaling that, of course, he wasn't. In fact, the rumor around the firm was that he was involved in a long-running affair with Helen Sharpe, the head of HR. Sandy was too unattractive for Jada to take seriously, married to some mythical wife, and had moved into California from some State no one could ever remember. And then there was Pete, with his passion for fishing. Fishing! No woman could ever compete with a Big Mouth Bass, for Pete's affections. Not that anyone would want to.

A couple of the associates were cute, but too young for Jada—and not a black man among them. And even if there were, it would not be smart for Jada to turn her sites on them. That would only get Helen on her ass, big time. So, at the end of the line, bottom of the deck, there was Ross Owen, with his Adrian Brody nose, crazy dark hair, lop-sided grin, five kids and a wife named Marcia.

Jada often reshuffled that dog-eared pack of Biltmore, Durham & Spears lawyers, in her head, imagining one of them might be mystically revealed as a better bet. But even after a fancy riffle shuffle and a couple of professional cuts, the answer always came up the same, like the ace of spades, the card of doom: her nemesis, Ross Owen.

There had been some interesting and good-looking black men in Jada's law class at Yale, but she'd foolishly ignored her mama's advice to snag one of them before graduation. Those educated black men had soon been snapped up, some of them by white women. Thank God her mama had not lived to see the life Jada was living now. Harvard undergrad, then Yale Law. After all the sacrifices and struggles and scholarships, to see her beautiful daughter, not only joining an all-white firm but having shameful liaisons with married white guys. For sure it would have killed her again.

Jada was thirty-nine, a hair's breadth from forty, the point of no return. 'Madame Ovary' was how she thought of herself, those dusty eggs of hers sitting on the shelf, cobweb-shrouded and rotting from within. She often wished she'd married someone, *anyone*, if only for a year, a month, a day. Even if the marriage failed, divorced women had an easier time hitching up with a new man, as if men perceived in them a woman who knew a few tricks about stain removal, throwing dinner parties and keeping up a guy's interest, sexually-speaking. Men didn't see divorcees as failures; they saw them as experienced, even exciting. It was all so damned unfair!

It was still early, not even nine a.m., as Jada considered the alternatives she had to amuse herself until Ross came by to get her for the trip to Simi Valley. She could do nothing. Or she could go into the office for a few hours, do nothing, pretend to do some work, or actually do some. Or she could do the laundry, vacuum, and scour all the appliances in her condo. It wasn't true that a girl's best friend was diamonds. Nor was it cigarettes, alcohol or drugs. A girl's best friends were Pine Sol and cleaning rags since those things would always be there for her, in the end.

Furious over the unfairness of absolutely everything in her life, Jada threw open her closet doors and began the thankless task of reviewing outfits to wear for her introduction to Derek and Audrey Owen, her never-to-be, future in-laws.

Chapter 4

The senior Owens clearly didn't think much of Jada. In fact, they barely acknowledged her for the first hour of the visit, during which Ross and Mrs. Owen chain-smoked, and Mr. Owen drank rye and ginger ale and blathered on about local politics and his high cholesterol.

The Owens' so-called 'country place' turned out to be their only place: a mobile home parked on the edge of Simi Valley. Audrey and Derek Owen were English, but not the quaint, whacky, dog-and horse-loving sort. They were just two unhealthy, bitter old people in a trailer home in the Valley. Derek's blood pressure had shot up in recent months, Mrs. Owen announced, as soon as she opened the door to Ross and Jada, then added that it was Ross's fault for abandoning his family and putting his Dad to so much worry.

Mrs. Owen was obviously shocked to see that Jada was black and had disapprovingly studied her outfit. '*A darky tart in a zippered trouser-suit,*' Jada imagined her thinking behind her mean little eyes. The flowers Jada brought went unnoticed, left to wilt in their cellophane sleeve on a table beside the door.

"Do you like kidneys, Ada?" Mrs. Owen asked, a while later, after Jada had followed her into the tiny kitchen, offering to help prepare the meal—an offer made at Ross's insistence. Jada would have much preferred getting drunk on the sofa with Derek.

"It's Jada," she said, "not Ada."

"Jada? Odd name isn't it?"

"Not to me."

"I suppose it means something? In Africa?"

"It's Hebrew. It means 'the knowing one'."

"Hebrew?" Mrs. Owen drew herself up.

"But I'm not Jewish, so go figure." Jada could see a wave of relief cross Audrey's sour wrinkled face. *Well, there's that, at least,* she had to be thinking.

"Kidneys on toast was Ross's favorite when he was a wee one," Audrey prattled on as she peeled potatoes. "Knees, he called them. I want knees on toast, Mummy. I don't expect Marcia ever bothered to make kidneys for Ross. She's much too lazy and selfish."

"Is that what we're having?" Jada was often horrified by the stuff white folks ate.

"Oh no, I've got a lovely pot roast. It was very dear, much more than we can afford, me and Derek being on a fixed income."

"Rad," Jada said.

After that, they abandoned further attempts at conversation, except for when Audrey asked Jada what on earth she wanted with all them zippers on her clothes—and inquired if they all worked—and Jada half-drunkenly invited her to try one and find out for herself.

Things threatened to liven up only once, when Audrey took some shots at Marcia. But Ross stood up for his wife, declaring that Marcia was doing her best with the heavy load he'd left her and that she wasn't to be picked on, especially when she wasn't there to defend herself.

Then Audrey wanted to know why Marcia was having such bloody great weekend parties if she was suffering so much—a question that was never answered. She then started picking on Ross's children. Jack was putting on too much weight, Obie was too old to be in diapers, the twins were going to fail second grade, and Kaitlyn was far too interested in boys. "You'll have no end of trouble with that one," she warned, many times over the evening.

Then she clicked her tongue and tut-tutted about her only son living in a bedsit. Ross informed her that it was actually an upscale Santa Monica apartment, after which Audrey pronounced that he was far too old to be in any sort of apartment, what with five kids and the mortgage on that big house that Marcia was using for her great bloody parties. Then she complained that Ross wasn't getting proper meals, throwing a sharp look in Jada's direction, obviously concluding that her son's money was being squandered on clothes and jewelry for his tarty black zippered mistress.

"I knew you'd hate them," Ross said, as they headed back to Santa Monica later that evening.

"Hey, don't say that. I had a bloody great time."

"I shouldn't have made you go."

"You didn't *make* me go. And they were fine. Though I'm not sure why you had to throw us together. I mean, your folks are still trying to deal with you and Marcia splitting up. So why hit them with me too? The *black* woman?"

"You're not just the *black woman*. And I'm tired of sneaking around, Jada. It's time to air things out. I'm sick of running away."

"We're hardly running. We work in the same damn office."

"The way you're talking, damn this and bloody that. It's not like you."

"No, it's *exactly* like me. You knew what I was about, knew what you were signing up for. I never pretended to be anything else."

Ross drove in silence for a few minutes, the muscles in his jaw clenched. He was making Jada nervous. She preferred a knock-down, drag-out brawl to jaw-clenching silence. "Look, Ross, I hope you're not thinking of making some sort of announcement about us, at the firm. Are you?"

"What if I am?"

"Oh no. It's such a bad idea! I'm not feeling it at all, Ross. Don't do it."

"Everybody already knows, are you kidding?" He pulled out a cigarette and lit it, steering with his elbows. Jada's eyes went wide with fright as the 405 rolled away, fast beneath them.

"You got five kids," she said, her mouth dry, "you can't be driving like this through the Sepulveda Pass in the dark!"

"Yeah? Watch me! Maybe I'll even turn my lights off!"

"Pull over then! Let me out! You got no right to kill me too!"

"Sorry." Ross still looked furious, but he slowed down.

Jada'd never seen him go crazy like that—he must really be on the edge. She pressed her lips together, afraid to say anything else, thinking it best not to over-react and throw gasoline on the fire.

"You're feeling some doubts about us," Ross said, "aren't you?"

Some doubts? *Some doubts?* "You could say that," she answered, carefully.

"You're thinking that we've got nothing between us except sex, right?"

"Well, no," Jada said, "not having that exact thought."

"So, what?"

"I was just wondering. Well, whether you and Marcia, I mean, if there's any hope? You know, after so many years together, so many kids, and now seeing your mama so upset and your daddy drinking like he is."

"He's always been a drunk. Derek always has a reason for a drink."

"But I'm just saying, to throw it all away? That nice big house you guys got, the whole family thing?"

"You want me to go back to Marcia?"

Everything inside Jada was screaming 'YES' but she couldn't say it, not right then, not after that horrible evening. Though she could hardly deny it either. She decided not to say anything at all, just twisted her mouth to one side as if she were deep in thought, leaning her head against the window of Ross's Jeep.

"I'm never going back to Marcia," he said. "I'd take the kids, though, as I know you would, too."

Jada just gazed out the window, at the dry scrubby landscape whizzing by in the dark. She didn't dare say anything.

"I want you to meet them," Ross continued. "In a couple of weeks, when things have settled down more. I was thinking of something casual, like taking them to McDonald's, then meeting you there. We could make it seem like a coincidence that we ran into you."

"I don't do McDonald's."

"Wherever you want, then," Ross said, exasperated. "Pick any place." He gave her a sideways look. "I just wouldn't want the kids to feel that it was all planned. But there's not much point, is that what you're trying to tell me?" Ross's eyebrows quivered, as they always did when he was being earnest, or confused, or both.

It was something Jada had found intriguing about him, at first: those shaggy expressive brows. Now, she wanted to shave them, pluck them out, stick them to his forehead with duct tape, burn them off with his cigarette lighter. She studied his profile. He looked—she cringed as her mind flailed around to produce the worst description she could come up with—*pussy whipped!* By no less than three pussies! And four if you counted his teenage daughter.

Even the way he was dressed revealed a man who had given up. Though it was July, and hot as hell, he was wearing grey flannels and a sports jacket handed down from his brother-in-law. Before Ross left Marcia, Jada had tried to dress him on the low, sneaking him elegant gifts like silk ties, cotton shirts, expensive sweaters (he gave her stuffed animals), hoping Marcia wouldn't notice and demand to see the bills.

For a while, it had been fun shopping for him. She'd loved the feeling that those who saw her—the salesgirls and other women shoppers—would assume she was married, that she *belonged* to some man. But instead, the other lawyers at the firm had started to notice Ross's upgraded wardrobe and begun teasing him about it. It was only a matter of time before Marcia got around to looking at her husband and asking the exact same questions.

Now that Ross was "free" Jada still thought about buying him things, mostly to preserve that feeling of being part of a couple. But after two pairs of dress socks and some jungle-patterned boxers, she'd abandoned the idea as being too pathetic. And Ross never seemed to notice or care what he had on anyway, several times passing Jada's gifts along to his kids—like the gorgeous cashmere sweater that thirteen-year-old Kaitlyn had thrown in the wash and shrunk to a pulpy felt mass that now wouldn't even fit little Obadiah.

"I think you and I have had an uphill battle," Jada said, carefully, her eyes fixed on the scenery. "I think we were doomed from the start. I should have left you alone, Ross. I made a mistake. You were a challenge to me—big game. You had a wife and family. Not to mention the whole race thing. I'm totally ashamed of myself."

"Well quit it. My situation was intolerable. You're the best thing that ever happened to me." His eyes were tearing up—Jada could see them glinting in the headlights of passing cars. "You did me a big favor by coming on to me the way you did. You helped me face up to things. Me and Marcia had nothing between us—we didn't even *like* each other anymore. It's better this way. The kids are doing great, and we're not tearing each other apart. I'm not going to let you destroy the memories of the last three months, so just shut up, okay?"

Since Jada had nothing else to say anyway, she closed her eyes and pretended to sleep. Ross pressed down hard on the accelerator, driving uncharacteristically fast, changing lanes with barely a glance in his side-view mirror. It occurred to Jada that he might be losing it, after the strain of that God-awful dinner with his folks. Their discussion in the Jeep might just be enough to prompt him to end it right then and there for both of them, crashing through the guardrails over the Sepulveda Pass.

"Ross?" she said, keeping her eyes closed. No answer. "We can talk about this later, okay?" Still no answer. "Why don't we just sleep on everything, see how we feel tomorrow?" Silence. "Ross?" She opened her eyes to look at him.

"Don't talk, okay? Don't say one more word right now. Or—I don't know what I might be capable of doing!"

Jada just sighed, and leaned her head back on the headrest, letting the Jeep's vibrations rattle further troubling thoughts from her brain for the rest of the drive home.

Chapter 5

B.M. Bradley looked a lot like a billy goat, Gillian thought, with his pointy little white beard, yellowish hooded eyes and perpetually hungry expression—like he could eat just about anything. From where she was lying on his scratchy polyester sheets, with his waterbed undulating beneath, she could see him watching *Homes Plus*, the real estate cable channel. Houses, condos and apartments popped up on the screen for fifteen seconds, just long enough to be described in wildly euphemistic terms by an ebullient voice-over. *'This fabulous property won't last long! Call Rocco Monteleone now to view this exclusive pied-à-terre!*

"Pied-à-terre!" B.M. hooted. "They don't even know what a pied-à-terre is!" He did a double-take at Gillian, as if startled to realize she was still there. "Come watch this with me." He slapped the sofa cushion beside him, raising a cloud of dust. "You've got to see some of these places." The picture on the screen changed again. "Oh God! How can people live like this? What grotesquely bad taste. Look! Flock-covered headboards!" Another picture. "And these slobs didn't even bother to pick up their *shorts* before their bedroom was photographed. They don't care if their stained underwear is syndicated across the country!"

"It's not syndicated," Gillian said, coming into the living room, "it's local cable. Though I hate to nit-pick." *Hate to nit-pick?* Nit-picking was her life! If it wasn't for nitpicking, she'd be out of a job. She yawned and rubbed her eyes. She'd hardly slept at all, in the heat, in B.M.'s uncomfortable bed, in his awful house.

B.M. rented a nondescript post-war bungalow, with no central air, on a street that bordered the Santa Monica airport. The planes started taking off early and were so loud that Gillian had to stop talking on her phone if one was overhead. And that was just the small planes. If a jet was taking off, it felt as though the entire house was being sucked up, up and away—with a noise so terrifyingly loud it made her want to vomit.

B.M. also had a raggedy dog—a mangy wire-haired terrier—that wandered in and out all night through the doggy door that B.M. had (ineptly) installed. It slammed shut with a bang, instead of closing softly, so every time the dog went in or out, Gillian was jolted awake, falling asleep just as the dog decided to go in or out again, with another bang of the door.

She hadn't intended to spend the weekend at B.M. Bradley's, which was not a *pied-à-terre* at all, since it was his only home. Fine example she was setting for Isadora, she thought, shacking up with a sometime poet and semi-recognized novelist. Her only comfort lay in knowing that her daughter wouldn't have worried—if she'd noticed Gillian's absence. If she'd even come home herself.

"Seriously, you should spend some time watching this channel," B.M. said, "since you're looking for a new house. We could get you an agent and start going around to see some tomorrow. It'd be a gas."

"I said I was thinking about moving. I haven't made a decision."

"We could snoop through all sorts of dives—and big fancy mansions too— peek into movie stars' closets and drawers. It would really help your writing."

"Assuming my writing needs help, I don't think snooping through some strangers' drawers would be my muse."

"Well, pardon me all over the place." B.M.'s looked hurt. "Where else do you think writers get material? Make it up? No! From life! Tacky and horrible and miserable and so very *there*, in our faces, if we'd only just *look*. As writers, we get so insulated, so detached from reality, from our material."

"I am quite sufficiently attached, thank you."

"You are less attached than anyone I know. And you need to get over that lawyer in your firm ripping off your poem. You're more of a novelist anyway. You're not a sprinter, you're a long-distance runner." He turned his gaze back to the TV. "So come on over here and get inspired about life and writing. Find yourself a real estate agent—and we can see all this shit up close."

"I'd rather get a literary agent," Gillian said, sulking.

"I'm working on that. I told you. It's hard to get one of them jazzed by telling them your book's about a dentist."

Gillian could see her manuscript for *At Whit's End* in the same grocery bag it had been when she brought it to B.M. a month earlier. And it was in the same place she'd put it: on the floor, leaning against a chrome leg of a kitchen chair, beside the table that also served as B.M.'s writing desk. B.M. had promised to put a bug in the ear of his publisher, call a couple of hot new agents for her. But, of course, he had to read her book first. B.M. Bradley was a *name* in the literary community; he was no literary whore. He couldn't just go off recommending *any* old first novel, could he?

"I have to go," Gillian said. "I need to see my daughter before the weekend is over." She yanked her tote out from under B.M.'s dog, who was snoring on it, beside the sofa.

"Ah, but does the enigmatic Isadora desire to see thee?"

When Gillian didn't answer, B.M. rolled off the sofa and bounced to his feet. "You're pissed because I haven't read your manuscript. Admit it.

All writers are super-sensitive. Come on. Let's go back to bed and talk about *feelings.*"

"No."

"Let's go into the kitchen. I'll make you breakfast."

Gillian followed him, then perched petulantly on a kitchen chair as B.M. turned another one around to sit facing her. *At Whit's End,* now deprived of all support, thunked over onto the floor.

"I *will* read your manuscript, Gilly. It's at the very top of my long to-do list."

Gillian could see his foot, with its long dirty toenails, just inches away from her manuscript. If he put his foot on it, if he dared even touch it with his stinky—

"Gillian?"

"What?"

"There is an easier way, you know. You could self-publish—just throw it up on Amazon, see if it sticks."

"I don't want to throw it up anywhere. I want someone to read it—a real publisher or agent, see if it's got a chance to be actually published and get reviewed. Why do I have to say all of this again? Don't you *get* it?"

"Okay, look. I've finally got some free time coming up. My new novel's got a saggy middle, according to my editor, so I'm going to take a few days off, step back, and let that comment gel in my head before I tackle the book again. I'm wildly excited about reading your novel. You know how much fun it is to anticipate a great read?"

Gillian did know.

"It's the same feeling I get when I realize you're going to spend the night with me," B.M. said, with a sly smile. His goat-like eyes looked, searchingly, into hers as he touched her lips with a nicotine-stained finger. "Gilly?"

"What."

"I really want to make love to you."

Gillian looked away.

"Okay, you don't have to say anything, I hear you." B.M. sighed. "But I'd at least like to give it another try. I mean, if you think you might be interested?"

Chapter 6

IN THE SMALL KITCHEN OF NUMBER SEVEN SIDNEY STREET, Gillian's daughter, Isadora, was drinking a Red Bull, her face obscured by a trashy romance novel called *Passion in the Night*. Funny, Gillian thought, how often the word 'night' appeared in the titles of the books Isadora bought by the boxful at a used bookstore, then sold back again after reading. *Blame it on the Night, Queen of the Night.* Those she couldn't re-sell, she tossed into the blue recycling bin at the side of the house.

As well as romance novels, Isadora read pulpy trash about modern-day vampires and werewolves. Those also frequently had 'night' in the title. *Children of the Night* had been lying on the floor in the front hall when Gillian came in, its cover warped, its spine broken. Despite her resolve not to pick up after her daughter, Gillian stooped to rescue the book. She'd always had a reverence for books, and though she disapproved of her daughter reading *Children of the Night, Night Walkers, Scream into the Night,* and so on, they were still *books* that somebody actually wrote, and reading them had to be better than tweeting her bare ass on Instagram or whatever people Isadora's age were wasting their time doing lately.

"I'm surprised you're up so early," Gillian said, a few moments later, as she poured water into the kettle.

"I'm not *up*. I never went to bed."

"Really? What did you do all night?"

"Read. What else would I be doing? Having sex?"

"I can remember when I was your age." Gillian smiled, ignoring the sex comment. "I used to stay up all night reading too. Or writing in my diary."

"Pancake from hell." Isadora didn't look up from her book.

"You made pancakes?" Fearfully, Gillian looked at the stove, expecting a blackened frying pan, blobs of batter on the counter, grease splattered all over the tiles behind it.

"I *meant* your make-up."

"What? No one wears pancake anymore."

"Duh."

Gillian frowned at her reflection in the side of the toaster. She had laid her foundation on a bit thick that morning. The fluorescent bulb in B.M.'s bathroom had been flickering in a maddening way. *Foundation.* What a word, she thought. Laid on with a trowel in a vain attempt to prop up a landslide.

"And you might want to, like, rethink the hair."

"Hey, I spent twenty minutes on this do," Gillian laughed. Her hair had always been long, blonde and pretty, but it was thinning noticeably, now that she was over forty. "So, what would you do if you had my hair?" she asked, conversationally, "since you're such an expert?"

"You mean, before or after I killed myself?"

"Hard to do hair when you're dead," Gillian said.

"Hair grows after you're dead," Isadora said, with the absolute authority of the young.

As she spooned instant coffee into a mug, Gillian wondered when it was that her daughter had begun to despise her; when Gillian's make-up and hair had ceased to be a source of delight and become objects of ridicule and contempt. At least Isadora hadn't made any acid remarks about her clothes today. Gillian was dressing younger: beads, scarves, cheap costume jewelry, short suede granny boots. It occurred to her that she might not look artsy and interesting at all, but only ridiculous: a forty-two-year-old patent lawyer done up like a Slovenian peasant from the middle ages, or a homeless person.

But women writers dressed in creative ways, and artists too, judging from the few Gillian had actually met: army boots and miniskirts, misshapen hats coupled with bad posture and cigarettes. In weak moments, she studied book jacket photos of women writers, trying to imitate their expressions: sneering, pouty, some of them even hostile. But the best looked sly, as though they knew something their readers didn't. Like how they got published.

So far, no one at Biltmore, Durham & Spears had commented that Gillian's clothing was becoming too peculiar for Santa Monica's Promenade, though Helen Sharpe was probably on it, making notes and capturing Gillian's sartorial misdeeds with her cell phone.

Gillian's bangles jangled as she stirred some milk into her coffee. Her clothing was a way of expressing herself, one she needed as she went about her business of drafting patents, with their rigid rules and formalities. And now she had the hell of having to do endless software patents for apps. Every one of her clients, and all of their friends it seemed, had come up with apps that were sure to be the next Uber, Airbnb or Whatsapp. Everybody had an app they were desperate to patent and protect, before even thinking it through. The days of whimsical patents with beautiful formal drawings (which Gillian had become very adept at doing) and arcane vocabulary, with words like 'chamfer,' 'detent,' 'gudgeon,' and 'spline' were gone forever, drowned in an endless sea of stupid apps.

The upside of her work was that she loved her clients (with a few notable exceptions) and got to meet totally wacky inventors. She had a lot of empathy for those creative types who found their way into her office to pay for her advice and expertise. Many of them reminded her—often painfully—of her father, also an inventor whose greatest achievement— Shower in a Sack—had been ripped off by a company in China just as he started to market it in the States. Also, like many of her clients, she knew the pain of rejection, and of toiling away in obscurity to create a product— in her case, her novel—that nobody seemed to want.

"So, I guess you were at B.M.'s for the last two nights," Isadora said, without expression. Her face was pale and wan; her greasy hair knotted and held in place with a grubby pink scrunchie.

"I left a message on your cell and sent a bunch of texts," Gillian said. "Didn't you get them?"

"What's that loser's actual name?"

"Well, number one, he's not a loser. He's been published a lot. And number two, I've never asked him that." Gillian stirred her coffee, thoughtfully. "Probably, he has some awful given names. Barnaby Methuselah, Beauregard Melville. That's what writers often do—use their initials. P.G. Wodehouse was actually Pelham Granville Wodehouse."

"Whorehouse?" Isadora squinted at her mother.

"Wodehouse. He wrote the *Wooster and Jeeves* books. You and I watched that series on PBS last winter, remember?"

"Nope." Isadora sank back into *Bring on the Night.*

"Are you angry about something today?" Gillian asked.

"Why do I always have to be angry about something?"

"That's what I'd like to know."

"Mother, can you just give it a rest? I want to finish this book before I die!"

"Why don't you come with me to B. M's some time?"

"Yeah," Isadora snorted, "that'll happen."

"You'd enjoy meeting him, since you're so interested in books."

"I actually don't *want* to meet Beauregard Prick-face whatever, okay? Not ever."

"So, what are you going to do with a whole Sunday of free time?" Gillian asked, anxious to change the subject. "Start writing your bestseller? Clean up your room? Why don't you go out and get some fresh air? Or go to the library and get something good to read? B. M's books are in all the public libraries."

Isadora's just sighed, heavily, and muttered something under her breath.

"Hey, you'll never guess what's up at the firm," Gillian said, happy to have thought of a safe topic her daughter might enjoy. "Kali—Kali Miller? You know Kali, one of my partners?"

"The one who's married to the dick-wad doctor that rollerblades?"

"Right." Gillian was pleased that Isadora remembered *something* she had mentioned. "So anyway, she's having a tea—a lingerie tea. You know, where a bunch of women get together and give a shower—in this case, fancy underwear—to the bride-to-be?"

"Who wants *underwear?*"

"Nice underwear. Things she probably wouldn't buy for herself."

"If she wouldn't buy them for herself she probably doesn't want them. "Anyway, it sounds disgusting. Can we please change the subject? Or just not talk at all so I can read?"

"But it's such a bizarre idea. I mean, nobody has tea parties anymore. And the woman who's getting married is our summer law student. Remember her, from the picnic? Ana? The really pretty Latina?"

"Nope." Isadora slouched deeper into her chair.

"And here's the big scandal, Izzy—"

"Don't call me that. Ever."

"Sorry, Isadora. We named you after a famous ballerina for a reason."

"She was ugly. And fat."

"No, she wasn't!"

"Did you ever see her dance?"

"Well no—she died in the 1920's. But listen to this, Honey, Ana's going to marry Alexander Spears."

Isadora squinted at her. "You mean that douche who tries to bonk every skirt in the office?"

Except for this skirt, Gillian reflected. "That's him." She was pleased that Isadora had listened to *something* Gillian had told her about her law firm, even if it was only about Alex Spears and his predatory tendencies.

"Assholes like him should be castrated." Hoisting herself up from the kitchen table, Isadora clomped past her mother to grab her jacket from a hook on the wall. "I'm going out."

"Will you be home for supper?" Gillian followed her into the front hall.

"Don't know."

"Need some cash?"

"Sure." Isadora looked down at the floor as Gillian took her wallet from her tote bag and pushed some bills into her hand.

"Well, see you when you get back," Gillian said. "Hey, I love you!" she added, as the door slammed shut in her face.

Don't let your last words be bad ones—that was Gillian's guiding principle. What had been her last words to Isadora's dad? *'You don't look that sick to me.'* She'd been annoyed with him for keeping her awake with his sniffling and hacking. They'd just gotten six-year-old Isadora to sleep and Gillian had been totally lacking in sympathy for Larry and what she thought was just a cold, and male self-pity and exaggerated helplessness.

Isadora had every right to be angry, Gillian thought now, growing up without a father, living on Sidney Street her entire life. Anyone could tell from the address that it was either a slum or 'slum-adjacent.' It was hard to imagine a row of upscale townhouses with shiny brass door knockers on a street called Sidney Street. The town planners must have run out of names by the time they noticed the short street that butted up against the underbelly of the 405 Freeway, in West L.A.

All day and all night the bright yellow sign of the Speedy Auto Glass across the street beamed in through the front windows of number seven. Gillian suspected her neighbors were puzzled about why a *lawyer*—a partner in a Santa Monica firm—would be living there, among them. Sometimes, Gillian herself wondered why she and Isadora stayed on Sidney Street, though, practically speaking, it cost next to nothing to live there. And it was a tribute to Isadora's dad that Gillian stayed in the house he'd worked so hard to renovate. She felt Larry's presence everywhere: from the back door—not hung quite flush—to the smear of blood near the skylight where he'd had an accident with a drywall knife.

Gillian's mother, Harriet, had cried when they first showed her their new home. 'Where are you going to do your shopping?' she'd wailed, her hot pink mules slap-slapping on the scarred wood floor as she traipsed anxiously from grimy window to grimy window. 'You said you were moving to L.A! This isn't L.A! Where are the palm trees? Where's the damn ocean? The movie stars?'

'Most of L.A. isn't like that, Mother.'

'But there isn't even a corner store! Nothing but an auto wrecker!'

'Auto *Glass*,' Larry corrected her. 'Shopping!' he'd later snorted to Gillian. 'Doesn't your mother have anything else in her head? Doesn't she have any *vision*? This neighborhood is going to evolve big time—we're going to make a killing when we sell this place.'

Though he'd been an architect, Larry hadn't been a very successful one. Not that his buildings ever fell down or anything, but he was a concept man, not so great with technicalities. And after he died so suddenly from that mysterious virus—sliding from flu-like symptoms, to a respirator, to a tag on his toe in less than twenty-four hours—well, Gillian hadn't been able to part with the house.

Maybe it was time to let it go, she reflected, standing in the front window, watching her daughter leaning on a lamp-post as she waited for her Uber. Moving into a fresh new condo might make Isadora feel better about herself. Perhaps the two of them could decorate it together, and the project would bring them closer. Living somewhere that Isadora wasn't ashamed of might motivate her to get a job or go back to school. It was either that or Gillian would have to kick her out, for Isadora's own good. She was twenty-four already, with no life plan, not even a vague idea of what she was going to do.

The Uber pulled up and Isadora slouched into it without a backward glance at the sagging little Sidney Street house or her mother. Could a condo really be the answer? Wasn't it bad enough that Gillian worked all day in Santa Monica, so removed from the throbbing heart of humanity which was the only place to find real, raw material for her writing? On the other hand, was it fair to Isadora to make her stay here, in this house of sadness and loss, with her father's blood staining the walls?

In Gillian's wallet was the scrap of paper from a fortune cookie she'd eaten many years before. 'The world is always ready to receive great talent with open arms,' it read. Thinking about it now, it struck her—and not for the first time—that it was not an omen at all, and not Gillian's talent to which the cookie, with its inscrutable wisdom, was referring. Maybe she should just give up on writing, stop wasting her time with B.M. Bradley and focus on helping her daughter.

Chapter 7

BY MONDAY MORNING, THE INTERNAL E-MAIL OF BILTMORE, Durham & Spears was full of updates about the Tie Party: a list of the lawyers going on Bert King's plane, details of the hotel reservations, and so on, ad nauseum. Dan and Alex, slammed with work related to a hostile corporate takeover, were scheduled to go over on the Catalina Island Ferry's first trip on Saturday morning.

There was only one e-mail Kali didn't delete right away, much as she wanted to. It was from Rick, requesting the names of the clients Kali was going to invite to Ana's lingerie tea. For a few moments, she indulged in some unpleasant free associations on the subject, then filed the request away in that crowded corner of her mind reserved for *things to be dreaded and avoided as long as possible*. Besides, it was 9:15, time to get out some files and start the process of dividing her day into hours, the hours into six-minute segments, and assigning seven-digit file numbers to each segment, all to be billed at her hourly rate. *Ka-Ching!*

She opened her computer to a nasty trademark opposition file that needed a formal Answer filed by the end of the day. The lawyer on the other side had submitted a phone book size wad of paper, complete with ninety-one tedious exhibits. Kali's client had banked everything he had on his chosen trademark and, not waiting for it to clear the lengthy registration process, had burst, full tilt, out of the starting gate with his brand. An opposition was the last thing he had expected, though Kali had cautioned him to hold off, in her opinion letter.

More and more lately, the fact that people asked, and paid for, her advice filled her with anxiety. *How the hell should I know what you should do?* she felt like demanding. But that would be looking down. Practicing law was like tightrope-walking: once you looked down, you might as well jump—or more likely, be pushed. Otherwise, like most lawyers, Kali figured she could just teeter along on that tightrope until she eventually dropped off on her own: slumped over in her Herman Miller Aeron chair with a *'do not resuscitate'* sign on the back of it.

From the adjoining office, she could hear Gillian thumping around, struggling to stuff her feet into a pair of kitten-heel pumps: metamorphosing from creative free spirit to patent geek. Gillian loved her office, she often said. A location on the gloomy north wall was actually an advantage. Who could get seriously creative with a sunny oceanfront exposure of catamarans bobbing around on winking waves? That kind of view made you think of Pina Coladas, not patents. So she was happy where she was. Of the three female partners of Biltmore, Durham & Spears, it was only Jada who regularly wailed on about her office and the 'pink ghetto' she claimed the three of them were stuck in.

There was no sound coming from Jada's office now. She'd been in before Kali, and gone out again, off to some divorce court or custody hearing. Kali could understand why she resented being 'banished' (as Jada put it) to the dead north side of the firm. She had long expressed her desperation to move out of family law and into something cleaner, more corporate, less personal. She wanted to be where that good type of action was, near the rainmakers, Rick and Alex.

"Hi there."

Startled, Kali looked up to see Ana in her doorway, carrying an armload of books. '*Hi there?*' Could the casual, offhand greeting have anything to do with Ana's recently-upgraded status at the firm—from summer law student to top billing partner's wife to-be?

"Don't just stand there, come in, come in! Have a seat. We heard the exciting news at Monday's meeting."

"I shouldn't really. I'm up to my whazoo in work." Ana nevertheless draped herself across one of Kali's client chairs. Casually, impertinently, she swung one leg back and forth. From her foot, a high-end, high-heeled shoe dangled. Her simple but elegant silk summer dress clung to her curvy body, leaving little to the imagination. Had Alex bought her the dress? Ana's clothes were the subject of some speculation at the firm, and a source of irritation to Jada since the day Ana showed up in a tailored suit identical to hers. 'How does a student afford Dolce & Gabbana?' she'd ranted to Kali and Gillian.

"I have to talk to you," Ana said, curling a dark lock of hair around her finger. "Alex told me about this tea party thing you're planning for me."

"Well, we—I—wanted to do something for you." Kali felt that some explanation for her blurted-out offer was expected. On the other hand, she realized, if she were cunning and careful, she might be able to use this private chat to get out of giving the wretched tea altogether. Hopefully, Ana was as appalled by the idea as Kali was herself. She got up and quietly closed her office door. "You know, Ana," she began, "I totally get that for a young person, this idea must suck. I mean, a bunch of older women sipping tea and eating soggy sandwiches? I think we can come up with something a lot more exciting for you and Alex. How about we throw you guys a Jack and Jill shower?"

"*Que ese so?*" Ana frowned, her pretty lips puckered in consternation.

"Oh, sorry. Maybe they don't have those in Mexico."

"Mexico? My parents were born here. Both of them. In Burbank."

"Oh. I didn't mean—well—"

"What's the problem with Mexico? Something wrong with coming from there?"

"No, I love Mexico! Puerto Vallarta, Cancun."

"You like the big tourist destinations? Are those the only places you would dare to go?"

"I was not suggesting anything bad about Mexico, Ana, not at all! But a Jack and Jill shower was something I thought you might prefer—a bridal shower that both men and women get to go."

"I know what it is, but I don't want one, thanks."

"Ana, what's the point in excluding the men? You get twice as many presents if they come. And forget about lingerie. That was a dumb idea. Everyone can bring a good *Cabernet* or *Pouilly Fuisee* to get you and Alex started on a great wine collection."

"Alex has too much wine already. He built a giant wine cellar in his house."

"Well, that was just one idea. It can be any kind of shower you want."

"I like the sexy underwear."

"Oh, well, if you *like* the idea. Sorry, I just thought—"

"Go for it. Forget about the men. They have their own thing going on with that *loco* tie party. I'm grateful you're doing something for me. And lingerie is cool."

Kali nodded, wondering what approach to try next. Jada's comment about Ana needing an intervention had struck her as right on point. "So, on a related matter . . ."

"What's that?"

"Well, Ana, you see, Alex and I go back a long way, you know? He was the partner who hired me, basically, here at the firm."

"He did not mention this." Ana straightened up in her chair then leaned forward, tipping her head as if to hear better.

"Yes, yes, the good old days," Kali chuckled. "Way back when."

"Interesting." Ana was staring at her, mouth twisted to one side.

Kali realized this was her chance to mentor Ana and stop this wayward young woman from making a decision that could ruin her life. "I'll just come right out and say this. I have a daughter myself."

"You want to invite her to the tea shower?"

"Oh, no, she's only three," Kali laughed. "Although she does love playing tea party with her stuffed animals and dolls."

Ana studied her, obviously wondering where this was going. "I should take these books back to the library," she said.

"Wait. Listen, Ana. I've known Alex for a long time, as I was saying."

"Were you lovers?" Ana's eyes went wide. "Did you have an affair?"

"Oh my God, no! That's not what I meant at all!" Kali laughed uncomfortably, feeling herself turn bright red.

"So, what do you mean you know him so very well? Just how well do you know him?"

"Not well at all, really. I just wanted to say that I hope you aren't rushing into this marriage. Speaking as a more experienced woman, marriage can be very hard work. And Alex, well, I adore Alex—"

"Have you made love with him? With Alex? My Alex?"

"No! Of course not! I'm a happily married woman with two children, Ana. I don't go around having office affairs." *Like you and Alex do*, she thought. *Or Jada and Ross do.* "I only meant that, and please don't get me wrong, but well, he has a reputation for having a roving eye."

"Something is wrong with his eyes?"

"No, I meant—well, it's an old expression, meaning that he, well, he likes the ladies. Does that make sense?"

Ana shrugged, then checked her cell. "He is very handsome. I am not surprised you tried to have a relationship with him."

"That's not what I said. Not what I meant at all."

"I have a lot of work to do, and then I'm meeting my fiancé for lunch when I will ask him about these roving eyes he supposedly has."

"I don't want you to do that," Kali said. "Please. I was just, well, warning you, as one girl to another, and having a daughter myself, you know?"

"I *think* I just heard you telling me that the man I love is going to fuck around on me, no? How do you expect that to make me feel?" Ana's dark eyes flashed. "Or to make him feel when I tell him?"

"I didn't mean any offense, Ana. Please."

"No? With this girl-to-girl talk like you're trying to help me out, so I don't make some biggest mistake of my life?" Her voice was rising.

"I'm sorry. I was way out of line. Please, forget I said anything. I was wrong, and you are one hundred percent right to be offended." All Kali needed was for Ana to take this up with Helen Sharpe, and Alex. "Why don't we just talk a bit more about the party I'm going to give for you? And the things you might like to get as gifts?"

"Okay," Ana shrugged. Kali was relieved to see that the fire in her dark eyes had died down. "It's a shower, right? The shower is the main event?"

"Yes, a bridal shower."

"It's not one of those deals where people have to try on stuff and then they are expected to buy it?"

"Oh no. Ana, we want to *give* you lingerie. It's not a sale. We're all so pleased about you and Alex—"

"You didn't sound so pleased a minute ago."

Kali picked some lint off her jacket sleeve, feeling prissy and tight-assed, not to mention shit-scared. "I am happy, Ana, for both of you. Everyone in the firm is delighted."

"Okay, I usually wear a size medium. I've got a whole drawer full of panties I can't wear because my mom thinks I'm a small. I hate it when they creep up between my butt cheeks, like wedgies."

Kali faked a chuckle. "I know exactly what you mean."

"No thongs either, okay? I save those for the beach."

"Of course." Kali nodded, desperately willing this conversation to be over. Where was a good five-alarm Santa Monica fire when you needed one?

"Go to Rio some time, if you want to see thongs on the beach. More like butt floss. We went there for spring break, and Alex had his tongue hanging out the whole time. I had to scrape the sand off it every night." Ana smiled at the memory, seemingly not bothered by her fiancé's behavior. "High-cut panties are cool. I like those."

"Look, why don't you give all of this more thought, write everything down and give me a list?" Kali didn't feel like continuing, item by item, through the intricacies of a lingerie wardrobe with such an appallingly frank young woman. Thongs? High cut panties? *Butt floss?*

"And I prefer silk," Ana said.

"Well, of course, who doesn't?"

"I know it's more expensive, but polyester makes me crazy."

"I'll make a note," Kali smiled. "But I should really get back to work right now."

"And I could use some sexy garter belts. Good ones, with a lot of snap. Alexander has a thing for them. A 'thing for zing' is the way he puts it."

Kali drew in her breath, feeling unpleasantly warm. Embarrassment? Sexual arousal? Or her first hot flash? "Look, Ana, I didn't mean to pry into your personal life—"

"You want my bra size too?"

"I can't honestly imagine anyone going out and buying you a bra."

"I'm a thirty-four C. But don't put it out on the office e-mail, okay?"

"Of course not. But look—if I don't call my client on this dog file I've got here—"

"—and I like short nighties," Ana went on. "Long ones get twisted up around my waist. Black is good, also pink. And I like light blue, and grey. But no red, okay? Alex thinks I look like a hooker in red." She paused, her brow furrowed. "I can't think of what else … I don't have a merry widow, a bustier or a bralette."

"Or a baguette?" Kali tilted her head and laughed artificially.

"What is that? You mean, like the bread?"

"A joke. It's just that our conversation is getting hilarious, don't you think?"

"No." Ana looked puzzled. "Why? You asked me what I wanted."

"I didn't, actually, but thank you for all this useful information." *Too much information*, she thought, as she stood up and moved around her desk. "Well, that should just about cover it. No pun intended." She smiled, to indicate an end to the discussion.

"You don't want a list of sex toys we want?"

"I'm sure you and Alexander can manage to get your own—of those." Kali cleared her throat.

"Okay," Ana shrugged. "I wasn't sure about the protocol—how broad an interpretation you were giving the word *lingerie*."

"Well, it doesn't include your contraceptives either."

"Oh, that's no problem. Alex got snipped. We don't want any kids."

Kali nodded. "Right. Good to know."

"But it's had zero effect on his ability to—"

Kali coughed, loudly. "Excuse me, Ana, but I really do need to get some work done today. The morning's just flying by!"

"Okay, I'm out of here." Ana flipped back her long dark hair and slid out of the chair, stretching her curvaceous body and yawning hugely. "It's sort of a retro thing, isn't it? A lingerie tea. It'll be a laugh. Is Helen Sharpe coming? The dragon lady?"

"Well, yes, I have to invite her." Ugh, Kali thought. Helen would be all over this, questioning the choice of shower theme for a young employee, reading all the latest bulletins and cases on sexual harassment in the work-place, not to mention activities motivated by race. Why pick a lingerie shower for a Hispanic girl? What message did that convey? That they were loose women? Unprofessional? Would Kali have offered to throw a lingerie shower for a non-Hispanic law student? There was a sort of greatness to the wrongness of it all, Kali thought, so much regretting her outburst at the meeting. But it was too late to turn back now. For sure, withdrawing the invitation—after Kali had gone out of her way to suggest that Alex was a philanderer—would initiate a fiery complaint by Ana to HR.

"If I think of anything else I'll shoot you an e-mail, or text you," she said, on her way out of Kali's office.

"Excellent. Good idea." Kali closed the door and sank back into her chair. Garter belts with zing, silk nighties, sex toys? Well, she had asked for it. Why should she be shocked that Ana was so brutally honest? Although, if their positions had been reversed, Kali would have blushed and mumbled that anything at all would be fine, mortified by the thought of her professional colleagues wandering through lingerie shops or cruising online stores, imagining what she might like to wear in the sack to turn on her man. But then, Kali was over forty. And she wasn't about to marry Alexander Spears, was she?

She thought about her husband, Matt, rollerblading close alongside her car that morning as she pulled away from the house. She wished he wouldn't do that. She was terrified that she'd run him over, that his wheels would slip under her car tires or he would bump against Kali's car door, to ricochet into the path of an oncoming truck. He'd laughed as he skated along, his boyish face beaming beneath the shiny black helmet. Matt enjoyed living on the edge, particularly now that he had turned thirty-five. And it was always a lot more fun if he could scare the pants off Kali while he was at it. Totally irresponsible, Kali thought, for a surgeon with a wife and two young children.

Kali would be meeting him for dinner at their usual place that night. Monday was their night to go out, have a meal, drink some wine and talk about the kids. Tonight, she might add a few more intriguing subjects to the agenda. Like thongs, and a 'thing for zing.' Except it might start giving Matt ideas. Which maybe wasn't such a bad thing.

Chapter 8

"Who says I want to quit work?" Kali stared at Matt, in disbelief. "What makes you think that?"

"Because you hate it so much. It's driving you nuts. You complain all the time, Kali."

"Did somebody say something? About me? About my work? Helen Sharpe? Rick Durham?"

"Hey, chill. No one's said anything—and I don't talk to people at your firm anyway. But your paranoid reaction is a perfect example of what I mean. I can tell how stressed you are—with all those hours you have to bill, the bitchy women."

"They're my friends, Matt."

"Well then, what about the sexist suits? It's getting to you, am I right? Or have you been complaining about something else, constantly, since before Harry was born?"

"I hardly ever talk about quitting. And I've been practicing law for over ten years. I'm a partner, making serious money. Why would you think it's too much for me now?"

"Because now you have two kids to deal with, on top of your job."

"I don't deal with them. Emilie does. That's why we hired her."

"Do you really trust her one hundred percent of the time with Harry and Molly? Or is it something you don't let yourself think about?" He checked the time on his cell. "Even now, I wonder what she's doing. Leaving them playing mindless video games while she sneaks outside for that vaping she's always doing. Yesterday Harry asked me if he could have an e-cig."

"But she's been with us for three years, and the kids have bonded with her. We hired her a week after Britta bailed."

"Hmm." Matt picked up the wine list.

"You don't think about Britta and wonder what she's up to now?"

"Nope." Matt glanced over the wine list, his lips pursed. Britta, the young, super-hot Swedish underwear model had almost destroyed their marriage—certainly, threatened it—while Kali was pregnant and then for the first few months after Harry was born. "Anyway, getting back to Emilie," Matt said. "After three years of being a nanny, why wouldn't she want to do something else? Move on with her life?"

"But the kids love her. And why should she leave? She's got a good thing going with us. And it's not like she's moping around our house every night. She has a very active social life."

"That's one of my concerns. She's hanging out with a bunch of creeps and dopers and becoming one herself, most likely. She seemed nice enough when we hired her. A bit naive, maybe, but not now."

"She does seem to have toughened up." At one time, Kali had thought it her duty to be more than an employer to Emilie, to take her under her wing, set her on the straight and narrow, encourage her to go back to school after a few years of nannying for the Millers. But Emilie had deflected any such well-intentioned efforts. "I don't think her friends are all that bad," she said. "They just like to shock people with their looks. Most of them are from decent homes." She traced a finger through the condensation on the side of her water glass. "So, what's this all about? Why are you trashing Emilie? If you don't trust her, we better talk about it. The kids adore her, especially Harry. She must be doing something right."

"You can't seriously expect good judgment from a five-year-old." Dark half-moons of sweat had stained Matt's shirt under the arms, and he needed a shave. As usual, he was over-worked at the hospital. His thick, wavy black hair was already tinged with grey at the temples; the laugh lines around his eyes had deepened to wrinkles. "Why don't we order a drink? Let's get a really good wine tonight, the best in the house."

"What's the occasion?" Had Kali forgotten his birthday? Her own? Their anniversary?

"The occasion," Matt said, waving over a waiter, "is that you're going to consider quitting work to stay home with the kids."

"What? I never said that."

"Kali, my practice is really taking off. We aren't going to need your income. That's what I've been trying to tell you for the past year."

"My walk-around money? My pin money?"

"I don't mean your income is insignificant. I'm saying that if you want the freedom to do other things, I'm able to give it to you—after all you've done for me and my career—being so supportive throughout my residency and fellowships."

"Tough times," Kali conceded, "especially with two babies." *Juggling on empty*, was how she'd thought of herself during those years.

"Think about it—that's all I'm asking."

"We'd have to sell the house."

"I doubt that. And even if we did, so what? You don't really like the house—you keep saying it's too big. Don't you miss Belmont Shore? We were happy there."

"That tiny house that was sliding into the ocean? We were lucky to get out of there alive. And all that trouble we had with Britta and my crazy client stalking us all summer—sitting outside our house in his car?"

Kali swallowed, anxiety overtaking her as memories of her pregnancy and Harry's first year flashed through her mind. "Where's that waiter? I need some wine."

"I remember those as happy times, even if you don't," Matt said. Kali said nothing as he signaled for the waiter and ordered the wine, but the painful memories came flooding back. She had accepted Matt's explanation as to why he had hired Britta, and she had forgiven him. And yes, she trusted him, but she was not sure she would ever one hundred percent TRUST him again. Relationships that went through a trauma as theirs' had, could be put back together, and might hold for years, even decades. But it was like broken china: it looked okay, it held together, and it 'worked' but there would always be that hairline crack, that inherent weakness and instability, way down deep, that you could only see if you looked really hard.

"Just imagine a life of almost total freedom," Matt said, snapping her out of her reverie. You could take courses at UCLA. You could entertain, like that tea party you're doing for your girlfriends. I was so proud when you told me about it."

"The whole stupid thing is for business development—I've been told by Rick to invite clients."

"That's my point. You'd be free of business obligations forever. Just think about it—but hold that thought. I've got to go take a piss."

As Kali watched him head across the bar, she thought about his offer. Without her job, they wouldn't be ordering the best wine in the house, and they couldn't afford dinners at The Glass House, their favorite place in Manhattan Beach. Was she selfish to want to keep things the way they were? Would the children be better off with their mom at home, twenty-four seven? Now that they were in school half-days, and next year Harry in full-time school, should she quit work to stay home? And do what? Laundry? Gardening? Cooking? Volunteering? And the kids' schools were great, not like those of L.A. Unified. People *killed* to get their kids out of L.A. Unified. They bought houses they couldn't afford and didn't like, just to be within the boundaries of the better schools, and were ready to pick up and even move their house if they had to, they were so desperate.

Matt returned to the table, grinning boyishly. "Well?" he said, as he slid into his chair.

"Well, what?"

"Are we ready to toast your freedom?"

"Matt. Hold on. You can't expect me to make a huge decision like this in the time it takes you to go to the bathroom."

"What's to think about? You could do anything that interests you, as long as the kids are looked after. You could finish decorating the house, start a small business of some kind, start working out again."

"You think I'm getting fat?"

"Not what I meant. Just think of the possibilities is all I'm saying."

Kali closed her menu. "You know, I'm really not hungry. I should have stayed at the office. I have a lot to do. Let's save the money, go home, make a sandwich and get a good night's sleep."

"Wait a minute. I don't get it. You're actually pissed off?"

"I'm not pissed off. I'm thinking about it, okay?"

"How many women wouldn't jump at the chance to give up work and live an interesting life of ease, pursuing whatever they wanted? But not Kali Miller. It's incomprehensible. I can't win."

Kali started to breathe and count, in and out, imagining she was in labor for childbirth. It hadn't done any good back then either. "Can we please just go home?"

Matt suddenly grabbed one of her hands, entrapping it in his. "If you don't want to consider quitting from a selfish point of view, why don't you think about Harry and Molly? You're yelling a lot, constantly on a short fuse. Your reaction right now is a perfect example of your unpredictable mood swings. I know you're under a lot of stress, but it can't be good for you, or the kids. You should see their little faces when you start to scream."

"I do not scream. I'm merely firm." Not scream? She thought, guiltily, back to that morning. She'd had an early meeting and been so short of time that she'd had to put her make-up on in the car. At every red light, another bit was added: a stroke of eyeliner here, a smear of lipstick there—at the same time on the lookout for the cops, fearing a traffic stop for careless driving. God only knew what sort of ridiculous kindergarten drawing of a face she'd had on by the time she met her client. Molly had been eager to do Kali's hair that morning, but Mummy didn't have time. 'You can do Mummy's hair tonight, okay, Honey?' Kali had said, desperately hoping to avoid her three-year old's meltdown. 'You can do a hamster hair-do on Mummy, or even a duck!'

'Can I do a parrot?' Molly's lower lip was protruding.

'A parrot? Sure! Anything you want, Sweetie. But tonight, okay? Not right now. Mummy's in a rush this morning.' *Mummy's got a headache, Mummy's very busy. Mummy isn't feeling well, Mummy has to go. Mummy hasn't got time.* That's all, it seemed, her children ever heard from her.

But she'd had no time for guilt that morning. She'd yanked a shirt from a hanger, sniffed the underarms, decided it would have to do for another wearing, and threw on a crumpled skirt and jacket. She'd flown down the stairs, to where she'd left her shoes the night before, only to discover than Cannon had chewed one of the heels off. 'What? Where is that dog?!'

'Are you mad at Cannon?' Molly had followed her and was looking up at her with big scared eyes.

'No, Molly. Mommy has other shoes, but it's not good for Cannon to eat shoes. He could get sick.'

'Is he going to die? Is Cannon going to die?!'

'Oh, Sweetie, no. Of course not. But I'll take him to the vet just to make sure, okay?'

'Can I go when you take him to the vet?'

'Kali?" Emilie had yelled from the powder room, 'the water in this toilet is brown!'

'So, flush it!'

'I did, but it's still brown. It's grossing me out. And the washing machine won't turn on!'

'Call me at work. I'll get a plumber to come over.'

'Can I change the wallpaper in my room, so it has dogs on it?' Molly asked, trailing after Kali into the kitchen.

'Sure, Honey.' Kali had yanked open the refrigerator door. 'There's no orange juice. Emilie? Did you forget to buy OJ?'

'It wasn't on the list!' she'd yelled from the powder room.

Kali had filled a glass with tap water and shook two tablets from a bottle of Tylenol she'd taken from a kitchen cupboard: the working mother's breakfast—when someone remembered to buy Tylenol.

When she'd arrived at her meeting, the client had, with obvious embarrassment, quietly informed her that she had a pink sponge roller in her hair. Thank God the client had been another woman. A man wouldn't have said anything—if he'd even noticed—and Kali would have gone around all day, up and down the corridors of Biltmore, Durham & Spears, and along the Promenade, with a pink roller nesting in the back of her hair.

As she studied her husband now, and the painful details of the morning re-played in her head, Matt's pager beeped. He pressed the button on it and read the number. "I have to pop back into the hospital to check on one of my residents. But I'm sure you don't want to hear about it." He grappled for her hand again. "Now, what were you saying?"

The truth, Kali thought, as she looked into his earnest brown eyes, was that she couldn't bear the thought of being supported. After putting him through med school, an internship, a residency and two fellowships, she wasn't about to hear him bellow over every penny she spent. And there was no 'taking time off' from the legal profession. The waters would close over as other lawyers quickly circled like sharks, to get her files and devour her clients. Once she left, there would be no getting back in.

Kali had tried a leave of absence, then going part-time during Harry's first two years, but the clock had quickly run out on the leave, and part-time flowed into full-time and then into all time, with pissed off clients calling her at home, or giving their work to another lawyer when they couldn't get hold of Kali. It was worse than just going into the office every day and having a predictable routine, with a full-time assistant. Those who dared attempt part-time were at the mercy of Helen Sharpe, who would seize the opportunity of re-aligning all assistants and parale-gals, assigning the best to the lawyers who billed the most. Part-time lawyers had no say in anything and were constantly being reminded of how much per square foot it cost the firm to keep them in their Herman Miller chairs.

In fairness, it wasn't Matt's style to bellow over money. But he would notice, oh yes, when those were his dollars Kali was handing over to store cashiers or clicking away online. His response was more likely to be that of the careful surgeon, taking the stainless-steel blade approach to the problem (her spending) the cause (her boredom) and the solution (cut it out). Once they were sharing one income, and that income was his, she couldn't just go out and buy toys for the kids or a new pair of shoes or clothes for any of them whenever she felt bored or depressed or both. And he would never understand how a shopping spree could lift her spirits in the first place. 'Don't you see?' he would argue, all male rationality. 'Once you're over that initial sugar high and the bills come pouring in, you'll be more depressed than ever.'

It wasn't that long ago, Kali thought, that Harry was an infant and Matt was a resident, earning less than Kali's assistant, and moonlighting on weekends doing house calls. No, Kali thought, she couldn't go back to worrying about money. And the children were much better off anyway, weren't they? Having a lovely home in a great neighborhood, top-rated schools and a mom who was happy and fulfilled, who enjoyed what she did for a living? Except that she didn't, not really.

But how was she supposed to let it all go, and turn her back on her profession? Matt wouldn't let go of *his* profession. And what would happen when he got bored with his stay-at-home wife who had nothing to talk about? Once the kids were in school full-time, what would Kali do? Probably drift around the Millers' enormous house, trying to pass the time watching TV or buying stuff online, snacking and getting fatter by the minute. Matt would soon get sick of her, then eventually dump her for a pretty young nurse or an OR tech.

"So," Kali said brightly, "let's change the subject. Alexander Spears got a vasectomy. Can you believe it? At his age? Because he's engaged to our law student. He must be nearly sixty. And guess what he likes Ana Valasquez to wear in bed?"

"No idea, and even less interest." Matt gave her a disappointed look, then called the waiter over to let him know they were leaving. "You're being incredibly selfish, Kali," he said. "But why should I be surprised?"

Chapter 9

THE VAPE ESCAPE WAS THE ONLY EATERY ADVANCED ENOUGH IN its thinking, and fearful enough of its clientele, to flaunt the city's bylaws and allow unrestricted vaping. It was decorated with industrial materials: hard rubber flooring, plenty of stainless steel, everything riveted together with bolts big enough to hold bridges together. It was hard-edged, aggressive decor. The waiters were also hard-edged and aggressive, but the service was grindingly slow.

"I think Kali's finally losing it." Emilie sat down and unbuttoned the top two buttons of her jeans. They were so tight it made Isadora hold her breath, made her own stomach hurt, just to look at them. On Emilie's T-shirt, in bold black letters across her boobs, it said: *JUST DO ME!*

Isadora couldn't be less interested in whether or not her mother's law partner was 'losing it' but Emilie loved to complain about being the Millers' nanny, and Isadora was too intimidated to let on how bored she was by the subject.

"I'll give you a perfect example," Emilie continued, turning on her e-cig. "She's sitting on the can, right? And I'm trying to get the kids to eat this gross cereal, and suddenly she yells out do I know how to make tea sandwiches?"

"What's a tea sandwich?"

"They're gross soggy sandwiches, with no crusts, and filled with cucumbers and other sick stuff and you have to eat, like about a hundred of them, to get full. And Kali's doing this tea thing because some old fart lawyer is getting married to their *law student*. Like, this chick is our age, right? You heard about them?" The pupils in Emilie's eyes dilated with pleasure. "Kali says the old goat had a vasectomy, too, like it's ultra-cool, like nobody's ever had one before."

"Yeah, I heard about that jerk-off douche bag."

"I told Kali I'd never made a tea sandwich in my life and I wasn't going start now, so she could stuff her cucumbers." Emilie sniggered. "Might do her some good since she and the doc don't do it anymore."

"How do you know that?"

"I get to wash their sheets. It's part of my fabulous job."

"You told her to stuff her cucumbers? You said that?"

"No biggie," Emilie shrugged.

"You're going to get fired." Isadora gaped in admiration as Emilie blew a stream of smoke across the table and looked at her through half-closed lids that were heavy with copper-colored eyeshadow.

"I'll never get fired. She knows she's got it good with me." She looked at her e-cig with distaste. "I guess you wouldn't know where I could get vape juice that isn't flavored like Twizzlers or birthday cake?

"No, I never buy that stuff."

"I'd suck off a homeless dude with leprosy for an Aloe hookup." Emilie opened her menu. "I feel like something humungously fattening. What about you?"

"Just a Coke Zero." Isadora wasn't hungry. She was wondering whether Emilie had brought *the book*. She couldn't tell by looking at

Emilie's backpack, since it was always bulging and loaded with stuff she'd shoplifted, or stolen from Kali Miller.

Isadora had met Emilie two weeks earlier at the Biltmore, Durham & Spears annual picnic. Emilie was there because Kali couldn't go and needed someone to take Harry and Molly to it, and she was willing to pay Emilie twelve dollars an hour to take them. On a weekend? To a law firm picnic? That was extreme danger pay! Emilie had demanded—and gotten—twenty.

Isadora was there because her mom made a big deal about her going. She was too old for kiddy picnics, she'd pleaded, mortified by the thought of hopping around in a sack, or three-legged racing with some four-eyed fuck of a lawyer. The picnic wasn't just for children, Gillian had argued, there would be lots of young people there—all of the firm's associates and junior lawyers, the paralegals and the summer student. Maybe she could make some new friends. Yeah, that was likely, Isadora thought. Tight ass twits and douche bags was who Isadora expected to find there, and she had not been disappointed. Hooking up with Emilie had been her revenge.

'You look like you want to be here as much as I do," Emilie had said, coming up behind Isadora in the crush for hot dogs and burgers. 'You vape?' She'd held out an e-cig.

'My mom's over there.' Isadora indicated the front of the line. 'She'd totally freak.'

'I noticed her right off. She stands out from the pack.'

Isadora shrugged, not sure if that was intended as a compliment or an insult to her mom. Emilie had more hair than Isadora had ever seen on one human head, and her jeans were so tight it hurt to look at them. She had long acrylic fingernails decorated with rainbows and stars and glitter.

'Want to grab a burger and meet me behind the boathouse?' Emilie asked. 'We can talk and vape back there. The kids I'm looking after went to see that stupid magic show. They won't notice if I take off for a bit. A law firm picnic,' she muttered, 'what could be deadlier?' She turned off her e-cig. 'I'm not supposed to vape in front of the kids. I'm a bad influence, supposedly.'

'Whose kids do you babysit?' Isadora asked.

'Kali and Matt Miller's.'

'Aren't they really little—their kids?'

'Don't freak out. They're good kids, they'll be fine."

'But they could drown, right?'

'They're not going to *drown*. Duh. I'm not a *total* fuck-tard when it comes to this nanny shit.' She'd fixed her eyes on Isadora. 'You look like you could use someone to hang with.'

Isadora shrugged.

'I might be looking for a business partner. I could use someone with your connections.'

'What does *that* mean?' Isadora was surprised and flattered.

'I'll tell you about it behind the boathouse.'

Chapter 10

"I'M QUITTING THIS NANNY BULLSHIT," EMILIE SAID AS SHE WAITED FOR the Super Nacho Meltdown with Triple Sour Cream Overload. "As soon as my dad comes through with the money he owes me and my brother. He never made support payments to my mom, but he's been like, totaling it up all along and he says it's our money. He was afraid my mom wouldn't spend it on us, which is why he never paid her anything. We hated him, but he was right. I can see her just blowing it on dumb stuff like clothes or a new car. I might even get my money by Christmas, he says, and then hasta-la-beach-ball nanny crap. He just has to cash in some bonds or something. He's like, super rich."

"What has this got to do with our business?"

"Izzy, chill." Emilie looked, with obvious pleasure, at the mountain of food the sullen waiter put down in front of her. "My dad's money is going to help finance the shop. *Our* shop. Don't go getting stupid on me. I hate stupid people." She balanced her e-cig on the table edge and shoveled up guacamole and sour cream with a taco chip. "And quit being so paranoid. Want some of this?"

Isadora shook her head, still thinking about *the book*. Emilie was supposed to have borrowed it from a friend of hers who had every book about witchcraft, the spirit world, the healing arts, cannibalism and other creepy and weird stuff.

"My dad's super cool," Emilie said, licking her fingers, "except that he and my mom named me Emilie. When I have kids, I'm going to make sure they have really cool names like Krystal, Amber and Tiffany. And the boys will be Tristan, Blair and Montana. I'd give anything to do a guy named Montana."

"I was named after a famous dancer," Isadora bragged.

"Yeah?" Emilie blew a vape stream her way. "Which one?"

"Isadora Duncan."

"That cow?"

"She was not a cow!" Isadora reddened.

"You ever see pictures of her? She was butt ugly, plus, she couldn't even point her toes right. I used to take ballet, so I know. I almost went pro. I could have gotten into any company I wanted, like even the New York City Ballet, but I got bored with all the practicing and sticking my fingers down my throat to puke and all that shit."

"She was not a cow," Isadora sulked.

"Okay, she wasn't a cow. I'm sure you've done your research since you were named after her." Emilie dug into her food as Isadora's eyes strayed over to her backpack, on the floor. "Speaking of our business, how much cash you got so far?"

"I got a twenty today." Isadora was still sulking over her name and the cow comment.

"So, the total is what?"

"Eighty-five."

"We're not going to get far on eighty-five bucks!"

"My mom doesn't just keep cash lying around, okay?"

"So, take it from her purse. Duh."

"Where do you think I'm getting it from?" Isadora flushed. She'd been expecting gratitude from Emilie. Even praise. "And besides, you never say how much you've got yourself. And you're the one with the fulltime job!"

"Okay, don't go psycho on me. I know you're doing your best. Here, look, I brought the book for you." She licked the sour cream from her fingers, wiped her hands on her very tight jeans, and pulled a big hardcover book from her backpack. "Don't be too shocked by what's in here. We're not going to jump right into genital piercing. Not at first."

Isadora opened the book and began turning the pages, aghast. There was a man hanging by a meat hook through a hole pierced through the skin of his chest; fakirs walking on knife points; women with elongated necks. "You said tattoos, like flowers and stuff."

"That'll be the start. Simple designs, simple piercings. But things have gone way beyond butterflies on butts. There was this picture on Instagram yesterday? This chick had mirrors implanted in her face, and this dude had all his hair replaced with real growing grass. How cool is that?"

"We can't do that stuff!" Isadora drew back from a particularly horrible and disturbing photograph. "And what do you mean by simple piercings?"

"General rule—if it sticks out, pierce it. If it doesn't, we don't."

"Sticks out?"

"Earlobes, noses, nipples…some unfortunate peoples' belly buttons."

"Yeah, what else sticks out?"

Emilie shrugged. "I need to do more research."

"Dicks?"

"Yeah, dicks stick out. At least when I'm around." Emilie laughed.

"I'm not sticking a stud through some guy's dick." Isadora closed the book. "That's not what we talked about."

"We *have* to do piercings. Nobody wants cute little hearts and ladybug tattoos. There's a lot of weird shit going down that you don't have a clue about. You worry too much anyway. If someone comes in and asks for something we don't know how to do, or we don't want to do, we just tell them to fuck off. They're not going to force us to do it. Guys are touchy about what happens to their dicks."

Isadora pushed the book over the table. "I don't need to borrow this." She wanted to wash her hands, wondering where that book had been.

"You should definitely read it. There's a lot of philosophy in there. Altering your physical body is consciousness-raising—a mental control thing. It's very spiritual. I know it's kind of a turn-off when you first see it, but remember, everything's very sterile now, very state-of-the-art. That's why we need to invest in good equipment, like an autoclave. Takes a lot of money."

Isadora thought suddenly, guiltily, about her mother. "I should get home," she said.

"You're not changing your mind, are you?"

"I need to think about it some more."

"Just take the book. Wrap your head around it. You'll get into it."

"I don't want to wrap my head around it!"

"Hey, whoa. Don't go getting put off before we even start, Izzie."

"Don't call me that! And I said I'm going to think about it."

"Excuse me, but your ingratitude is a little hard to take."

Isadora looked uneasily towards the glass and steel doors of The Vape Escape, desperate to get away from Emilie.

"Are you going in with me or not?" Emilie demanded. "I need to know right now. There's other people interested, if you're going to wimp out." Her long fingernails flashed as they tapped a pissed-off staccato on the steel table top.

"I guess so. Probably. I don't know for sure. You're throwing a lot at me that I'm not ready for."

"Okay." Emilie heaved a deep sigh. "Take your time. I can wait." She paused, studying Isadora. "I didn't mean to scare you, okay? I'm used to seeing this stuff, and I keep forgetting you're not, and that you're a lot younger than me."

"Three years. Big deal."

"I brought some other good stuff for you to read, too." Emilie dug deep into her backpack to pull out half a dozen paperbacks. *Wait Until Night, Night Stalkers, The Night Visitors.* "This one, *Night Visitors?* Don't read it when you're alone. You can keep them. I don't need them back." She smiled. "Look, Izzy—I mean Isadora—I know it's a bit heavy when you first see some of this." She picked up the book and wedged it into her backpack. "But what's in here will start looking pretty tame when you see what's really going down these days. Not that we'll do it all. We can just stick to basics, okay? At least for a while." She dabbed at her lips with a crumpled napkin, took a lipstick from her backpack and applied it without using a mirror. "Chanel. Brand new, straight out of the box. I'm not that jazzed about the color but hey, it was free."

"You actually really steal stuff from Kali?"

"She never misses anything. She's too distracted. Besides, the Millers are rich—they deserve to get ripped off. So anyway, if you need to go slow at first, with our business, that's totally cool. We're partners. We're in this together. Right?" She waited, frowning. "Right?"

"I guess so," Isadora said, unhappily.

"Don't look so thrilled about it. Jesus. Like I said, I have other people interested if you want to wimp out. But I'm keeping the money. It was my genius that got it. Okay?"

"Okay," Isadora sighed, "but I should go."

"Sure." Emilie watched her slouch out the door of The Vape Escape. *The ingratitude of that little twit,* she thought, turning on her e-cig again.

Chapter 11

THE SMALL PRIVATE PLANE THAT WAS TO HAVE TAKEN RICK, PETE Ross and Sandy to Catalina was a Beechcraft Baron, twin-engine, with two propellers. It had been purchased by Rick's client, Bert King, for just over a million dollars. One of its propellers would eventually be salvaged from the waves of the Pacific and later, part of a wing. Not much else would be recovered.

"I was getting ready to go out," a shaken Jada told the reporter in front of her condo. "I wasn't going to answer the door. I was running late— but there was something in the way the buzzer was ringing—I knew it was urgent. But I never expected the cops!" She'd looked steadily into the young reporter's eyes, determined that no one would ever know what she'd really been doing: lying on her chaise lounge, wearing her ugliest and most comforting pajamas, eating Haagen-Dazs straight from the carton and watching back to back episodes of *Game of Thrones*. A wet cloth had been draped across her forehead, and she was thinking she had a brain tumor, the pain in her forehead was so intense.

The night before, she and Ross had their biggest brawl ever, this time about whether he should go to the Catalina tie party. Ross didn't want to go. In the first place, he liked all of his ties, didn't think any of them were ugly, and had no desire to give any of them away. Money was tight, and he was happy with the ties he had. But the best reason for staying in Santa Monica was that he could spend the *entire weekend* with Jada. They could finally talk things out, really *talk*.

'*Talk?*' Jada had demanded, her hands on her hips. 'What kind of man wants to *talk?* Are you really a damn woman?'

It was the perfect opportunity, he'd explained, especially since he had a ten-day business trip coming up after that (Jada knew—she was counting the days!) and wouldn't see her for a while. Of course, they wouldn't be able to *go out* anywhere. He'd never told Marcia who the 'other woman' was, and if they ran into her—or anyone else who knew Ross—in Whole Foods or at the beach or wherever, when Ross was supposed to be in Catalina, it could be extremely unpleasant and embarrassing for all concerned. But they could still have fun, he'd argued—holed up in Jada's condo, drinking, role-playing and having tons of sex.

'Holed up? Jada had cried, 'you mean like Hitler and Eva Braun in the bunker? You think that would be *fun?*' Rage had flared up inside her like a pan of forgotten grease under a broiler. Stay inside her condo all weekend and *talk?* Like two convicts, two mental patients, two shut-ins with some highly contagious disease? Not even able to go out for cigarettes without wearing big hats and mirrored sunglasses? And then Ross would make her put on the chef's hat and paddle his white ass with a spatula while they waited for a delivery of order-in food since they couldn't go out to an *actual restaurant* where they might be spotted together.

Her immediate response to his idea of staying in for the weekend had been barely articulate, and not very polite. Besides, Rick would have his ass if he didn't go to Catalina. It would arouse suspicion, and they were already on edge with their office affair. Out of only six seats, there was one with his name on it, reserved on that plane. Why would he want to piss off their Managing Partner and insult a big client like Bert King? And what if Marcia called the Catalina hotel only to hear that Ross had gone missing? She'd call the cops, and they would track Ross down, and find him, holed up like a criminal in Jada's condo—and they would search the place too, just in case Jada had drugs or illegal firearms lying around, which they would just naturally assume, her being black, and holed up in there with a white man. But she might as well have saved her breath for the pack of cigarettes she would smoke after Ross finally left.

'If I go to Catalina it's only because *you* don't want me *here*,' he'd said, his expressive brows quivering, 'not because of Rick Durham and Bert King.'

Jada could still hear his footsteps clanging down the emergency exit of her condo, then see him look furtively around before climbing into his Jeep in Guest Parking. The belt of his trench coat had gotten trapped in the Jeep's door as Ross slammed it shut, and it trailed along on the road as Ross turned onto Lincoln Boulevard, then disappeared into the traffic.

By the time the police showed up on Saturday afternoon, Jada was panicking about her empty weekend and had hurried to answer her door, overjoyed that Ross had changed his mind and decided to stay in L.A. She *would* wear the chef's hat and the schoolteacher spectacles and even come up with some exciting new humiliations for him. And, did she mention that she was *dying* to try out a couple of new food delivery services?

"The business and legal communities have reacted with predictable shock to the devastating loss of four brilliant legal minds," the reporter said, clipping a microphone onto the lapel of Jada's bathrobe. "Apart from your own personal reaction, can you tell us what effect you think this tragedy will have on Santa Monica's legal community?"

Jada accepted the tissue he pressed into her hand, sniffed, then grabbed his mic. "How can I answer that? I can't even deal with this myself. I can't even really think yet, it's such a shock."

"Would you expect it to make people take a step back, take a long look at their lifestyles? Lawyers especially?" The reporter's eyes had urged her to agree.

"I suppose so. We—they—my partners and me—all work—worked, I mean, much too hard."

Passers-by gawked at the camera crews and mobile units clogging the circular drive, and at Jada, shivering in the oversized bathrobe under the glare of the lights. The afternoon had been cooled by a flash thunderstorm, complete with hail, which had compounded the problems faced by police divers between Long Beach and Catalina. "I'd like to see all attorneys spend more time with their families," she said, trying not to think specifically about Ross and his kids, and hoping to avoid a meltdown on national television.

"There's been very little found, so far, of the plane, and the search continues for the bodies," the reporter said into the camera. "Police divers only found the site because of a heavy oil slick on the water."

"An oil slick? Say, what?" Jada stared at him.

"Hold on," the reporter was listening to something through his earpiece. "I believe that was a *gasoline* slick, not oil. My apologies. Police say it's too early to say whether foul play can be ruled out." The reporter paused, holding the microphone out for Jada's reaction.

"Foul play? Who would want to kill four lawyers?"

The reporter cleared his throat. "Attorney Tyler, we very much appreciate you giving this interview since the shock must be devastating. Do you think your firm will recover? I understand it's a small firm. Four lawyers must make a pretty big dent in the bottom line, would that be fair to say?"

Jada lifted her chin to face the nation. "We've survived a lot, our firm. It's over fifty years old, though it doesn't look it. There are many fine lawyers left, the undersigned included. I do corporate work, very high level." She looked straight into the camera, with what she hoped was a piercing, lawyer-like stare. "We will come through this. You can be sure of that."

"One of the deceased men—the pilot—was also a client of your law firm, I understand. Can you confirm that?"

"I can't speak about our clients. That's confidential. And I can't talk anymore right now. Please, get these cameras away from me."

'GET OUT OF MY FACE! HYSTERICAL LAWYER SCREAMS AT MEDIA' was reported by TMZ later that day.

Jada had yanked the microphone off her bathrobe and, turning her back on the reporter, promptly tripped over a snarl of cables and wires. Then, someone was taking her arm, helping her to her feet and towards the front door of her building. "Dan!" She'd blinked up at him over the wadded tissue she had pressed to her nose. "What are you doing here?"

"I was passing by and thought you could use a shoulder or two."

"You weren't on that plane?"

"Alex and I stayed back—we were supposed to take the ferry over in the morning." He put his arm, protectively, around her.

"Are you also with Biltmore, Durham & Spears?" The reporter shoved the microphone into Dan's face.

"No comment. I'm not talking, except to my partner here." Dan eased Jada out of the path of the reporter, encouraging her to lean against him, and they shuffled together towards the door of the condo.

"Thank you for coming over, Dan." Jada leaned into his over-pumped arms, acutely aware of the size of his biceps. "Oh, God, look at me! I should have put on something else. Here I am on national TV, in *some man's* bathrobe. I was just getting ready to go out when—when all this shit went down!" She pulled out the balled-up tissue and pressed it into first one eye, then the other. "How are we ever going to get through this, Dan?"

"I'm not sure," he said, grimly.

The doorman pulled open the door, giving them a sympathetic smile. He would later give a series of exclusive interviews to KTLA cable news: *REMAINING LAWYERS FEAR FIRM WON'T SURVIVE!*

"You seem much taller," Jada mumbled into Dan's shoulder as they traversed the lobby. "Up close."

"Can we go to your place for a while? I could really use a drink."

"Yes, yes! I don't know how I'm going to make it through the night. Thank God you're here! You absolutely can't leave me now."

LAWYER ADMITS TO NIGHT TERRORS FOLLOWING FATAL CRASH! Buzzfeed reported the next morning.

"What about Alex?" Jada said. "Does he know?"

"Yes, but he's hiding out somewhere with Ana. Poor you. You were the only one the media could track down."

"And I was about to go out. As I was saying, I had a date." An innocent enough lie, she thought. And it was almost true. She would have had a date if Ross had not gotten onto that plane. Did Dan know about her and Ross? Doubtful. He always seemed kind of dense. "Poor, poor Ross! Let's get upstairs," she sniffed.

SURVIVING LAWYERS IN SECRET MIDNIGHT TRYST! Fox News was first to break the story, the next day.

Chapter 12

K ALI NEVER HEARD THE URGENT MESSAGES JADA HAD LEFT ON HER cell. At the exact time of the crash, she would later calculate, she'd been standing in the playground of a park, trying to keep a fix on Molly, who often vanished with heart-stopping speed behind pieces of playground equipment.

Meanwhile, Harry had been hanging upside down from a spidery network of cables and ropes, yelling, 'What is your will, O Evil One?' at her.

Matt was at the hospital, called in for some emergency, and Kali had nothing planned for the kids since she'd been counting on Matt to take them for a couple of hours. She'd had a hectic week and been looking forward to a little personal downtime.

'Take them somewhere," was Matt's advice, as he backed his Prius out of the garage. "Get out of the house. It'll make the day go faster."

Kali had stood on the front lawn as she watched his car disappear around the corner. The neighborhood was silent, apart from the heavy-artillery in-ground lawn sprinklers that spun and rotated and fired in carefully randomized directions. Most of the neighbors were away, as they were every weekend, as if the prestigious, tree-lined street was something to be escaped from as often as possible.

After half an hour in the park, storm clouds had started to roll in, sudden and black off the ocean. Kali had gathered up the kids, their toys and Molly's stroller, and made a dash for her car. As huge leaden drops began to plunk down onto them, Kali installed both kids in their car seats, then turned to tackle the stroller. It was supposed to collapse easily into a compact umbrella shape, but Kali had never been able to bend it to her will. It took several futile efforts before she finally managed to stuff the thing into the trunk, and she was soaked to the skin by the time she heaved herself into the driver's seat.

The children squealed with delighted terror over the thunder, lightning and rain, then roared with laughter at Kali's wet hair. "You look like Cannon after his bath!" Harry jeered, making Molly giggle uncontrollably.

As the car crawled through traffic, the kids grew restless and started slapping each other for amusement. Molly, as usual, got the worst of it and was soon screaming, kicking the back of Kali's seat, and wailing that her mother didn't care about her, or love her anymore.

It wasn't until after the kids' supper, baths, and five bedtime stories that Kali noticed all the messages and missed calls on her phone. But before she could listen to them, Molly had fallen out of bed, and Kali had rushed to her rescue. A moment later Harry threw up his Happy Meal and Cannon bayed at the back door to be let in from the yard where it was later discovered, he'd suffered a serious bout of diarrhea.

In the end, it was Kali's mother, Marina, who got hold of Kali. She'd heard about the crash on the local news. It was such a tragedy! How could a plane just fall into the ocean? It was a ball of flames, they said on the news. And with all those lawyers from Kali's firm dead, was Kali going to lose her job? And what about the guy who was getting married? Was he dead too? Was Kali still throwing that lingerie tea?

Kali called Jada, but her call went immediately to voice mail, and Gillian didn't pick up and neither did Alex or Dan or Helen Sharpe. Then, in a daze, she wandered through the house, picking up balled-up socks, plastic ponies and miniature gargoyles. Finally, at a loss for what else to do, she crawled into bed beside Harry and snuggled up against him, one arm around him as he lay—his firm round belly gently expanding and contracting in a comforting way. Staring at the wallpaper in the dim light from his night light, Kali lay there, in total shock, longing to hear the reassuring sound of Matt's car in the driveway over the patter of rain that had suddenly started up again.

Chapter 13

GILLIAN'S MORNING HAD STARTED OUT WELL ENOUGH. ISADORA was off to a friend's place for the weekend, leaving Gillian with an entire day of uninterrupted time to get a solid start on her new novel. But first, she'd gone out for a latte, then read the latest book reviews online, sitting in a Starbucks six blocks from their house on Sydney Street. Satisfied that her book would be far superior to any of those reviewed, she went home to make a sandwich for lunch before settling in to write.

While searching for Dijon mustard in the cupboard, Gillian realized that it was not condiments, but chaos and filth that were mostly to be found in there. They would soon have cockroaches and rats! She had no choice but to take immediate action. As this was a *bona fide* emergency, writing would just have to take a number.

The first time her cell buzzed, she'd had her nose in a bag of dusty brown leaves that were either ancient oregano or pot. Whatever it was, she had managed to live without using it for a few decades, so she tossed the bag into the trash.

The next time she heard her phone, she'd been trying to get a grip on a slippery mass of rotting onions in a pool of sludge under the kitchen sink. It was B.M calling, she was sure, but she was in no mood for the parade of homes he found so hilarious. His book having a saggy middle was no reason he should expect to make inroads into her precious creative time. She set her phone's ringer to mute. That would teach him that if he wanted to get together he would have to make plans with her, in advance.

While she was under the sink she noticed a slow leak just above the u-bend. The last person to do anything major to the plumbing in the house had been Larry. Dear sweet, well-intentioned but incompetent Larry, she thought, a few minutes later in the garage, pushing aside bags of clothing marked for the Goodwill, and dust-covered cartons of Christmas ornaments, to find the toolbox. Back in the kitchen, after twenty minutes with a pipe wrench and pliers, Gillian gave up on the leak. She would just have to call a plumber.

The cupboards! She hadn't finished that job and here she was starting on another! Out came all the food and dishes, and off went the stained and crusty vinyl-backed shelf paper. By the time she'd scrubbed and re-papered the shelves, organized the dishes and replaced the boxes, cans, and jars of food—in alphabetical order—it was three o'clock.

It was her obsessive need for organization and precision that had drawn her to the career of a patent lawyer, she reflected, morosely, and that same obsessive compulsiveness was now *killing* her as a writer. It was what made her interested in prosaic types like dentists and their equipment; it was what led her to write about the procedures they performed with painstaking, reader-losing detail.

By now it was too late now to do much by way of creative writing about dentists or any other boring thing or person her imagination might send her way to write about. She changed into a mini-dress, vintage denim jacket with *SAVE THE PLANET* embroidered across the back (from the good old days when that was believed possible) and took an Uber downtown to The Last Bookstore, where she bought a selection of books on writing: *Use That Writers Block to Your Advantage! What Happens Next?* and *You Too Can Write a Bestseller!*

She felt a surge of self-loathing as she stood waiting at the cashier's counter. None of the writing books were written by anyone she'd ever heard of. They were all people like her: wannabees who couldn't get their novels published.

Only after she got home, did Gillian finally notice the number of text messages and missed calls on her cell. B.M., she thought, now begging for her company or, even better—way better—dying to tell her how much he was loving *At Whit's End.* But the first of the many messages and missed calls was the only one she listened to, since it sent her into a tailspin. It was not from B.M. but from B.M.'s literary agent, telling her to come and get her manuscript for *At Whit's End* since the agent didn't have room to store it and, honestly, couldn't think of a publisher who would find it right for their list. Gillian could try to find a home for it with one of the small presses, but she didn't need an agent for that! And if Gillian couldn't come to get her manuscript well, *At Whit's End* would, sadly, be tossed into the trash. The agent had only a small pied-à-terre; storage space was a big problem, L.A. being what it was. And B.M. owed her some 'pages' so if Gillian had a chance to speak to him, the agent would appreciate it if she would tell him to call her. Gillian stopped listening then, and erased the message, amazed by the woman's rancor.

Nobody had *forced* the agent to take *At Whit's End* and she'd supposedly been delighted to have a look at a manuscript written by B. M's "special friend." Clearly, the woman had *hated* Gillian's book, if she'd read any of it at all. Unnerved and upset, Gillian grabbed a bottle of tequila from the gleaming, freshly-papered kitchen cupboard and flopped down onto the sofa. So, here she was, still with half a weekend to spend however she liked. She didn't feel like writing anymore; she was totally deflated. Well, she supposed, she could always get drunk. Wasn't that what writers were famous for doing anyway?

An hour later, she was lying on her sofa, still sulking about agents and publishers, her hapless dentist hero and her novels, both written and unwritten. By the time Jada finally reached her, Gillian was completely zonked. She grappled for her phone and was jolted unpleasantly back to reality by someone (Jada) popping up in an area of Gillian's life (a weekend) where that person had no business being. It was a struggle to make sense of the call, and that was just at 'hello.'

"It's me." Pause. "Jada." Pause. "Your law partner?"

"You okay?" Gillian ventured. "You sound weird."

"Well, spending the day with reporters and cops will do that to a girl."

"You've been busted?" Gillian perked up a little.

"Haven't you been watching the news?"

"I never watch the news."

"So, are you sitting down?"

"Lying down. Prone, as we writers would say."

"Listen to me! I've got some bad news. Worse than that. Something *devastating*. So tragic—"

"You broke a nail?"

"You're drunk!"

"What if I am? It's Saturday. I'm entitled. And I've got to get to bed anyway—I've had a brutal day of writing. So, can we talk Monday?" Gillian's eyelids were heavy, the room blurry and out of focus.

"Now you listen to me, Girlfriend! Sober up! You and Kali and I have just become senior partners of Biltmore, Durham & Spears!" Jada waited, sucking on her cigarette. "Are you too in the jar to understand what I'm telling you? They're dead! Rick, Pete, Sandy and Ross! And Bert King! They crashed and burned. They never got to Catalina! (pause) Are you still there? Gillian?"

Gillian's cell phone dropped from her hand and clunked onto the floor. A second later, the tequila bottle followed—rolling under the sofa where it would remain, home to a dozen dust balls and an extended family of cockroaches, for the next six months.

Chapter 14

There were three reasons for holding an inquest. First, was to get answers to questions that needed answering. Second, was the community interest: the nosy public's right to know. The third was to get recommendations to prevent similar disasters in the future. No one argued that an inquest was needed for the Biltmore, Durham & Spears disaster, for all three of those reasons.

But even after a four-day hearing, the jury could not say for sure what had made the Beechcraft Baron plunge into the ocean. How were they supposed to conclude anything without physical evidence? There was virtually nothing left of the plane: tiny parts of the control panel, a section of one wing and a single propeller blade. As for the bodies of the four lawyers and their client, forensic experts agreed that any fragments of the corpses would have bobbed to the surface of the water and been snapped up by gulls before the search and rescue attempts got fully underway. Two life jackets were also found, along with bits of a Styrofoam cooler and shards of plastic drinking cups. None of it was of any probative value.

The best the jury could do was blame the crash on a combination of human error and poor visibility: the usual hideous combination that caused small planes to crash. It had been a gloomy morning, with dense clouds squatting low over the ocean and a wind rising from the east. The owner and pilot of the Beechcraft Baron, Bert King, was a loud aggressive type who liked to tell macho stories about near brushes with death while out in his private plane: running out of fuel in thunderstorms, flying upside down through fog.

Kali, sitting in the observers' gallery at the inquest, could imagine Bert chuckling as he overloaded the plane with cases of beer, anticipating how he was going to give the four lawyers the scare of their lives. 'All these brews better be downed before we land, ya pussies!' he would have shouted into the wind that whipped across the tarmac at Long Beach airport. He would have been half-pissed already. But no one getting on that plane would have challenged Bert or pointed out that he was in no shape to pilot it. The boys being boys, would only have expressed their eagerness to get the Tie Party 'off the ground.' Except for Ross Owen, who might have hung back, trying to light a cigarette in the wind as he tried to figure out how to sneak back to Santa Monica, and Jada.

Once airborne, Bert would have ignored the storm warnings coming in at 119.3 megahertz from Long Beach and LAX. 'Bunch of wimpy fags!' would have been his take on the air traffic controllers. Within thirty seconds of take-off, his drink-sodden brain would have gone into overdrive as the plane shot into dense fog and clouds and Bert's spatial orientation was lost. Without a competent co-pilot, and a bunch of half-loaded attorneys on board, he must have panicked, incapable of pulling the plane back onto course.

The jury estimated that, spinning downwards, the Beechcraft Baron would have hit the surface of the Pacific at around 300 miles per hour. And that the five men on board were dead within a few seconds of impact.

Everyone came away from the inquest unsatisfied. Some new

regulations about small plane safety and improved take-off procedures would be put into place, but that was little consolation to the families, friends and the law firm left bobbing around in the wreckage.

The relatives of the dead lawyers had organized private funerals, but Alexander, on behalf of Biltmore, Durham & Spears, arranged for a public memorial service to be held at the Metropolitan United Church, in downtown L.A.

'Choose comfortable shoes. You may be on your feet for a long time today, talking with other mourners,' advised *The Survivor's Guide*—a book Kali started reading the day before the service. 'If your eyes are red and swollen from crying or lack of sleep, dab some witch hazel onto cotton wool and apply gently. Pack extra tissues in your bag.'

If Kali had read through to the end of the chapter, she would have come to: 'And be sure there is enough gas in all the cars that will be used today.' That might have made her think about having her car cleaned as well, but she'd been interrupted by Emilie stomping in the front door, looking sulky and put-upon and clearly peeved by having to work on a Saturday. Then Cannon came barking in from the yard and the children burst out of their rooms, laughing and shouting to swarm their beloved nanny and their dog.

Chapter 15

Kali, Jada, and Gillian were late for the memorial service. It was Kali's fault, for failing to anticipate the snarl of traffic in downtown L.A, then making everything worse by running out of gas. At least, that was the opinion of Jada and Gillian, and they would express it often during the days, weeks and months that followed.

Kali had offered to do the driving, wanting the others to come with her. They would need each other for moral support, she'd said—now was the time to stick together, put aside their minor differences. Not that they had any. Not that any of them couldn't otherwise be put aside.

Gillian, who didn't drive, readily accepted the offer and Jada, who'd mentally calculated the cost of parking and the annoyance of driving around downtown L.A. on a Saturday afternoon, accepted as well.

"Will you look at this?" Jada said as they chugged around the church in Kali's car, for the third time. She was still in a fairly good mood at that point. "This is some turn-out, isn't it? I'd never get a crush like this for my funeral."

"There are *four* dead people," Kali reminded her, thinking that Jada could find something to envy almost anywhere.

A sort of carnival atmosphere prevailed in the streets, and the traffic was jammed for at least a half mile in every direction. Although Metropolitan United was a magnificent venue, its location was not the best. Pawn shops with flickering neon signs and jewelry marts fought for space on the bordering streets; homeless people with tents and filthy blankets slept on the edges of the church's tidy lawn, and its flower beds were littered with cigarette butts, beer cans, bongs and condoms.

As Kali turned her BMW into its fourth circle of hell and watched Metropolitan United recede again in her rear-view, she realized that parking anywhere near it was going to be impossible. The service was scheduled to start at 4 p.m. In exactly three minutes.

"What were you planning to use for a parking spot?" Jada finally demanded.

"I don't know."

"Jesus Christ, Kali. It's already four."

"No, we've still got three minutes."

"She's doing her best," Gillian said, supportively. "I'm just glad I'm not driving."

"We need a contingency plan." Jada leaned over the front seat. "This is totally fucked up."

"We'll make it," Kali said, with more conviction than she felt, as she glanced, anxiously at the gas gauge. The needle had been in the red 'empty' zone since they'd merged onto the 10 Freeway, a half-hour earlier. "Or maybe," she licked her lips, nervously, "I could let you both out here, right in front. Then all of us won't have to be late."

"No way," Gillian said. "We stick together. You were right, Kali. We're going to need each other." She was toying nervously with the edge of her hat that was perched, like some large nesting bird, on her lap. It was made of black lacquered straw: an elaborate structure known as a 'cartwheel' hat.

She'd bought it at a used clothing store called Second Hand Rose. The hat smelled faintly of dog. Jada was nauseated by the smell of it and desperately counting the minutes until she could get out of Kali's car.

Gillian, was, of necessity, used to suffering the driving habits of others, and believed she had no business complaining when someone else was good enough to give her a ride, but really, she thought, she would have made better time if she'd *walked* from Sidney Street. And it would certainly have been less stressful. Not to mention cooler. For some reason, the air conditioning in Kali's car was not working.

"Christ, it's hot in here!" Jada complained, as if reading Gillian's thought bubble. She felt like she was in hell already—a place she was sure to be headed. At least being pissed off at Kali gave her mind a focus: a distraction from contemplating those she was about to face. There was Marcia Owen—the woman whose man Jada had stolen; the five Owen kids—whose daddy Jada had stolen, and Audrey Owen, whose son Jada had not only stolen but practically pushed onto that plane, resulting in his almost immediate death. She should have worn a hat, she thought, envying Gillian in her dog-smelling, partial-face-concealing cartwheel. She adjusted her Pradas—the biggest shades she had—on her face. In this intense heat, they were sliding all over. It was not much of a disguise, but it was better than nothing, and she could always keep them on throughout the service since everyone would assume she was trying to hide her eyes that were red and swollen from crying. Disguising the fact that she was black was a much bigger challenge, of course, especially as she was sure to be the only person of color in the whole damned congregation. Audrey Owen, with her sharp beady little eyes, would spot Jada immediately, her racism trumping her grief, in the moment.

The traffic suddenly cleared, and Kali accelerated, feeling a surge of optimism. Then, abruptly, she had to hit the brakes again. Six long, hot and miserable blocks north of Metropolitan United, the BMW's gas tank finally ran dry. There was no choice but to leave the car where it was—in a tow-away zone—and walk all the way back to the church. Jada, for one, did not accept this news gracefully.

"Are you going to swear like that all the way to the church?" Gillian asked, as she got out and slammed shut the car door. "Because if you are, I'm not walking with you."

"Don't you worry about me. You've got all you can handle with that *thing* you got on your head." Jada also slammed her door.

"I happen to be a widow!" There was a catch Gillian's voice as she said the word 'widow.' This day was reminding her, so painfully, of Larry—dead at the ripe old age of thirty—and his funeral, and how Gillian had to explain it all to six-year-old, hysterical, Isadora. Larry's funeral had not been a big one, like this. It had been small, private, with folk songs and poetry. A 'hippie affair,' according to Harriet, just like Gillian's wedding. Widowed at twenty-eight, she was surely owed a modicum of respect now, she thought. She marched away down the sidewalk, the brim of her cartwheel hat trembling with hurt, anger, and grief.

"Hey, Gilly, wait up!" Jada ran after her. "Come on back here. I didn't mean that about your bonnet! I wish I had one! I was just feeling pissy because of Kali's sorry ass car."

Feeling horribly guilty, Kali followed her partners, anxiously clutching her bag to her chest as if afraid of being assaulted. Her black, bias-cut, skirt swirled around her ankles, making walking hazardous and threatening to trip her with every step. And, by the time the three women reached the church, she could feel the pinch of a blister on one of her heels, despite the comfortable shoes she'd chosen to wear.

Gillian's face was crimson from the heat, her emotional journey, and the long walk on a very hot day. Perspiration trickled down her temples and formed tiny rivulets on her upper lip. And Jada, Kali saw—eyes wide with dismay—had a melted M&M smeared across the back of her white and navy silk dress, courtesy of either Harry or Molly. Or Emilie. She didn't feel like drawing it to Jada's attention, just then. "Look you guys," she said, as they reached the wide stone steps of Metropolitan United, "I'm sorry about everything. I meant to fill the tank yesterday, and have the car cleaned. It just slipped my mind, like most things in my life lately."

"What are you doing here?" Gillian demanded, as B.M. Bradley, notebook in hand, pen behind his ear, popped up from behind a shrub. "I *specifically* told you *not* to come!"

"Gillian, forget it." Kali pulled her arm. "We've got to go in—we're already late!"

"This is a public event," B.M. said. "A funeral is not an invite-only affair. And, as I explained to you, I need material. Be fair, Gilly. This is what writers do."

"Show up to places where people are in mourning and insert themselves, just to snoop?"

"If we have to, yes." He pulled on his little goatee. "Everything's material—you're a writer, you know that. And the more intense the experience, the better. Hey, is one of the dead guys the one who ripped off your poem?"

"How dare you bring that up now?"

"So, who the fuck are you?" Jada was in his face.

"I'm your partner's paramour," B.M. said.

"His what?"

"Lover. Stud. Boyfriend, if you will."

"I won't!" Jada looked him up and down, her expression conveying what she thought of him as stud material.

Gillian was horrified, mortified and close to tears. "I didn't invite him, I swear!"

"We've got to go in," Kali took her arm. "Come on, forget about him."

"Yeah, Gilly, forget about me," B.M. taunted.

As the three women climbed the steps of the church, Jada suddenly stopped. "No," she moaned, "I can't do this. No way I can go in there, see his wife, and his million kids. And it's all my fault," she said, struggling to hold back the tears, "that he's—that he's—"

"Dead?" B.M. offered. He leaned over the railing of the church steps, to peer at her, pen poised and notebook open. "Do you feel like you personally killed him?"

"You get out of my face!" Jada cried.

"Listen, Jada," Kali gripped her by the upper arms. "If you weren't having an affair with Ross, he would have been on that plane anyway. He was a partner, and he would have been glad of an excuse to spend a weekend away from his responsibilities."

"That's true," Gillian nodded. "It's not your fault, what happened to him. Rick would have made him go."

Jada sniffed into her tissues. "You're right, I guess. He would have gone. But I could have prevented it right?"

"We can't talk about this now, Jada," Kali said. "We've got to tough it out through this service. And if you don't show up, it'll be so obvious what was going on with you two. Do you want to add public humiliation to his family's grief?"

"No! I just feel so bad for them, is all."

"We all do. So please, let's just hang in there and help each other through this, okay?"

Jada nodded. Then Kali and Gillian each took one of her arms, and the three partners proceeded, a little awkwardly, towards the front doors of Metropolitan United.

"Hey Lady," B.M. jeered, "looks like you got shit on the back of your dress!"

"WHAT?" Jada struggled to look over her shoulder at the back of her silk dress, as Kali and Gillian pushed her into the church. Moments later, a tow truck driver whistled happily as he put 'the hook' on Kali's car.

Chapter 16

After the bright blast furnace of the afternoon, Jada, Gillian, and Kali were momentarily blinded by the dimness inside the ancient cathedral.

What a sight they must be, Jada thought, stumbling in, squinting like the three blind mice: hot, rumpled, bedraggled and bitching at each other. Or like three demented bridesmaids, unsure of whose wedding they were supposed to be attending. And that car they'd been forced to ride in! Vile sticky stuff on the floor, the seats crunchy with crumbs, windows foggy with fingerprints, that chocolate on the back seat that had ruined the dress that she would have to wear, embarrassingly, for the entire afternoon and into the early evening. Surely common decency dictated the cleaning of one's car for the funeral of one's partners! It wasn't something that could ever just slip a person's mind, no matter how busy she was. Kali liked to blame her mental lapses on the fact that she had two kids—it was so convenient. Like she was the first person on the planet ever to have more than one kid, plus a full-time job. And besides, she had a nanny to do everything anyway.

Amazing Grace was piping softly through the great organ, not nearly loud enough to conceal the sound of their entrance. All eyes swiveled around to gawk at them. It was obvious that the service had been delayed just for them. Everyone else in the packed church was already seated; the guest book in the foyer had already been closed and whisked away.

The first rows of pews were reserved for the lawyers of the firm, and families of the deceased. Alexander Spears sat in the front row, Dan on one side of him and Ana on the other. A couple of rows behind them, Helen Sharpe—all in black—frowned disapprovingly at Kali, Jada and Gillian. She was sure to write up their lateness in the burgeoning HR file she had on each of them.

Kali slid into the pew, juddering in along the wooden bench to take the spot beside Dan. His eyes were closed, his head tilted back, and he seemed to be praying, as was Alexander. It struck Kali, suddenly, how alike they were: same well-cut suits, edgy haircuts and sharp, corporate profiles. Dan would be giving the eulogy on behalf of the firm. He had wanted to. No one else did, so everyone was glad when he'd stepped up. Plus, as the most junior partner, he really had no choice. He opened his eyes, gave Kali a sorrowful smile and touched her, briefly, on the arm. Alexander had his hand on Ana's thigh—a little too high up to be decent, Kali thought, in a church. Alex didn't bother to acknowledge the embarrassingly late arrival of his three female partners.

Taking a deep breath, Kali pulled a tissue from her bag and dabbed at the perspiration on her upper lip. The church was gratifyingly full. That had to be some comfort to the families. Many of the firm's clients were there, and lawyers from other firms. She also recognized several State and Federal Court justices.

At the front of the church, positioned among large sprays of white lilies, were painted portraits of the deceased lawyers. Their expressions were stern but sincere: lawyerly in the most traditional sense. What handsome, successful men they'd been, Kali thought—what an incalculable loss to their families, friends and, yes, the law. The portraits had been painted from professional photos of the lawyers, as once posted on the Biltmore, Durham & Spears website. The website photos had been removed and replaced with solemn black boxes and an '*in memoriam*' notation, above the lawyers' biographies. It had been Alexander's idea to have the four partners memorialized on canvas by a local artist who'd had to work very quickly but had done an amazing job.

It was a shock, being confronted with the faces of the four dead men. Kali had been trying for days to remember—really remember—what each of them looked like. Though she'd seen them almost every day for five years, she hadn't been able to picture them, accurately, in her mind, once they were *gone*. As a flush spread over her face, she dug her fingernails into her palms, and swallowed. Her jaw ached. Crying was allowed, she reminded herself, but once she started, there'd be no stopping it. And she was sure to get everyone else going as well. *Buck up*, she told herself. No one had more right to cry than the families, and they were all holding it together. At least for the moment.

The one direction Kali couldn't look was the children. She hoped none of them was going to speak as part of the service. She wouldn't be able to get through it: the clear innocent voices and sweet little faces of the children—like Harry and Molly—who would never see his or her daddy again. She would dissolve into a helpless mess on the floor; the church's janitor would have to mop her up after the service.

Gillian kept her eyes down, not able to look at anyone, let alone the children, and picturing, with disgust, B.M. in one of the back rows somewhere, busily scratching away in his notebook with his Bic pen.

The cavernous church, the enormous crowd, the heavy scent of lilies, were giving Gillian a strong sense of her own mortality. She glanced sideways at Kali and Jada, seeing them with X-ray eyes—as grinning skeletons floating above the bench they were on. Her heart pounding with terror, she forced her eyes away. *Look at something ordinary*, she told herself:

find some everyday normal, comforting thing! Or a stronger person at least. Alexander—dry-eyed, cool and in control—was whom her eyes alighted on for reassurance that she was never going to die, or not soon anyway. Though she could never *like* the man after what he'd done to her, he appeared now as a life-affirming force, sitting there with his hand resting possessively on Ana's thigh—so carnal, so human, so alive and pulsing with sexuality.

Ana's dress, Gillian noted, feeling calmer now, was one she herself would have been pleased to wear: floaty layers of midnight blue chiffon with a glitter of jet at the neck. Ana was even wearing delicate lace gloves, the same deep blue as her dress. The sight of her made Gillian feel chunky and ordinary in her bulky linen blouse and dirndl-style skirt. Her hat was all that saved her from looking totally unremarkable. She only hoped that whoever sat behind her wouldn't ask her to take it off. Funeral etiquette would dictate she comply— unless she could plead religious reasons for keeping her head covered, which, in good conscience, she couldn't. But should she take it off anyway? In the crowded pew it seemed so brimmy. It made her feel like a lamp. Not cool or artsy at all. She could practically feel B.M. behind her, and the thought filled her with rage. This was *her* funeral for *her* partners. If anyone had a right to it as material it was her. Why, oh why, hadn't she thought to bring at least a scratch pad along? She had no business calling herself a writer.

The rector was approaching the pulpit, his black gown flapping officiously behind him. For a youngish man, he had a surprisingly stiff gait (*a poker up his butt,* Jada would later say). His head was bald on top and what little hair remained hung long and dispiritedly to his shoulders. Wire-rimmed spectacles were perched pedagogically on his nose; on his feet, sandals with crisscrossed leather thongs—the classic 'Jesus boots"—as they were called back in the 'sixties. After fussing with the folds of his gown, he puffed up his chest, gripped the edges of the lectern and gave his audience a baleful stare.

"Before we begin," he began, "I must remind everyone that we are in the House of God." He paused, glaring down at them. "Therefore, there must be no taking of photographs, nor sketching." He eyed the reporters at the back of the church, with a fierce and threatening look. "No scribblings in notebooks of any kind, in any manner." Gillian bit her lip, almost sure she could hear the sound of B.M., suddenly taking a pause with his Bic. "I'm not going to comment on those few who have arrived so late for this important event," he continued. "It's a busy warm Saturday and I'm certain the traffic is quite congested." His chilly smile took in Kali, Jada, and Gillian and pinned them for a moment, making them squirm with embarrassment. "One of the joys of our Metropolitan United, known to some of us, affectionately, as 'the Old Met,' is that it is located in the beating heart of our wonderful, vibrant Los Angeles. But there are times when, outside its doors, there is a devil of a traffic jam." He waited, allowing the congregation a moment to appreciate his wit. "Now, again, to those *three* who have arrived late," his voice reverberated, "I say only that I am certain no offense was intended and wish to reassure them that none has been taken!" Another sardonic smile, and a glint of gold dental work. "But would the lady under the large black hat kindly remove it during the service so that others' views are not obstructed?"

Gillian glanced around, then, mortified, reached up and yanked off her hat. Her hair would be hideously flattened now, glued to her head from the heat, humidity and the weight of the hat, but she didn't dare fluff it, or even touch it, with hundreds of eyes on her. She shrank lower into her seat, hot with humiliation.

"What an asshole," Jada whispered, giving her hand a reassuring squeeze. Kali also threw her a sympathetic look.

"Now then," the rector said, "I shall begin the formal service in a moment. But first, I would ask all of you to notice something striking." Gillian crossed her legs self-consciously. He wasn't going to draw attention to her hair now, was he? "And that striking—dare I say, amazing—thing is that a well-known Santa Monica law firm, in concert with the families of Richard Durham, Ross Owen, Sandy Krupnik and Peter Johnson, has chosen this wonderful historical building, Metropolitan United Church, this magnificent house of worship, in which to remember the four fine men who have so suddenly shuffled off their mortal coils. Look around you, at the person to your left, then to your right. How many of you attend church regularly? How many of you have ever been inside a church? And I don't mean to attend a wedding or a funeral or a baptism. I mean, because you have felt the need to talk to God?"

Pews creaked as people rearranged themselves: examining fingernails, adjusting neckties, smoothing skirts and checking watches and cellphones. The rector shook his head, pityingly. "Just as I thought. Not very many. Perhaps none." There was an uneasy clearing of throats. "Well then, as you look around at one another, and look into your own souls, I want you to ask yourselves why!" His voice rang out, accusingly. "Why have you turned away from the Lord, just when you need Him the *most*? And then I want you to think about it even more. And then again. Ask yourself *why* until it hurts! Until you find the answer which you know in your heart to be God's truth!"

From behind Kali, came a wheezing sound. It was old Mrs. Biltmore, widow of one of the firm's founders. She was making an adjustment to her hearing aid. Turning it off, Kali thought, if she was smart. At the moment, she envied the hard of hearing.

"I challenge each of you," the rector continued, his voice increasing in intensity, "to look to your right, then look to your left, and ask each other *why?*"

People looked uneasily at each other. There were a few mumbled and embarrassed 'whys' uttered in low voices.

"Where did we find this nit-wit?" Jada whispered to Kali.

"He comes with the church. Package deal. No substitutions."

"Now, would all who can remember the words, please rise and join me in a recitation of the Lord's Prayer?" The rector seemed satisfied that his congregation was now thoroughly humiliated and humbled. "Those who cannot remember those inspiring, yet comforting, words will find them in the front of the hymnals which have been generously donated to the Old Met by the surviving partners of Biltmore, Durham & Spears."

How much had this cost the firm? Jada picked up the one in front of her. They were inscribed, on the front page, in memory of the four deceased. Then she was flooded with shame over her pettiness—thinking about pinching pennies when it was her fault that one of them—dear devoted family man, Ross Owen—a man who had really and truly loved Jada—was now at the bottom of the Pacific or floating around in bits and pieces.

"And for those of you who don't know—or have forgotten—what a hymnal is," the rector continued, "it's that lovely red book in the front of your pew. And I expect everyone must know what a pew is since you are all seated in one or another."

"When is the show going to get started?" Old Mrs. Biltmore demanded, mostly to herself, as she continued to fiddle with her hearing aid. Someone cracked their knuckles, loudly. There was some clearing of throats, here and there, and Gillian could have sworn she heard B.M. snicker, from way back at the rear of the church. She didn't dare look, afraid she would pop an aneurysm, or have a stroke if she saw him back there, pulling on his beard.

Finally, the congregation rose with a great groaning and creaking of wooden benches and the rustling of hymnal pages.

Chapter 17

"Our Father, who art in Heaven," Gillian read, her head down and her voice quavering, "hallowed be Thy name."

As Kali joined in the prayer, she looked apprehensively around her. She had trouble with funerals and memorials, even when, as here, there was no coffin or corpse as tangible evidence of the deceased. Death was a part of life, Matt always reminded her: he saw it every day in the hospital. Besides, who did she suppose *liked* going to funerals? He had promised to try and make it to the service, but Kali knew he probably wouldn't. He was kicking off a colon cancer clinic that afternoon—an idea his Chief of Staff had come up with to boost the hospital's profile in the community—and Matt was expected to show some enthusiasm for it. He was also on call, and no one would have appreciated the buzz of his hospital pager in the middle of a hymn or eulogy.

Boris and Marina were a few pews behind Kali. They would have arrived early, to be sure of getting a good parking spot and an unobstructed view inside the church. Boris was very anal that way; he hated to be inconvenienced and liked to plan ahead. Marina was totally the opposite—a chill-out, don't sweat the small stuff, kind of gal. Kali was a conflicted mixture of both.

High above, in the great vaulted ceiling, three puny fans rotated, creating barely a breath of air. The twelve stained glass windows of the church depicted scenes from the Bible: Moses smashing the tablets; the sermon on the mount; Adam and Eve. At the top of each was a hinged window that had been pushed open, which was stupid, Kali thought. If they had been left closed, the church might have retained some of its ancient coolness.

Though Gillian had been a partner with the men who'd been so tragically killed, she was realizing now how little she knew about any of them. The firm didn't do much socializing. There was the obligatory 'winter holiday' dinner for professionals and significant others, and the summer picnic that was sporadically attended, and only by those with kids. This year's picnic had been the last for her and Isadora, Gillian had decided, after hearing that her daughter had spent much of it vaping with Kali's nanny behind the boathouse. Gillian had felt obliged to pass that intel along to Kali, but it gave her an uneasy feeling to know that Emilie and Isadora now despised her for ratting them out.

She was also furious with B.M. but what pissed her off the most about him showing up was that she wanted the funeral scene as material for something she might eventually write. It was *her* material to claim, as a former partner of the four deceased, not B.M.'s! She took some deep breaths, to calm herself and remember why she was there: to honor and mourn her four partners, not seethe about B.M. Bradley, whom she would never speak to again, she decided. "For Thine is the kingdom," she recited, "the power and the glory, forever and ever. Amen." She sat down and was startled to find Isadora suddenly beside her in the pew. "Oh! Thank you for coming, Sweetie. I didn't think you would make it." She gripped her daughter's hand in a loving and grateful squeeze. Isadora would have had to have taken a bus, all the way in from West L.A. It choked Gillian up that she had come.

Looking at her, though, Gillian almost wished she hadn't. Her jeans had huge ripped holes in both knees, and her sloppy T-shirt had B.U.M. written across her chest. "You couldn't have put on a dress?" Gillian whispered.

"Nope!" Isadora said loudly, then slumped down in the pew, arms folded defensively across her chest. "Why am I here, anyway? It's not like you actually *needed* more people."

"Keep your voice down, Honey," Gillian whispered, "please. And you're here because I asked you to come, and I'm so glad you did." She glanced fearfully at the rector, hoping he wouldn't hear her. She looked sideways at her daughter. "What did you do to your ear!?" she demanded, forgetting all about the rector.

"What does it look like?"

"It *looks like* a dozen holes! Can they be filled in?"

"You're one to talk! You had your nose pierced twice"

"Ten years ago!"

"Do you want me to leave, Mother?"

"What else did you get pierced?"

"You obviously care a lot about the dead guys!" Isadora shouted.

The congregation gave a collective gasp, as all eyes turned, in horror, to Gillian and Isadora.

"I don't need this bullshit!" Isadora hoisted herself to her feet, slouched out of the pew, and shuffled back up the aisle towards the front door. The rector coughed loudly as the congregation watched her retreat. In the silence, Isadora's chunky, denim-clad thighs rubbed together with a sawing sound as her heavy Doc Martins clumped on the wooden floorboards.

Kali leaned over to Gillian and squeezed her hand. "I can't wait for Molly to get to that age," she whispered, to be supportive.

"But she was reaching out," Gillian said. "It was a big step for her, and all I could do was criticize!" Her eyes were filling. Kali and Jada looked at her, sympathetically.

"We're here for you," Jada whispered loudly. "We know where you two are at with this mother-daughter teenage shit. It'll be cool."

"We'll go and talk to her after," Kali said. "Maybe we can help somehow."

"Excuse me?" It was the rector. "Excuse me? Would it be too much to inquire if all that commotion in the front pew might soon be over? Surely, out of respect for the deceased and the bereaved?"

"Why don't you just take yourself on down to hell?" Jada demanded. The congregation gasped. Jada stared at the rector, eyes wide. She hadn't intended for her words to carry like that; they had just popped out. The stifling heat of the church, the stress of being late for the service, the mess on the back of her dress, the sanctimonious lecturing by the rector, the scene between Isadora and Gillian—all of it was making her crazy. But that was no excuse. Mother of God, Kali thought, her hand to her mouth. Here it comes, fire and brimstone.

But the rector only cleared his throat, allowing the gathered assembly to murmur its disapproval of that person of color. Then, holding up his hands for silence, he reminded everyone that emotions were running high and that God's forgiveness would be available to the woman who had blasphemed before Him. He pushed his spectacles further up on his nose and took a pocket watch from beneath his cassock. "Perhaps now would be a good time for all talking to cease, and for us to observe a minute of silence for each of the departed? I will announce their names, in turn, and I would ask that all of you reflect on each of them individually, on their brilliant careers, their families, their hopes and their wondrous achievements. And on what they meant to each of you, in the context of your own lives. I will begin with Sbitozan Serhiy—known to most of you as Sandy—Krupnik, whose likeness appears to my far left."

"Why not do the right side first?" Audrey Owen demanded. "That would be only natural! Who starts with the left? That's my Ross on the far right! Why not Ross first?"

The rector ignored her, his eyes on his pocket watch. Clearly, he was not going to suffer any further interruptions to his service.

Sandy … Sandy, Jada said to herself, forcing her thoughts away from Audrey and Ross. *Think about Sandy Krupnik.* She gazed at his portrait, at his round face and sincere brown eyes. He'd always been one of those guys whose thoughts you could never read. He was a loner; his marriage was said to have been on the rocks. His widow, Natalie, sat glumly in the pew, not making eye contact or conversation with anyone. What was it that was wrong with her? It was supposedly the reason she'd given up her work as biochemist though she was said to have been a brilliant researcher.

"Peter Johnson!" The rector seemed to have recovered some enthusiasm for his job.

From across the aisle, Audrey moaned another complaint about Ross not being next, as Jada switched her thoughts over to Pete. He loved fishing, was practically obsessed with it. That fact alone had created a gap in understanding between them that Jada had never been able to bridge. Fishing! So-called sport of morons, the obese and the comatose. But now, with Pete's sudden passing, it seemed endearing: a touching human foible. What else did she know about him? Nothing, really.

"Ross Owen!" the rector's voice rang out.

"It's about time!" Audrey wailed.

Jada hastily retrieved some tissues from her bag as she prepared to contemplate her dead lover. Then, fearfully, she glanced over at Ross's widow, Marcia, and their five children. Behind the granite-faced Marcia, Ross's parents clung together, Audrey sobbing loudly. The youngest of Ross and Marcia's children, Obadiah, looked around with a bright expectant expression, seeming delighted to be in a strange place with lots of new people. Jada choked on a sob as pity, shame, and dread overwhelmed her. She had taken that boy's father away—first destroying Ross's marriage, then his life! If there really was a hell, there had to be some prime real estate reserved for a sinner like her!

"Richard Durham!"

"Wait! No! That wasn't a full minute!" It was Audrey again. "That was barely thirty seconds! I checked my watch!"

Rick's widow, Leighton, and his children—two boys and three girls, all in their twenties—sat cool, blond and impassive in their pew. What amazing composure, Kali thought, they were like Kennedys, or kids from a Ralph Lauren clothing ad. You might think they were there to watch a boring lecture—they showed so little emotion. Leighton as well. Kali turned her gaze to Rick's portrait. In the pose, he was leaning forward, as if in a hurry to be off to someplace else. The artist had managed to capture his essence: Rick the rainmaker, always ready to dash off to court or to meet with a client, roaring around L.A. in his vintage Porsche. He was the most energetic man Kali had ever known: a top biller, tireless promoter, and Managing Partner for the past four years. Of the deceased, Rick was the one whom she had most deeply admired. She closed her eyes, feeling again the pain of his loss, not only to her, personally, but to the firm. How would they carry on without his tireless business-development efforts? It almost served them right; they had let him shoulder too much of the load for too long. There was no obvious second in command.

"And now," the rector continued, "before the eulogy is delivered by Dan Chatwell, would everyone please rise and join me in one of the most beautiful hymns known to the Christian church, 'Nearer My God to Thee.' This hymn is of particular relevance to those of us gathered here today, for it is said to be the last hymn that was played by the orchestra of the Titanic as the great ship sank, in 1912. So many innocent lives were tragically given up to the waters of the vast Atlantic, as the four lives commemorated here today have been given up to the Pacific. 'Nearer My God' may be found in your hymnals, at page ten." He gestured to everyone to rise again.

Kali was trying to remember the last time she'd been in a church. A wedding, she guessed—but whose? And when would the next occasion be? Boris or Marina's funeral? Harry or Molly's wedding? Would Ana and Alexander still be getting married now that all this had happened? And would she still be expected to host the tea? Hopefully, they would decide to put off the wedding. It would be in poor taste to expect the survivors to get cranked up for a big society function so soon after such a tragedy, wouldn't it?

She watched Alexander's hand on Ana's thigh, feeling a tingle of envy and sexual arousal. Such carrying on, and at a memorial service! But since when was Alex ever concerned about poor taste? Since when was Ana, for that matter, Kali thought, recalling the embarrassing conversation they'd had about lingerie. Was Ana wearing anything under that chiffon dress? Her long, bronzed legs were bare, and she was wearing strappy high-heeled sandals. A single dew-drop of perspiration glittered like a diamond on her upper lip as she sang.

"Nearer, my God, to Thee, Nearer to Thee!" The congregation warbled out the last lines of the hymn and then everyone sat down again. The rector, satisfied that he had finally flailed his errant flock into some humiliated order, gathered his gown about him and strode, self-importantly, down from the pulpit.

Chapter 18

DAN STOOD UP, ADJUSTED HIS TIE AND TWEAKED HIS JACKET INTO place. From all over the church came scattered sniffling and the sound of noses being blown, as the assembly prepared itself for a cathartic experience. The pews creaked as backsides settled deeper into them. The only movement of air came from the ineffectual waving of the printed pamphlets—the Orders of Service.

Dan's shiny shoes—obviously new for the occasion—squeaked as he strode towards the lectern. A sense of expectation hung over the crowd as he took a sip of water and cleared his throat. He smiled slightly, sadly. "To paraphrase Shakespeare," he began, "their lives were gentle, and the elements so mixed in them that Nature might stand up and say to all the world these were men!" His voice cracked with emotion, and he turned his head from side to side, allowing the congregation to appreciate his perfect profile.

Well, he had the right to a certain amount of vanity, Jada thought, gazing at him. Ross had disliked Dan, for some reason. Maybe it was envy.

Dan was younger, smarter, cuter and single. She pulled a fresh tissue from her bag and dabbed her nose. Even if Ross hadn't been on that plane, and were alive today, he wouldn't be there beside her, she thought. He would be in the pew opposite, casting longing looks at her from beside Marcia and their children—where he belonged, in other words. Guiltily, she realized she didn't feel all that sad about Ross's death. It was actually a relief to not have to suffer weeks, if not months, of arguments and fights as their relationship suffered through to its tortured, bitter end. And if that thought damned her to hell, well so be it—not much she could do about anything now.

"Wherein does greatness lie?" Dan was asking, rhetorically, his voice ringing in the cavernous cathedral. "In the head?" His finger grazed his temple. "Or in the heart?" An open palm rested, briefly, on one immaculate lapel. "Greatness knoweth itself." The dimples on either side of his mouth deepened. Jada caught her breath, wishing she hadn't kicked him out of her condo quite so fast, that night after the plane crash. The man looked damned good, she thought.

"I'm not a very creative guy," he continued. "I've borrowed a lot from William Shakespeare today." He bowed his head as if acknowledging the greatness of the bard, and the extent of his own limitations. "But who else has the words?" he asked. "The words we may borrow to pay tribute to such men as we, gathered here today, have lost? Who else has the words that may do justice to a sunset?" Among the gathering were sad smiles, heads nodding in agreement, and short, broken sobs. "Be not afraid of greatness," Dan continued. "Some are born great, some achieve greatness, others have greatness thrust upon them." He paused, for dramatic effect. "But I would add that still others have greatness torn away from them. Along with their very lives!" Kali, Gillian and Jada exchanged looks. Who knew Dan had this flair for the dramatic?

Then, there was then a longer pause as Dan allowed the impact of his words to sink in. Someone blew his nose violently—a great Canada

Goose honk—from the back of the church. Others scrabbled for more tissues. Audrey wailed loudly, her shoulders heaving, as Derek ineffectually patted her on the back. "Yes," said Dan, "greatness torn away, with their very lives! That is what has tragically befallen our most excellent friends, Richard Dusome Durham, Peter Elliot Johnson, Sbitozan Serhiy Krupnik and Ross Geraint Owen."

Geraint? Jada looked away, willing herself to show no reaction.

"Whether you are here today to honor these men as lawyers, or simply as men, you are among friends. Welcome, all. Those of us who remain, to carry on at Biltmore, Durham & Spears, share your enormous grief. We have all lost four trusted friends and four valued counsellors. They can never be replaced."

"You'll never know! You'll never know!" It was a shriek, the voice torn off in a ragged sob. Audrey again. Those whose attention had been wandering in the torpid atmosphere of the old church snapped back to appalled attention. Order of Service cards stopped waving. Audrey leaned into Marcia's pew to jab her daughter in law in the back. "And fat lot *you* cared about my son! Waltzing out on him like that!" She was fanning herself vigorously with a blocky red hymnal and it looked as though she might clobber Marcia with it.

"He left me, you fool!" Marcia cried, her face scarlet. "You're even stupider than I thought!"

The congregation drew in a collective, horrified breath, Dan looked as though he'd been slapped, clearly at a loss for an appropriate Shakespearean quote.

"Not as stupid as *your* carryings on!" Audrey countered, eyes sparkling with fury. "You pushed him out—pushed him right on that plane! He had no choice!"

"Believe whatever you want, you miserable old cow! Ross always said you were soft in the head!"

"That's telling her!" came a man's voice from the rear of the church.

"Not *my* son!" Audrey cried. "He would never say that! He was a decent, good man! He adored his mum! And he was a great father to his kids too!" Then, after snatching the handkerchief from her husband, she buried her face in his shoulder. "*She* killed our Ross! Marcia done it!"

If she only knew, Jada thought, fumbling desperately in her bag for more tissues as Obadiah began to whine and Dan looked down from his pulpit, blinking rapidly, his face a perfect mask of tragedy. "Please, Mrs. Owen and Mrs. Owen. On such a sad day, can you not think of the children. Marcia? Audrey?"

"We don't need your bleedin' input!" Audrey cried. "We need our Ross back!"

Kali almost wished for that pompous ass of a rector to get back behind his pulpit and shepherd his unwieldy flock into peaceful order again. Jada was biting her lip, hard, her shoulders shaking. Gillian, totally exhausted from all the emotion, and still panicking about Isadora, was pretending to be engrossed in reading her hymnal.

"Perhaps we should all take a few moments to collect ourselves," Dan said, kindly. "Ladies? Please." His hand shook as he reached for his water glass. "This is a terrible strain, for all of us." He waited, patiently, clearing his throat and sipping water, for the murmuring in the hall to subside. When it seemed that a further disturbance was unlikely, he continued.

"Now, if you will all permit me, there are some words I would like to say on behalf of those of us who have been left behind." He fumbled with his notes, obviously thrown off course by the disturbance. "I've been talking a lot about greatness here today. As Thackeray wrote, and I'm giving Shakespeare a break now—to endure is greater than to dare, to ride out hostile fortune, to be daunted by no difficulty and to keep heart when all have lost it. Who can say this is not greatness?" He was rushing his lines, Kali thought, obviously anxious to get through them. And who could blame him? She would have passed out by now from fear and embarrassment if she were the one delivering the eulogy.

"Those of us who must now carry on—are we not as great as those we have lost?"

"No! Never! Not like Ross!"

"Oh, for God's sake, Audrey, shut the FUCK UP!" With a loud hiccup, Marcia got up. Her eldest daughter rose too, taking her mother's arm, and together they made an unsteady progress towards the side door of the cathedral. The middle children—twin girls and a boy—tried to hang onto a thrashing little Obadiah as Marcia moaned something, her words garbled, until at last, her voice faded, and the side door of the church swung shut with a soft *whump*. The children looked confused. Then one of the girls burst into tears and was quickly imitated by her sister. Eventually, they all trailed miserably out of the church after their mother.

Gathering up her bag and gloves, and clucking and muttering, Audrey followed them, prodding Derek along in front of her. The side door creaked open, then thudded shut again. "Why my Ross? Why him?" came Audrey's strangled question, tiny and helpless, from outside the church. "Why?!"

Why him indeed? Jada thought. Because his hideous *mistress* let him know he would not be welcome at her condo for the weekend because she wanted to go out. Party! Dance! Indulge! Show off! Troll on Tinder and Match. How she prayed the agony of the service would soon be over and that she would somehow escape without further torment.

"Now, it used to be," Dan was saying, "that greatness was considered exclusively a male domain. Webster, in The Duchess of Malfi wrote the following. Whether the spirit of greatness or of woman reside in him, I know not. I owe him much pity."

Kali, Jada, and Gillian exchanged looks.

"Back in Webster's day," Dan continued, "it was an either-or equation. If one were great, one could not also be a woman. Fortunately for all of us, things are different today. The face of the law has changed, and much for the better. It certainly has become prettier." He smiled at Kali, Gillian, and

Jada. "Biltmore, Durham & Spears will carry on," he proclaimed. "Make no mistake. From nine partners, we are now but five. And three of us, the majority I am proud to say, are women, and eager to prove just how wrong Webster was. Let us remember that *justice* is always portrayed as a woman. We are privileged to have in our firm three truly great women partners. Kali Miller, Jada Tyler, and Gillian Lawrence." He looked expectantly at the pew where they sat.

"Hear hear!" Alexander clapped his hands together, the sound ringing loudly in the vaulted hall. Ana looked at him, adoringly. The organist began to play, softly.

"What are we supposed to do now? Get up and curtsey?" Gillian whispered to the others.

"Don't ask me." Kali turned to the congregation and nodded, then raised a hand in a limp wave.

"Who do you think you are?" Jada demanded. "The freakin' Queen Mother?"

Overwhelmed, suddenly, by a surge of courage, Gillian got to her feet. "I have a quote too!" she said, her voice startling her with its resonance in the old church. "It's from Charlotte Bronte. If you don't mind, Dan?"

"Please." He smiled, beatifically, from the pulpit. "We would all be honored."

"Charlotte was writing about someone close to her who had passed away at a very young age." Gillian swallowed. "I have to paraphrase a little." She took a deep breath. "I do not weep from a sense of bereavement, but for the wreck of talent, the ruin of promise, the untimely dreary extinction of what were four burning and shining lights." As abruptly as she'd stood up, she sat down again.

"That was beautiful," Kali said, as she squeezed Gillian's hand.

"Charlotte Bronte had four guys keel over?" whispered Jada. "She knew four guys who died young?"

"I *said* I was paraphrasing." Gillian looked down at her hands. "I've always loved that quote."

"That was my partner, Gillian Tyler," Dan said, "for those who don't know her."

"Lawrence," Gillian corrected him.

"One of my great woman partners. Thank you, Gillian Lawrence." He lifted his head and calmly regarded the assembly again. "Although we will never fully recover from the ross of loss—excuse me, I mean, the loss of Ross—and Rick, Sandy, and Peter, we must remember that they died in the service of the law, and in the service of our firm's esteemed clients."

Kali, Gillian, and Jada exchanged looks. A drunken boys-will-be-boys weekend was the service of the law?

After a moment of silence, Dan nodded to the organist and the music swelled. He raised his arms and invited everyone to join in a recitation of the twenty-third Psalm.

"What? No loaves and fishes?" Jada muttered.

"Those will show up later," Kali said, "when that rector returns to walk on water."

Chapter 19

IN THE OFFICES OF BILTMORE, DURHAM & SPEARS, THINGS LOOKED pretty much as they always had. There were fresh-cut flowers in the reception area; the Keurig machine was warmed and ready to dispense caffeine by 8:00; the cleaners still came around at night with their carts, dusters and vacuums. The man in the white coat continued to come by to check the quality of the air, and the pony-tailed adolescent still watered and pruned the plants every week.

The most perceptible change in the firm was in its sound. The relentless twitter of phones, like dozens of exotic birds, had stopped. The air inside the conference rooms was dead and the marble foyer echoed when anyone walked across it. People stopped saying 'thank God it's Friday' on Fridays, though Mondays still brought the usual gloom. There was lots of whispering going on and the sounds of heavy doors being discreetly closed. No one seemed to find anything funny anymore.

A few days after the memorial service, Kali, Jada and Gillian were in Kali's office for a quick meeting, at Kali's request. Alex and Dan were out, and their assistants claimed not to know where they'd gone or when they'd be back.

"Ladies," Kali began, "I've got some bad news and some worse news. Which do you want first?"

"Let's have the bad," Jada said, "I need a lift right now."

"Let me guess," Gillian said. "Four of our partners have died in a plane crash and nobody knows the cause? No, you're right. It's too far-fetched."

"Well, okay, here's the bad news," Kali began. "Ross, Sandy, Rick and Peter each had two million dollars of accidental death coverage, with our firm—us partners—as the beneficiary."

"That's bad news?" said Gillian.

"Sounds like fine news to me," Jada said.

"It would be great news," Kali said, "if we could collect it. But there's an exclusion clause in the policy that no more than three partners were allowed to travel together by air."

"How's that?" But Jada didn't really need clarification. In her mind, the memory of the belt of Ross's coat, trailing from his Jeep, formed itself into a huge dollar sign, then became a noose which was now available to her for hanging herself.

"Hold on. It can't be that cut and dried," Gillian protested. "Nothing in law ever is. We can get around it somehow." She pressed her hand to her forehead.

"Are you receiving messages from the spirit world?" Jada asked.

"Shut up. I'm thinking." Another pause. "Okay, I've got an idea. The exclusion clause was never drawn to our attention. The insurance company had a duty to highlight that very important exclusion. There was no disclosure made to all partners of the firm."

"We're lawyers," Kali sighed. "We can hardly plead we didn't read the fine print. We write that stuff."

Jada was now recalling, miserably, the ease with which she might have stopped Ross from leaving for Catalina. A single encouraging word would have done it. Five little Owens, now with no father; Marcia with no husband, and the firm (herself included) losing out on what would have been six million dollars. She gazed out at the sky through Kali's office window. What would be the best way to do herself in? Pain was out. She was not into that stuff. How many Ambien were left in her bathroom cabinet? Not enough. She'd been popping them like crazy lately.

"Well, how about we argue that they weren't actually *traveling* by air?" Gillian continued. "I mean, it was hardly what you could call *traveling*, was it? They barely got off the ground, did they, before the plane crashed?" Jada and Kali avoided Gillian's eyes. "Okay, so it's not the greatest legal argument, but at least I'm trying to find a creative solution."

"Travelling by air is not really subject to interpretation," Jada said. "The thing was off the ground when it crashed, since it fell into the ocean. A hot air balloon would have qualified."

"Of course, we'll fight it," Kali said. "Alex has already retained the best insurance litigators in L.A."

"You talked to Alex about this?" Gillian gasped.

"*Before* talking to *us?*" Jada's dark eyes flashed.

"I did speak with him, yes. Last night. And Dan."

"You got together with Dan and Alexander, *without us?*" Jada repeated.

"This is a little hard to take," Gillian added. She and Jada looked at Kali in hurt silence.

"It was no secret meeting—it was just a Skype call. And I tried, but I couldn't reach either of you. You should be glad I was around to represent your interests. Gillian, where were you? Off at some poetry reading?"

"No." Gillian thought, guiltily, about where she had been: slumming with B.M. and an exuberant real estate agent, through depressing houses where desperate owners pretended to watch TV and not notice the three people assessing their cupboard and closet space.

"And you?" Kali turned to Jada. "What were you up to? Now that Ross is gone?"

"Excuse me? What has Ross got to do with anything?"

"Come on, Jada. Everyone's known about you and Ross for months. You must have realized that."

"Actually, I didn't."

"It was so obvious."

"How was it so obvious?"

"Forget Ross for a minute," Gillian said. "I want to get to the bottom of this secret meeting Kali had with Dan and Alex, behind the backs of her women partners. And friends."

"It wasn't a secret meeting—I just told you. It was a call and I had no prior notice." Kali was exasperated. "Look, I don't need this. I've got a husband who's begging me to quit work. I could just walk out of here right now, forget this whole mess, put it behind me. Live on easy street."

"That's where you live anyway," Gillian shrugged. "Manhattan Beach. On a *cul-de-sac*."

"With a rich doctor husband, two cute kids and a dog from a puppy mill," Jada added. "You don't need this shit."

"Cannon is not from a puppy mill," was all Kali could think of, by way of quick retort. "And we'd have to sell the house, for your information, take the kids out of their private schools and fire our nanny."

"Wah, wah," Gillian said. "Such terrible problems the rich have. You're breaking our hearts, Kali."

"So, go for it," Jada said. "Just walk away. I would." The women looked at each other. No one spoke for a moment.

"Of course, I'm not going to quit," Kali said. "I didn't mean that. I only wanted you both to start thinking about the future of this firm. We've got a real opportunity here to turn things around. Biltmore, Durham & Spears now has five partners, three of them women, as Dan said. It's fair to say this is a woman-driven firm now, right?"

"So what else went on at this meeting?" Jada asked.

"Well," Kali hesitated. "Now don't get pissed off, okay?"

"What?" Jada demanded.

"Well, he—Alex, well, he wants Ana to join the firm."

"To do what? She's not even a lawyer."

"As soon as she passes the bar."

"We won't know until Thanksgiving," Gillian said, "when the bar exam results come out."

"He wants us to make the offer, so she doesn't go somewhere else, considering the problems we're having here. And it gets worse." Kali cleared her throat.

"How could it?" Jada demanded. "Not?"

Kali nodded. "Partnership," she said.

"WHAT?" Jada and Gillian demanded together.

"I'm not sure he was serious, and anyway, nobody can be made partner without a unanimous partnership vote and we have three out of the five."

"So, what if we don't vote for her?"

"They might go somewhere else, the three of them, break up the firm."

"There's no way they can fire us," Jada frowned, "is there?"

"Of course not," Kali said, "we're still partners."

"Is the wedding still on?"

"As far as I know."

"Are you still be doing the tea?"

"I don't see how to avoid it."

"That'll be quite the gruesome affair," Jada said.

"It was always going to be," Kali said. "Not much has changed there."

"I want to hear more about your secret meeting with Dan and Alex," Jada said. "Does Dan have any similar requests? Like he wants his mother admitted to the partnership? Or maybe his pet rabbit?"

"Laugh all you want," Kali said. "But while we're sitting around bitching, what do you think they're doing? Dan and Alex?"

Gillian checked the time on her cell. "Lunching."

"*Power* lunching," Kali said. "With the firm's clients—with *our* clients, while we sit around here clucking like a bunch of hens. They're making sure the business stays with them, no matter what happens to the rest of the firm. To us."

The women shared a moment of deep paranoia. Then, Kali's assistant, Alicia, tapped on the door. "I've got a call on my line for any partner." She dropped her voice, looking totally freaked out. "It's Mrs. Owen. I don't know what she wants. Should I ask her?"

"Marcia," Jada asked. "Or is it Audrey? Old English lady?"

"She doesn't sound old," Alicia said.

"Well, I'm not talking to her," Jada said.

"Take a message please, Alicia," Kali said. "I'll call her after our meeting."

"You're not going to be able to avoid Marcia forever, you know," Gillian said to Jada, after Alicia had gone. "She'll be around for a long time, picking up Ross's things, straightening out his *affairs.* And she'll be there at Kali's tea."

"Well, maybe I won't go to the damn tea myself," Jada said, defiantly.

"Oh, you're coming," Kali said. "That's not even up for debate, my friend."

The Alicia was back. "She's insisting on a personal meeting." She looked, questioningly, at Kali. "Is that okay with you?"

"Oh, sure," Kali said. "I'd be happy to see her. And it's not like I'm that busy these days."

"She asked to have lunch on Monday."

"That's fine. Book it for Tender Greens at noon."

"What do you think she's after?" Jada asked, after Alicia had gone again. "Money?" Her thoughts turned to the millions they would have had if she hadn't practically *pushed* Ross onto that Beechcraft Baron. "Me?"

"I'm sure it has nothing to do with you," Kali said, though she was not sure at all. "She might have some questions about Ross's estate or need to make some arrangements. Maybe she found his will, or just wants someone to talk to, or needs some things from his office."

"Yes," Jada brightened. "That's probably it. I'll just be out of the office on Monday, in case she comes up here with you after your lunch."

"You don't suppose Ross left you anything, do you?" Gillian asked. "Something weird and revealing or seriously unpleasant?" Her writer's brain was galloping wildly over the field, so rich with possibilities.

"We had a brief, ill-conceived and silly liaison. That's it. Besides, he didn't have much to leave. A big mortgage. Five kids. Lots of orthodontist bills."

"You should be prepared though, Jada," Kali said, "because it could be awkward if he did leave you something."

Jada's eyes met Kali's, then Gillian's. What if Ross had left her something intimate and embarrassing, like a long confessional letter that Marcia would have found while going through his stuff?

"What if he changed the beneficiary on his life insurance policy from Marcia to you?" Gillian said.

"No way he'd do that!" Jada said. Though, how could she be sure? He had been desperately in love with her sorry ass.

"I'll talk to you after I see her," Kali said. "Otherwise, as for the so-called secret meeting, the only other thing I talked about with Alex and Dan was the four offices of the—well, our deceased—partners. Alex wants to go through them on Saturday, clean them out. He thinks we should all be there for that."

"I'm not going through their personal things!" Gillian was horrified. "I can't even look at those offices, knowing our partners are still out there, somewhere... maybe pieces of them floating around, bobbing up and down on the waves."

"Cut it out," Jada said. "You're talking weird creepy shit."

"I'm never going to the beach again," Gillian said. "That's all I need, to be sitting there on a rock and see one of Pete's eyeballs looking up at me from the water."

"There aren't any floating body parts," Kali said. "You've got a science background, you know that. So please, try and stop with that kind of talk. The bodies are at the bottom of the ocean, buried with the wreckage of the plane. Or else there's nothing left of them because they've disintegrated already. Think of it as if they've been cremated and buried at sea. They aren't going to bob up to the surface. Not ever."

"I must be losing it," Gillian sighed. "It's Isadora's books all over the house ... vampires, corpses climbing out of coffins."

"We're all having morbid thoughts," Kali said. "It's common for people to need counseling after a tragedy like this. But I've been thinking about what we need to do now, about our practices. We're going to have to think serious damage control. The good ship Biltmore, Durham & Spears is springing a hundred leaks."

"Right," Gillian said. "The associates have nothing to do—they all leave early every day, to hit the bars. Resumes are flying all over the internet. The word on the street is not good. Sick jokes, mostly. Know what I heard yesterday? What's the biggest defect with the Beechcraft Baron? Not enough seats."

"Sick," Kali said, shaking her head. "But dead lawyers jokes have been popular since Shakespeare."

"Oh, way before," Gillian said. "Since the profession started—like with the Etruscans, or whatever."

"I guess we should be relieved about the slowdown of work," Jada said. "We couldn't handle the files of those four guys, not right now, not with our own clients to look after. Assuming we keep them."

"Without Ross, we're losing all the real estate work," Gillian said.

"Without Sandy, the bankruptcies. Excluding our own, of course," Jada said.

"Without Rick, the litigation," Gillian added.

"Without Pete ..." Kali paused. "What did Pete do, anyway?"

"He always seemed busy," Gillian said.

"We're lawyers," Jada rolled her eyes. "We all learn to look busy in law school."

"I think he was in tax shelters," Kali said. "No, wait, securities."

"Really?"

"I guess we'll find out when we go through his files."

"Please, leave me out of it," Gillian begged.

"We have to do it," Kali said. "We can't leave their offices untouched, like shrines. Space here is sixty dollars a square foot. We might have to look for another building, with lower rent. Plus, we've got four assistants with nothing to do but gossip and worry about their paychecks bouncing and Helen Sharpe sending memos around that we need to ax them all."

"Can we ax *her?*" Jada said.

"I would *love* that," Gillian said.

"Well, maybe, but not right now. We'll have to give the associates and assistants severance packages. It'll be tough. Especially since we've got no insurance money coming to the firm." She glanced at Jada, then looked away.

Jada looked at her shoes wondering how Kali knew that she had metaphorically stuffed Ross, kicking and screaming, onto that plane.

"I bet Ana tries to grab one of those big offices now," Gillian said.

"Over my dead body," Jada said.

"Couldn't you *please* use some other expression?"

"Those south-view offices are ours. As senior partners, we get our pick, and we can finally move off Baltic Avenue and onto Park Place."

"I'm staying where I am," Gillian said. "There's no way I'm going into an office with an ocean view, so I can sit there every day watching the water, thinking, wondering."

"If you're prepared to sit and stare at the water all day, you can find someplace else to work," Jada snapped.

"Hey, I'm a senior partner here, same as you."

"We're all going to have to bust our butts or we'll be going down with those four men. I apologize for being blunt, but no shit, Gillian, there are times when I have to wonder if you're all there."

"I've been thinking along those lines too," Kali said. "Not about you, Gillian," she added quickly, "but about how we're going to survive. We'll have to get down and get dirty. We can't afford to turn away any kind of work. We all got referrals from the four guys when they were alive. But there's no loyalty owed to us just because we still have the firm's name. In fact, it's a liability. Biltmore, Durham & Spears is now synonymous with tragedy, disaster, and death."

"And we don't even do wills and estates." Jada was feeling discouraged, thinking about all the unpalatable types of legal work that could come in off the street: personal injury claims, mortgage enforcement, tenant evictions, false arrests, shoplifters, assaults and elder abuse.

"By the way, Gillian," Kali said, "I'm sorry to say this, but you're going to have to get a lot tougher on your inventors. Your receivables are through the roof."

"But then I might not get any work at all," Gillian protested. "Lots of brilliant inventors can't afford the up-front costs. They have to wait until their product gets onto the market."

"Then you'd better re-tool," Jada said.

"Excuse me?"

"We're not a bank. Or a charity. You need to get work that pays, like the rest of us. And if you don't like the ocean view from your new southern exposure, shut the damn blinds."

"So, what about you?" Gillian demanded. "You're pretty good at figuring out what everyone else should be doing. What are you going to do to survive?"

"Business development. I'm going to play hardball, get work any way I can. Just like one of the boys. We're all going to have to start thinking like men. And we can start by getting rid of all the plants. Do we have any idea what the cost of maintaining those oxygen-eaters is?"

"They actually make oxygen," Gillian said, "in the daytime, anyway."

"Whatever. They're history. And how about the cut flowers in reception? What's wrong with fakes? And what about the free coffee and cookies all day long for the staff? It's going to be vending machines now, and we'll make money on every bag of Fritos and every cup of coffee. And what about the pilfering that goes on in the mail room? Everybody sticking their personal mail through the postage meter, filling their pockets with pens and paper clips. I've been watching, oh yes, I have, and it's been an eye-opener. We're being bled dry with that shit—tape, legal pads, envelopes. A man wouldn't put up with plants and cookies. Ask Alex and Dan. I know they're thinking exactly like me."

"But those little things, like the coffee and cookies, make a workplace human," Gillian said.

"Yeah? But they don't make money. They suck it. Listen, we either shape up around here or we sink, and go down with our four partners. There's a couple of other guys with football cleats ready to trample us into the ground on their way to the big touchdown."

"They certainly seem to be busy ... Alex and Dan," Kali admitted.

"And don't forget Ana," Gillian said. "Lady Macbeth."

"We may be getting paranoid," Kali said. "I mean, we haven't seen them do anything directly against our interests, right? And okay, maybe Dan got a little carried away with his memorial speech—that woman lawyer justice stuff."

"It wasn't a good day for anyone," Gillian said.

"You've got that right." Jada glared at Kali, thinking about that melted M&M on the back of her silk dress, the cost of having it cleaned and how everyone must have thought she'd shit herself the entire time she was at that church. "But okay. Let's quit all this bitching in the kitchen and work with the boys, come up with a business plan, be co-operative. But let's not totally forget that pithy old chestnut."

"What pithy old chestnut is that?" asked Gillian.

"Just because you think you're paranoid, doesn't mean someone isn't watching you."

Chapter 20

Rick Durham's office looked as though its component parts had been put into a gigantic box, given a giant shake, then tossed back into the room. There was little evidence of the efforts Leighton had made over the years to decorate it, though she was a professional decorator, with her own business.

An elegant chintz slipcover (hand-sewn by Leighton) on the small sofa was mostly obscured by boxes of depositions and other court transcripts. Against one wall was an antique roll-top desk, with brass locks and trim, that Leighton had meant for Rick to use as a mini-bar but had become home only to his sweaty gym shorts and squash racquet.

"Unpleasant though this is," Alexander said, stepping over a box of files, "we have to go through everything that belonged to our partners. The personal stuff goes to the families. Anything related to their law practices stays with the firm. Assuming we still have a firm, when all the dust settles."

"It's a good thing old Mr. Biltmore passed away before all this," Kali said, sadly.

"He would have gotten his office back," Alex said, drily.

Mr. Biltmore, when he found himself with nothing much to do—his practice having dwindled as he lost his edge and neared his eightieth birthday—was allowed to keep coming in every day, as a courtesy extended to him by the active partners. He drifted, forlornly, up and down the carpeted corridors, looking remote and confused. Since he was producing no revenue for the firm, his office was, by necessity (according to HR) reduced from a big corner one with a spectacular ocean view, to an inner office with no window, to a cubicle and then, finally, to a desk at one end of the mailroom. He had passed away a few months after the last move.

Dan started constructing a cardboard carton, reinforcing its seams with packing tape. The tape gun shrieked as he dragged it down one side, across the bottom, then up the other side. 'RDD-PERSONAL' he wrote on the side of it, the thick black Sharpie squealing loudly. The others watched in riveted silence, as people with nothing to say to each other pretend to be enchanted by the activities of a hyperactive child or a dog. When the first box was taped and labeled, Dan started on the next.

"Look, I don't mind if you want to go through these offices without me," Gillian said. "We don't all need to be here. So, if nobody minds? I'd like to go now."

"What, exactly, is your problem?" Alexander demanded.

"It just seems like such a horrible invasion of privacy."

"The dead have no privacy. And you have to be here. You're a partner. Nobody *wants* to do this. You think I wouldn't rather be out at the ball game, or off somewhere penning a sonnet?" He and Gillian exchanged looks of extreme dislike.

"This is harder for some people than others," Kali said. "We can do this without her."

"No," Gillian said, "Alex is right. I'll be fine." She turned to look over Rick's bookshelves which were jam-packed with ragged binders, untidy bundles of papers, law books and a collection of unrelated objects.

"Everything relates to one case or another," Jada said, picking up an athletic shoe. "Oh, I remember this one! A product liability case, for one of the Lakers. Something to do with the treads on the bottom—like he lost a big game or broke his ankle or something."

"Why would Leighton want all this junk in her perfect house?" Gillian asked rhetorically. She pushed aside a plastic coin bank to read the title of a book wedged in behind it. "So this is where the *Annotated Patent Digest* went! I've been looking for this for a year. I must have asked Rick a hundred times."

"He must have needed it for something. Check inside the front cover," Alex said. "If it was Rick's, it goes to his family."

"It's not his. It's from our library." She put it on a wing chair that had the same patterned fabric as the sofa. Apprehensively, she took down another book and opened it. "This one has his name in it. *Persuasion — The Key to Success at Trial.*" Reverently, she placed it in one of the boxes Dan had constructed. "He was such a great lawyer, Rick."

"One of the best," Alex agreed.

"And look!" Jada said. "Here's his 'SUE THE BASTARDS' commemorative desk toy. I remember when he got this—from one of his clients. It's even got 'To RDD' engraved on the bottom." She sighed. "I guess we have to do this sorting out, but I agree with Gillian. Doesn't it seem too soon? Sort of disrespectful?"

"If we're going to get weepy over every book and knick-knack, we're never going to get through this," Alex said. "We've got three more offices to do, and I feel as bad as you do, but we've got to hire more lawyers and fill these offices with revenue-producing butts. I only hope we don't find something that puts us straight into a lawsuit. God knows what we're liable to discover. People keep strange things in their desks. We might come across something that could compromise the firm."

"I don't keep anything strange in my desk," Jada said.

"Not what I've been hearing," Alex retorted.

He had lost a lot of weight, Kali thought, noting the loose hang of his jeans as he moved around behind Rick's desk. If he really was out power-lunching with clients every day, he wasn't getting much to eat. Either that or Ana was wasting him with her sexual appetite and things that zing or whatever it was she'd said. The weight loss made him more attractive, Kali thought. He looked younger, even though there were hollows in his cheeks that were shaded by the blue-black of a five o'clock shadow. "People keep stuff in their offices that they can't keep at home," he said, "for one reason or another."

"Alex is right." Dan's marker squealed across another box top. "We might find something that would embarrass the families. We don't want to add shame to their grief."

"There seem to be a number of locked drawers here," Alex said, trying a desk drawer. "Fortunately, I thought ahead, and got the keys from the company that made this desk." He pulled a ring of keys out of his jeans pocket and tossed it onto Rick's desk. The clank of metal made everyone start. "Who wants to start on them? By my guest."

"I'll keep going through the books," Gillian said. "What's the worst I can find on a bookshelf?" She glanced at the ocean beyond Rick's windows, and shuddered, her imagination running away with her. "Anybody mind if I pull down the blinds?" Without waiting for an answer, she scrolled down the grey mesh blind, dropping a gloom over the room that gave it the atmosphere, suddenly, of a rainy day.

"Okay, let's get our asses in gear. I've got a date tonight," Jada said. It wasn't true, but she grabbed the keys anyway. "I can handle Rick's secret locked drawers. Ain't nothing this girl ain't already seen." A few minutes later, she pulled open the last of the drawers. "I hate to speak ill of the deceased," she said, "but our Managing Partner was a total pack rat. There's nothing in here worth keeping—dead felt pens, sticky notes, chewing gum wrappers. A box of cigars … I didn't even know he smoked. Did anyone bring trash bags? Most of what's in here can just be dumped."

"I'll get some from the kitchen," Gillian said, glad of an excuse to leave.

Alex selected the smallest key on the ring, unlocked Rick's credenza doors and slid them open. "This is weird," he frowned, peering into it. "Why would he keep files locked up in here instead of out in the file room?"

"A yo-yo, a shoe horn, a jar of loose change…" Jada was itemizing more stuff from the drawers. "I guess we give the change to Leighton. Looks like about twenty bucks' worth."

"He owed me a lot more than that," Alex grumbled, looking over the first few folders he'd pulled from the credenza. "He was always bumming lunch money, never seemed to have his wallet on him."

"And I thought I was the only one he hit up for cash," Dan smiled, shaking his head.

"Trash bags!" Gillian called, cheerily, re-entering the room.

"Come on over here, Dan," Alex said. "Take a look at these."

"Here," Jada directed Gillian, "hold a bag open beside this drawer. I'm making an executive decision. All of it goes, except the change."

"But is it art?" Dan said, looking over Alex's shoulder, with a shocked expression.

"Is what art?" Jada looked up, midway through the drawer dump.

"It's porn," Alex sighed. "All neatly filed and labeled. He was an organized guy—I'll give him that."

"So, what's the big deal?" Kali said. "If It's porn, just toss it. No one expected him to be a saint. Leighton doesn't need to know."

"The porn happens to be labeled by client name."

"Those are porn pictures of our *clients?*" Jada bounded out from behind the desk, tripping over an empty box in her haste. "Let me see that." She grabbed the file from Alex. "This is that bank president! What's his name?"

"Conrad," Alex said. "John David Conrad—Rick's biggest client. He pulled all his work out of here yesterday."

"So, who's this with him?" Jada demanded. "You can't really see her face, but it looks a lot like—"

"Angela," Alex sighed.

"Rick's assistant?" Kali was stunned.

"At least Conrad's with a human being in that one. Don't bother looking at the rest," Alex said.

"Does Angela still work for us?" Kali asked.

"Helen fired her last Friday."

"There's no way these could just be fun photos, is there?" Gillian suggested. "Maybe Rick and his clients were into some kinky stuff together, or planning a skit or something?"

"Richard Durham is notably absent from any of these photos," Alex said.

"How many of those files are there?" Jada asked.

"A dozen, maybe more."

"So, this was Rick's big business development tool," Gillian gaped. "Blackmail."

"And it looks like he kept that tool nice and sharp," Jada said, "as he always used to tell us to do. Are we liable, as partners, for Rick's extortion? For his criminal acts? Assuming he was blackmailing our clients?"

"What if the firm—the partners—derived financial benefit from his ... activities?" Kali said. "We'll have to go back through all of his accounts, see what kind of money he was taking in, compare it to the hours he clocked and return any money he didn't legitimately bill for. But even that won't tell us if he actually *worked* those hours he billed. What a nightmare! We're going to have to hire a forensic accountant."

"And we can't destroy those photos, can we?" Gillian said. "They're evidence of a crime."

"Why can't we?" Jada demanded. "Rick's dead. Who's left to prosecute?"

"You're assuming there's no backup. No negatives, copies on Rick's computer, cell phone," Alex said. "And that no one else around here was involved."

"Like who?" Kali said.

"Pick anyone," Alex shrugged.

"So, let's just burn it all, and sweep his devices," Jada said.

"You mean, spoliation of evidence?" Alex frowned.

"No, I guess we can't do that."

"I'll get Ana to look into our potential liability, do some research. One of these clients might press charges. I'm not sure what criminality might accrue to the firm."

"Wait. Hold on. We don't need outsiders involved," Kali said.

"She's not an outsider, and she's going to be my wife."

"Well, she's not your wife now," Jada snapped.

"Let's keep Ana out of this, Alex," Kali said. "None of it goes beyond this room."

"We three do represent a majority of the partnership here," Jada reminded Alex. "Get used to it."

"I'm not worried about that. The three of you couldn't agree on what color this chair is, or which way is up."

The women gasped, collectively.

"Whoa, whoa, everyone," Dan said. "Let's take the temperature in here down a few thousand degrees. This is very tough for all of us. Let's not turn on each other. It's a terrible shock. I, for one, always respected Rick."

"We all did," Kali said.

"I also owe him my life," Dan said. "If it wasn't for all that work he dumped on me at the last minute, I would have been on that plane. He had a ton of work for Ross too, but Ross said there was no way he was staying in L.A. He was all in for the tie party. Funny, I thought. Poor old Ross."

Jada looked away, just then, avoiding the eyes of all of her partners.

Chapter 21

Sandy Krupnik had been a transfer from another Los Angeles firm. None of his partners seemed to know that much about him, other than that he was a reliable and heavy biller, with a portfolio of international clients he'd brought along when he'd jumped ship and changed firms. His office was very neat, and therefore unlikely to be hiding unpleasant surprises, Kali thought, with relief.

On the other hand, there was Gillian's point of view. "Tidy offices creep me out," she said, as the five partners clustered in Sandy's doorway. "It looks like he knew he was never coming back."

"It always looked like this in here," Jada said, impatiently pushing past her. "Come on. This'll take five minutes, tops. Look at his books. They're alphabetically arranged by title. And look over here. He's even labeled one shelf as his personal library."

"That makes our job easy," Kali said. "Who can get weepy when there's no sign of a personality?"

"Sandy had a great personality," Dan said, defensively. "He was a super nice guy."

"I didn't mean it like that," Kali said.

"Okay," Dan smiled. "I get where you are coming from. It's the stress. It's hitting all of us, especially now." He began his cardboard box construction, his tape gun and Sharpie squealing in the room that was silent, but for the sound of the partners flipping through and piling up Sandy's many books.

"A lot of these are in foreign languages," Gillian said. "Where was Sandy was from originally?"

"Croatia," Alex said. "Or Serbia."

"Aren't they the same thing?" Jada asked.

"No, Jada," Alex sighed. "They're not."

"I get all those countries confused too," Kali said, in Jada's defense. "Slovenia, Slovakia…"

"That just shows your gigantic ignorance, doesn't it?" Alex said.

Kali didn't answer. What was up with him? He'd always been a bully but lately had become an obnoxious one as well. "So, how are the wedding plans coming along, Alex?" she asked, as she placed a bunch of hardcover books in the box marked 'Sandy-Personal.'

"Good, all good," Alex said. "Ana's really something. She was so funny last night." He chuckled to himself. "An amazing woman."

"Can she put her legs up behind her head?" Gillian asked.

The others looked at her, shocked.

"What?" Gillian said. "I was just curious about what's so fun about her."

"I'm not going to answer such an offensive question," Alex said.

"Desk keys please?" Jada said, eager to change the subject to anything else, even a dead lawyer's files.

Alex tossed her the keys and she pulled open the first of the drawers. "Lots of personal files, as expected." She started flipping through the many file folders. "Insurance stuff, paperwork on his car, junk from the State Bar.… Where was it that Sandy got his Bar originally?"

"Delaware," Alex said.

"I thought it was Minnesota," Kali said. "But his California license is on the wall. We know he was licensed here, right?"

"But who frames his license?" Alex said, going over to check it out. "Sbitozan Krupnik. Weird. It's like hanging up your high-school diploma. So junior league."

"Maybe in Minnesota they do things differently," Gillian said. "Maybe they're prouder, back there, of becoming lawyers."

"It's not like he had to prove to anyone that he was a lawyer, right?" Jada said.

"Unless he wasn't," Dan said, looking nervous.

The room was silent as they considered this real but unpleasant possibility.

"Well, I doubt he counterfeited this license," Alex said. "And he would have had to pass the Bar—there's no waiving in from anywhere, not into California."

"Right," Jada agreed. "We can't get totally paranoid about everyone, just because of Rick's extra-curricular activities."

"However," Alex said, "looks like there are some other intriguing documents in here." He plopped a thick file onto the desk.

"Not—?" Kali said.

"No photos. Personal stuff though." He flipped through a stack of papers, then pulled one out. "A Notice from the District Court."

"What for?"

"Denaturalization hearing."

"Who? ICE?"

"DOJ. Alleging that he participated in persecution or genocide—"

"What?" Kali demanded, shocked.

"Or had been involved with the Nazi party, the Communist party, or a terrorist organization." Alex looked up from the document. "He had thirty days to respond, which deadline passed last week."

"Wait, come on, that's ridiculous. Sandy was too young to have been a Nazi," Kali protested. "Come on."

"Terrorist organization is pretty broad. No one is saying he was a Nazi."

"Shabby old Sandy, with the white socks and sandals?" Jada said.

"Maybe Natalie was going to be deported too," Gillian said. "Maybe that's why nobody ever sees her anywhere."

"Natalie's all American," Dan said. "I was over at their place once. She's from Chicago."

"Maybe it was a green card marriage," Gillian said. "Maybe that's why nobody ever sees her anywhere. She doesn't have some ailment or disease—it's a phony marriage. He paid her to get married and they don't even live together. That's why the memorial service was the first time anybody's seen her in like a year. Makes sense, right?" She looked around at her four partners.

"Hey, what happened to the presumption of innocence?" Jada said. "We're all presuming Sandy guilty—and now his wife too. As a person of color, I'm sensitive to that bullshit."

"She's right," Kali said.

"Okay," Dan sighed. "I'll put a call in to the DOJ on Monday, let them know he's passed away, if they don't know already. Let's get on with Pete's office and then we can all get out of here. Peter, God love him, was an unmade bed. If anyone's got a roach motel, better bring it along."

"Fishing lures, fishing flies, books on fishing. A rubber salmon." Kali plopped the fish down on the ink-stained and much-scribbled-upon blotter of Pete Johnson's desk.

"That's a Kokanee," said Dan, "that salmon there."

"Whatever," Jada sighed.

"Wonder where he got it. Maybe up in Canada." Dan was examining the fish. "Pete was a great fisherman. He won a Big Mouth Bass tournament last year."

"And here's the prize to prove it." Gillian was lugging a large trophy of a jumping fish, thickly covered with dust, from Pete's equally dusty bookcase. "There's more fishing trophies at the back there."

"So, where does all this fish stuff go?" Kali asked.

"Goodwill," Alex said. "Unless any of you likes to fish, in which case, you could buy this junk from the firm."

"Is his mom still alive?" Kali asked. "Any relatives that we know of?"

"His mom has passed but I'll talk to Helen, see if she knows," Dan said.

"Or maybe he has a fishing buddy that would want all this stuff." Kali took down some books from Pete's shelves. "Bass Myths Exploded," she read. "The Scream of The Reel."

"And look here, behind his door," Gillian said. "There's about a dozen rods, rubber boots, hats, tackle boxes, some kind of net. The cleaners must have *hated* doing this office."

"I wouldn't mind first dibs on this baby." Dan was casting an imaginary fly with a wooden rod. "It might be a Pinky Gillum."

"If it is, you're not getting it," Alexander said.

"This lure could be worth a bundle too."

"Ugh," Jada said. "Somebody swat that thing."

"It could be a genuine Bumble Puppy trout fly, hand-tied by Theodore Gordon," Dan said, still admiring it. "If it is, it's worth about a grand."

"Did I ever tell you how much I *love* feathered buggy things?" Jada ran over to look.

"How do you know so much about fishing, Dan?" Gillian was looking through a tackle box that she thought might be perfect for storing writing paper, pens, and inks.

"We had lunch together a lot. He used to drool over catalogs of rare and unusual rods and lures. I was going to go out fishing with him one day, up to some lake he liked."

"We need to call in some fish gear appraisers," Kali said, "assuming there is such a thing."

"I'll find out," said Dan. "I've got to know if I'm right about the Bumble Puppy."

"I'm going to start on the desk, so we can all get out of here sometime today," Jada said. "Keys, please."

"Looks like Pete was a closet snacker." Dan was peering into Pete's credenza. "There's bags of cookies in here … chips, nachos …"

"Let's hope there's no bugs. Throw it all out." Kali passed him a trash bag.

For a few moments the room was silent, but for the sounds of fishing gear being moved around and the rustle of snack bags and cookies being tossed into the trash.

"Oh my God!" Jada slammed shut the desk drawer. "It's alive!"

"What?"

"Where?"

"In there! I can't look. It's some hideous rodent!"

"Stand back," Alex warned.

Dan grabbed a fishing net and approached the desk. "Careful. It might be rabid."

Cautiously, Alex pulled open the drawer. No one moved. He opened the drawer wider. "It's not alive," he said, finally. "Everybody relax."

"So? What is it?" Jada demanded.

Alex pulled a floppy mass of brown curls from the drawer and tossed it onto the desk. "A wig," he said.

"Well, why would Pete keep a wig in his desk?" Gillian said. "I mean, he had enough hair."

It's a *female* wig. And digging a little deeper into this drawer we find …

a pair of heels. Size 10 would be my guess." Alex placed a pair of high-heeled pumps on the desk. "There's some kind of slinky dress in here too, but I'm not touching it."

The room was silent of a few moments as all of the partners contemplated the secret life of Peter Johnson.

"No wonder he never got married," Jada finally said.

"Poor old Pete." Dan shook his head. "Hiding behind the macho veneer of a champion sports fisherman."

"Maybe he used the wig to lure Muskies," Gillian mused.

"So what about the dress and the heels?" Kali said.

"His mom's? Maybe after she died, he couldn't bear to part with any of her stuff," Gillian said.

"How can you joke about this?" Jada moaned. "We've been partners with a blackmailer, a Nazi and a cross-dresser! Is no one in this firm *normal?*"

"I like to think I am," Alex said drily. "As is my wife-to-be."

"We don't know that Pete was a cross-dresser or a transvestite," Gillian argued. "He could have been a female impersonator. For fun, you know, doing drag shows or whatever."

"What's the difference?" Jada demanded. "He dressed up in women's clothes, a wig, and high heels! God knows where he went in that getup, or who might have seen him."

"They were all probably in women's clothing too. It's really not that big of a deal anymore," Gillian said.

"It happens," Alex shrugged. "There were a couple of Federal Court judges last year, caught on video. Nobody cared that much, except for their wives." He was stacking cartons of books on top of each other. "Personally, I can leave forever unanswered the question of Peter's sexual orientation. We'll get the cleaners to dump whatever else is in that drawer. It can all go to Goodwill. Unless one of you ladies wants it?"

"Or you do," Kali snapped.

"Or your *fiancée* does," Jada added.

"Wouldn't fit her. She's a size four. Except in the chest, where she's a six."

"Good to know, Kali," Jada said, "for your lingerie tea, right?"

"A thirty-four C. She told me already," Kali said.

"That's my girl," Alex smiled, proudly.

"Hey Alex," Gillian said, "how's that accidental death payment coming along? The eight million? That would help with all of this, wouldn't it?"

"We're screwed," Alex said. "But if those four guys knew about the exclusion and went off in that plane anyway, I'd kill them again. If just one of those guys had enough sense of responsibility to have stayed off that plane..."

"Well, one of them didn't," Jada snapped, "so why don't we get out of here and get on with our lives and stop talking about this bullshit?" She wouldn't have to kill herself, she thought. Alexander might well save her the trouble.

Chapter 22

"At least we can count on this office not having any skeletons in its closet," Dan said, opening the door to Ross Owen's office. "He was such a regular guy."

A half hour later, everyone sighed with relief as the last of his drawers was opened and searched. Jada was the most relieved, having spent the time dreading they might find something to incriminate her—like, maybe a pair of her silk panties (used) in one of Ross's drawers. She could deny ownership, of course, but what if they found something that pointed incontrovertibly to her? Or they had some DNA test done for some creepy voyeuristic reason? Sure, everybody seemed to know about her affair with Ross (a shock, actually, though she should have guessed, since Kali and Gillian were both such horrible gossips) but they weren't entitled to all the humiliating details!

"He sure took enough pictures of his kids," Dan said, looking sad as he sorted through the junk in one of the bottom drawers.

"How many did he have again?" Alex asked. "Six?"

"Five," Jada answered, a little too quickly. Her partners exchanged looks. "At least, as I recall..." she added, vaguely.

"Wow, here's a whole series of the kids at all different ages." Dan pulled a stack of photos out from the rest of the things and piled them neatly on the desk. Some were framed, others were in pocket-sized albums or photo folds. "Wonder why he didn't just keep them on his phone like most people do. Anyway, I guess we box them up, send them over to Marcia. There's not much else in here. Some popsicle-stick art...a couple of yogurt containers with glitter and stones all over them."

"Oh, how sad," Gillian said. "I remember Isadora's stones and glitter phase."

"You mean last week?" Jada said.

"You shut up." Gillian snapped. "You're pissed because you'll never have a child, you're so selfish."

"Sorry," Jada said, in a rare moment of contrition. And she really was sorry.

"He was a real family man," Dan said. "Even with all the traveling he did." He took a handkerchief from his pocket, shook it out, and blew his nose. "Those poor little fatherless kids."

"And look at these sweet lumpy clay things they made," Gillian wailed. "Oh my God." She picked up the children's art and gently placed them into an empty box. "For sure Marcia will want these treasures. We should wrap everything up in newspaper, so nothing gets broken."

The mail room can do it Monday," Alex said. "I'm not spending my weekend gift-wrapping kiddie art. Let's get going with the rest." He looked at his watch. "If we get moving, I can catch the last few innings of the ball game.

"I'm seeing Marcia for lunch tomorrow," Kali said.

"Really?" Alex said. "What about?"

"No idea. She wants to talk."

"Well, be careful. You don't want to say anything that might put us straight into a lawsuit."

"She likely just wants to talk, a shoulder to cry on."

"She may be wearing a wire."

"A wire? She's a grieving woman who just lost her husband and the father of her five kids. Besides, we have nothing to hide with Ross, do we?"

"Just saying, Kali. Be smart."

"I always am, Alex."

"O-kay, right! Dan said. "Looks like a wrap here. A few little surprises, but nothing we can't handle if we hang tough, keep a tight lip and contact our insurers asap. Why don't we all just head for the nearest bar? Drown our sorrows? I know a super watering hole we can walk to from here."

"No, Ana's waiting from me," Alex said. "Sorry my friend."

"I don't have a sitter," Kali said. "Emilie's off today and Matt's home with the kids."

"I have a hot date," Jada lied.

"Isadora shouldn't be alone," Gillian said, "she's taking this whole thing pretty hard."

A moment later, Alexander pulled the door closed and locked it. No one felt like talking anymore. Silently, the partners retrieved bags, cell phones and jackets from their offices and left the building, each heading off, immersed in his or her own gloomy thoughts, in their separate directions.

Chapter 23

T HE NEXT DAY, INSIDE FRESH GREENS—A SMALL RESTAURANT ON the Promenade—Kali scanned the crowds of lunching office workers, trying to spot Marcia. Alicia had arranged for them to meet there at noon. Marcia said she didn't like fancy restaurants and was only interested in a quick bite. A relaxed atmosphere, and somewhere dark and secluded would have been Kali's choice, particularly when unpalatable matters (Jada?) might be on the table for discussion.

"You Kali Miller?" A very large woman in a bright flowing dress tapped her on the arm.

"Hi. Um, do I know you? I'm sorry—"

"Just tell Kali to look for the fat lady, I should have said," she laughed. You could hardly miss me, right? Everyone around here is so *skinny*. Though how's anyone supposed to stay thin, working in a donut shop her entire life?"

"You're not . . . fat," Kali faltered, still wondering who she was talking to.

"I'm your lunch date, Grace Owen! And I'm sorry I'm late. I got totally lost, then so frustrated trying to find parking around here."

Kali's eyebrows went up. "You're Grace Owen?"

"*Mrs.* Grace Owen. That's how widows are supposed to call themselves. You'd know that, being a lawyer."

"Let's grab a table," Kali said, now totally confused. After they had settled into the molded plastic chairs at a small table near the back, Kali leaned over to her lunch date. "You were Ross's wife?" she asked, her voice low.

"Grace Owen. I just told you. Ross's wife. Widow now."

"Oh my gosh," Kali said. "Uh, do you know about Marcia?"

"Do I know about her? I know so much about her I could puke."

"I don't mean to pry or suggest anything, well, untoward."

"What's that supposed to mean?"

"Just, please don't be offended."

"You can't offend me. I'm easy-going, ask anyone." Grace took off her dirty glasses and wiped them with a fold of her dress.

"Were you and Ross ... really married?"

"Ring, license, the works. What kind of girl do you think I am?"

"I didn't—I wasn't—"

"That question was too easy. Ask me something else."

"Why don't we get some lunch? On the firm, of course."

"Sounds good to me!"

Kali picked up her menu and pretended to be absorbed by what was printed on it, though she felt on very unsteady ground, not sure what line of questioning to pursue, if any.

"There's nothing like this place back in Riverside where I live," Grace said. "Ross has a real estate developer client out our way. That's how I met him. He stopped in for a half-dozen Krispy Kremes one day, and the rest is history, right? He loved his Krispy Kremes. And, he loved me too, Mrs. Miller." She jambed her glasses on her face and picked up her menu.

"Of course he did," Kali said. "Have anything you want. Please. A drink maybe?"

"I don't drink—I'm a recovering alcoholic. I'll have whatever you're going to have to eat. All this stuff looks pretty weird. Ancient grains?" She made a face. "Who wants to eat ancient grains? They'd be moldy, right?"

"The Caesar salad is good," Kali said. "Why don't I order a couple of those?"

"Sure, whatever. And a Coke." Grace closed her menu, and Kali waved over a waiter and ordered.

"We knew Ross had another family back here in L.A.," Grace confided after the waiter had gone, "and we knew he couldn't always be with us. But we were fine with sharing. It seemed selfish for one family to claim him all to themselves. He was such a great guy and a great dad. I don't think he meant to do anything wrong by having two families. I think he just loved kids."

And wives, Kali thought. *And mistresses.* "So," she nodded, "you had children with Ross?"

"Four. And I have two from my first marriage. They thought Ross was their dad—I never bothered to tell them different. I know kids are supposed to be told the truth, but why screw up their little world? It'll get screwed up soon enough anyway. So, you got kids, Mrs. Miller?"

"You can call me Kali."

"Great, Kali. I bet we're going to be good friends," Grace smiled.

"I have two children, Grace. A five-year-old and a three-year-old."

"Ooh, you must be busy. Those are active ages."

"Tell me about it."

"So, who looks after them when you're at work?"

"We have a—nanny."

"That's the way it is now, I guess, with you working women. Nannies and what-not."

"But you work, right? You just said so."

"In a Krispy Kreme, three shifts a week. My mom takes the kids those nights. I only do it because I need the money, not because I like it. And I sure don't need the free donuts. I mean, look at me, right?"

Fortunately, the waiter arrived with their salads before Kali could answer. Grace frowned at hers and immediately started picking out the anchovies. "Who puts smelly *fish* on a salad?" she grumbled.

"So, how many years have you and Ross been together?" Kali asked.

"Twelve, this October. I'll show you some pictures." Grace hoisted her handbag onto her lap. It was a crazy quilt patched thing, made from scraps of leather, crudely zig-zag-stitched together. She dug through it until she found an envelope that she handed over to Kali, before she turned back to her salad. "That's Brad, Jake, Melissa and little Gracie. All Ross's."

Kali looked through the photographs, an agreeable, interested expression on her face, despite her growing alarm. There was Ross, holding a baby up to the camera; Ross steadying a teetering little boy on a bicycle; Ross holding a beer and laughing, feet up on a lawn chair, two little kids on his lap.

Grace dug her cell out of her bag and held out a photo to Kali. "Here's Libby and that one's Carmella." Carmella looks like Ross, don't you think?"

"Yes," Kali nodded. "She sure does."

"Funny, right? 'Cause she's not his. These two little monkeys are from my first marriage. They're almost teenagers now." She sighed. "Where does the time go?"

As Kali continued looking at the photos, she had a flashback to the day before. Ross's open drawer, then Dan's question about how many children Ross had, and his comment about the photos and children's art as he piled everything onto the desk. All of it had then been boxed up by the mailroom and was on its way to . . .

"Uh, Grace? Did Marcia know about you and your children?"

"Good question. Ross kept saying he was going to have this big talk with her, but I don't think he ever got around to it. I've been waiting for that big talk for twelve years."

"I have to make a call. Would you excuse me for one minute? It's kind of private."

"Oh, sure, I know, you must be so busy." Grace waved her fork at Kali. "I've got all the time in the world. I never have any important calls to make—or anywhere to go, really, after this trip here today."

Kali stood up, wondering where she could make a quick private call. The Ladies room? No, Grace could walk in anytime. Better to go outside, where her conversation would be partly concealed by street noise. "I'll just be two seconds. It's important. I'm really sorry." Kali hurried out of the restaurant, fumbling in her bag for her cell phone.

Chapter 24

"Gillian!" Kali said as soon as soon as she picked up. "I'm so glad I got you!"

"Aren't you having lunch with Marcia?"

"Yes—no—it's a long story. Look, I need you to go to the mailroom and get that box that was going out to her today. I'll wait."

"What's so important?"

"Just go get it. Please."

"You not going to say why?"

Kali dropped her voice. "I'm having lunch with her now."

"I know. So, what? You want to give it to her? You want me to lug that box downstairs?"

"Not Marcia. *Grace* Owen!"

"Mother? Sister?"

"His *other wife!*"

There was a silence. "Wow. That's intense."

"And he had *four children* with her."

"Ross had *nine kids?*"

"And two teenagers who *think* he was their father!"

"Ross had *eleven* kids?"

"That we know of. So far."

"And all those cute kiddie pictures and artwork are being sent out to—"

"Go to the mailroom. Run!"

Through the restaurant window, Kali could see Grace pick listlessly at the salad on her plate. Then she sat back and gazed around, sipping her Coke, not seeming very comfortable.

"Too late," Gillian said, breathlessly, back on the phone. "The box went out rush FedEx, first thing."

"Can we get it back?"

"It was probably delivered already. Poor Marcia."

"Poor Grace."

"Maybe Marcia won't bother opening it—just stick it in the attic or the garage or someplace. Too emotional to deal with. That's what I did after Larry died."

"Could you put a trace on it anyway? Maybe Marcia wasn't home when it got there—and she would have had to sign for it, right?"

"I think so."

"If we're lucky, it's on its way back here. Or to some Fed Ex storage place."

"I'm on it."

"Oh, and maybe don't mention any of this to Jada, for now. It wouldn't help."

"As if."

"Well now!" Grace said as Kali slid into her chair a moment later. "I hope whatever it was got all sorted out."

"I hope so too, but I somehow doubt it." Kali looked uneasily at her.

"That's the business world for you. It's very stressful, isn't it? But donut shops have tough moments too. Everything does. Work, husbands, kids."

"That's for sure."

"Well look, I don't want to waste much more of your valuable time, so I better get to the point."

"Sure," Kali smiled awkwardly, afraid of what might be coming next.

"I wanted to meet someone else from Ross's—my husband's—firm. Let you all know that hey, here I am, right out in Riverside, Grace Owen. In the Krispy Kreme. Come out and see me sometime." She smiled at Kali from behind her dirty glasses. "I'm thankful to you for meeting me, and to the Lord for helping me find my way here. It was Him who told me to ask for your help."

"Oh, well, I don't know how much help I've been," Kali said uneasily. "Maybe just talking to someone about everything, after all these years, finally being able to tell your story. It just shows how poorly we all really know one another. I mean, here I was a partner with Ross for years, and I had no idea, about anything really, about his personal life. But you feel better now, don't you? After talking about it?"

"A bit, I guess." Grace twisted her mouth to one side. "But there was one thing I wanted to ask you, so I better just spit it out." She leaned forward, conspiratorially, across the table. "Well," she began, her voice low, "now that Ross is gone, I've been thinking I need a lawyer. To handle things . . . the estate, right? Isn't that what it's called?"

"Yes, the estate." Kali nodded and took a sip of water.

"I don't want to make trouble, you know, but I do want my fair share. For the kids' sake, right? And then Marcia, I guess. I'm going need someone to handle Marcia."

"What do you mean handle her?"

"Well, at first I was really upset by the accident. Oh, what a dumb thing to say! I was a total mess! My Ross, somewhere at the bottom of the ocean! And then having to tell all the kids."

"I can't imagine." Kali put her hand on Grace's, and squeezed it, supportively.

"But then I got mad." Grace pulled her hand back. "How would *you* like to be part of the *other* family? The *other* wife? Not even invited to that big downtown service you guys had for Ross?"

"It was for all four lawyers, Grace. And it was mostly just other lawyers who went. And business types. And we didn't know about you, none of us did."

"Was Marcia there?"

Kali nodded.

"Audrey too?"

"Oh, yes," Kali sighed.

"Marca arranged the actual funeral for Ross. 'A small private affair' it said in the paper. But I didn't get to go to that either. She's the status wife, the one everybody feels so sorry for now." Grace grabbed a napkin and dabbed her eyes with it. "The *other* family never counts for squat. It's Marcia and *her* kids who get all the attention. It's been like that from day one."

"Grace, be fair. We didn't know about you. No one did." What if Grace and her children *had* shown up at the memorial service? It had been enough of a debacle as it was. Then Kali's mind fast-forwarded to Marcia, opening the door to the Fed Ex guy, signing for the box, taking it into her kitchen, slicing through the packing tape . . . and surprise!

"That's another thing the status family gets," Grace said, "protection from the truth. It was all very well for me to know every detail about Marcia and little Obie and the rest of them. Nothing against the kids— they're innocents and Jesus loves them like he does all children. I'm just saying, in the eyes of the world, us—me and my kids—way out in Riverside? A bunch of white trash nobodies."

"Oh no! Don't say that. I'm sure you weren't nobodies to Ross. I'm sure he showed your kids' pictures around to everyone. I'm sure he loved you, and all his kids." Kali winced inwardly, imaging how Grace would feel if she found out about Jada, on top of all this.

"Well, I'm not so sure anymore, about anything."

"It wasn't easy for Marcia, the service. It was awful, really. You're lucky you weren't there."

"Oh, you must mean Audrey? Yes, I know all about that Audrey. That's the one saving grace with being the hidden wife. I never had to be nice to Ross's mother, and neither did my kids."

"There! You see?" Kali beamed at her. "That's a big plus right there."

"They never got Christmas or birthday presents either. Never talked about Grandma and Grandpa, or even met them. They've only got my mom." She blinked, rapidly. "Oh, sure, it was a real bonus, never meeting Audrey and Derek. What do they call it? The booby-prize? With me as the prize booby!" Through teary eyes and smeary glasses, she gave Kali the look Kali knew she deserved.

"Did Ross have any other, uh, any other entanglements?" Kali asked, gently. "That you know of?" She had to know if Jada was on Grace's radar.

"Is that what we are? An entanglement? Is that some legal term?" Grace zipped her crazy quilt bag shut. "Fat Grace and her brood from the boonies. You probably wonder what Ross saw in me."

"I don't wonder that at all. You seem like a wonderful warm person. And what was between you is none of my business anyway."

"Well, there weren't any other *entanglements*, as you put it. That I know of."

Except for Jada, Kali thought. How had Ross found the time and energy for three strong-willed women and eleven children? No wonder he'd always looked so wasted. No wonder he was so skinny. He was running for his life most of the time!

"So," Grace cocked her head. "Will you take my case, Kali? Will you be my lawyer?"

Kali should have anticipated the question, but she was caught off guard. "I don't do estates work," she said, feebly, "or family law." How ironic, she thought, that Jada was the only lawyer and Biltmore, Durham & Spears who could have helped Grace. "And, ethically, I, well, I couldn't represent you. Ross was my partner. And he was, well, kind of a bad guy, as we now know. I don't mean bad, like evil."

Grace's face had settled into a look of angry determination. All those years of feeling shame and being hidden away, with just her mother for emotional support, except for the odd time that Ross swung by. "It would be a conflict of interest for me to act for you," Kali added. How despicable she was, she thought, doling out this preachy, insensitive pronouncement, hiding behind the law.

"Which one is the illegal one? That's what I want to know. My marriage to Ross? Or Marcia's?"

"I'm not sure, Grace. Or that I should say anything about it, really." Kali looked at her unhappily. *Sure, hide behind a conflict of interest, you wimp!*

"Which one is legal? I have a right to know."

"Well, uh, speaking in generalities, of course, since I really can't advise you, the first marriage would be the valid one, in law. But that doesn't mean you wouldn't have any rights, as the mother of Ross's children, and maybe in respect of the two girls from your first marriage, since they thought of Ross as their father."

Grace nodded, visibly perking up.

"You yourself may be entitled to something, Grace. You would have all the rights of a common-law spouse, assuming you were with him for seven years." Kali was in it now, she thought.

"Twelve. A lot more than seven. And who says I came second?"

"Pardon?"

"What makes you think I'm the common law wife? How do you know my marriage to Ross was the second one? And that is wasn't legal?" Behind her glasses, Grace's eyes had become sharp.

"I don't know that," Kali said, "I have no idea when Ross and Marcia were married, or you and Ross."

"So, it will be pretty interesting to find out, won't it? For inheritance purposes and all that?"

"Yes," Kali said, "I suppose so."

"Has anyone found a will?"

"Not that I've heard."

"Didn't think so." Grace settled back in her chair, triumph on her face. "Ross wasn't that organized."

Around them, the hum of voices had all but disappeared and most of the tables had been cleared, but for some plastic trays and a litter of paper cups and straws. It was two o'clock. "Are you going to eat the rest of your salad?" Grace asked. "'Cause if you're not, I'll take it home for the dog."

Chapter 25

"Is she gone?" Jada stuck her head around Kali's office door. "Coast clear?"

"She's gone," Kali said. "And she never came up here anyway."

"You mean I hid under my desk for nothing?" Looking relieved, Jada entered Kali's office and perched on the edge of her desk. She was in black leather: pants and a form-fitting jacket over a dazzling white shirt. "What are you doing here?" she said to Gillian, suddenly noticing she was there. "Haven't you got some widget to work on? I need to talk to Kali, confidentially, about her meeting with Marcia."

"Too bad she didn't see Marcia." Gillian said. "You're a hard person to feel sorry for, you know that, Jada? But I do. Almost."

Jada adjusted herself on Kali's desk and crossed her legs, with a creak of expensive leather. "You feeling sorry for me is not a good sign. What's going on?"

"Tell her," Gillian said to Kali.

"Well, Jada," Kali began, marveling at the number of 'careful' conversations she was having that day, "you were not the only woman in Ross's life. I mean, not the only other woman."

"No shit?" Jada examined her fingernails. "So, who else? You?"

"Of course not."

"Grace Owen." Gillian jumped it. "Ross had two wives. That we know of. So far."

Jada looked unfazed. "But I was still the only other woman. There was a wife, and another wife. But I was the only *other woman*, right?"

"As far as we know," Kali said.

"I can live with that."

"And his other family has *six kids*," Gillian added, "four of them Ross's."

Jada nodded, digesting the news. "Busy guy."

"Is that all you're going to say?" Kali asked. "You don't want any details?"

"I don't know," Jada shrugged. "What does she look like? The other wife? Better looking than me?"

"No."

"White?"

"Yes."

"But not better looking?"

"I said no."

"So she's a dog? Makes pit stops at every hydrant?"

"Would you feel better or worse if she was?"

"Not sure yet. Need to cogitate on that."

"Well, she's pretty, actually, in a girl-next-door kind of way. But, with all those kids, and working in a Krispy Kreme, like she does—"

"She works in a Krispy Kreme?"

"In Riverside."

"Yeah, Ross had a big client out that way."

"I guess that's how he met Grace," Kali said.

"Donuts," Jada said. "Wow."

"You'll probably never have to meet her," Kali said. "She wants a lawyer and I told her the firm can't represent her since Ross was our partner, not to mention a bigamist."

"I'm just wondering about one thing," Jada said, "in terms of guilt, assuming I have any. Does this Grace Owen compound my guilt? Or make it less?"

"Makes it less," Kali said.

"Definitely." Gillian nodded. "Ross was mentally ill."

"You were a pawn in his very sick game," Kali said.

"You're right. You know, I'm feeling better now, knowing about Grace. This is good. Good for me. I didn't take Ross away from his wife and kids because he already had another wife and kids doing that."

"Right," Kali said.

"And if he didn't want to go to Catalina, he could have gone to Riverside. Should have, in fact, since he had all those kids—and not been on my ass to stay holed up in my condo all weekend."

"He didn't want to go to Catalina?" Gillian asked. "First I'm hearing this."

"Oh, I don't know. I didn't say that. I couldn't read his damn mind. Well, I got to go, Girls." She creaked to a standing position. "Time is money. Thanks for the intel on Grace. It's been a slice."

"Ross didn't want to go to Catalina," Gillian repeated after Jada had gone. "He wanted to stay here. She basically *pushed him* onto that plane."

"Eight million dollars," Kali moaned, putting her head down on her desk.

Chapter 26

Like her mother, Marina, Kali was missing the 'good hostess' gene. She and Matt rarely entertained, preferring to take people out rather than have them at home, especially with the kids being as young as they were, with early bedtimes. Now, a month before the tea, the details of it were making Kali crazy. Plus, she was totally drained by the end of every stressful day during which she and her partners beat the bushes for work and struggled to keep the firm afloat.

After picking up the invitations from a trendy stationery store, Kali stopped in at the party rental place, to see what they had in the 'afternoon tea' department.

'Rent? Are you kidding?' Marina had said, during their last phone conversation. 'Who rents that shit? We've got a garage full of that crap that I never use. I can bring anything you need.'

'I don't want you and Dad having to clean all that stuff and lug it over here.'

'We won't be lugging, Kali. We have a car.'

Kali had hoped to keep her mother's involvement in the tea to a minimum. Not only was Marina an old hippie who couldn't possibly get into the idea of a tea party, she was cheap. Kali could hear it already: *'These lemons aren't fresh—how much did you pay for them? Ninety-nine cents? Each!? In California? Are they gold-plated?'*

'There some things I'll have to rent,' Kali had said. 'Like a samovar.'

'Samovar? Are we in Czarist Russia all of a sudden?'

'Lemon forks, sugar tongs. Bun warmers.'

'I have all that from your grandmothers—on both sides.'

'I was thinking of hiring a caterer.'

'For a fucking tea party?'

'There are ten women coming, maybe more.'

'Tea's a cup, a bag, and hot water. Jesus, Kali. Let's get real.'

'It has to go off without any major embarrassments.' Kali could hear her mother drag on a cigarette, or, more likely, a joint.

'I hear you." Marina held her breath, then exhaled. "I guess an underwear party's embarrassing enough as it is, right?'

Harry and Molly were still at school when Kali got home, and Emilie was on her way to get them. Grateful for a few minutes to herself, Kali dumped her shopping bags on the stairs, grabbed the mail and collapsed with it onto the living-room sofa.

Among the flyers, fast-food coupons and bills was the latest *Katherine's Mail Order* catalog. *Katherine's* advertised the sort of undergarments that women got as gifts from men but rarely appreciated, being then obliged to wear the itchy, lace-encrusted synthetic stuff to bed. It should be called *male* order, as Jada once commented.

But could there be something in *Katherine's* that Ana would like?

The prices were reasonable. Could Kali justify buying something for another woman that she would never wear herself? The answer occurred to her with surprising speed. Why the hell not?

At the back of the catalog was a section called *Kate's Kosy Kountry*: all fly-fishing motifs, flannel robes and bed socks. She flipped through the section, wondering if Ana would appreciate something comfortable (read: *unsexy*) to curl up in with Alexander? Maybe when they went on some ski vacation?

Kali kept flipping, then stopped at a page where a model posed before a roaring hearth, one foot up on a horsehair settee. The garment she had on was described as a 'romantic nightdress.' It had lace-trimmed patch pockets, a deep ruffled hem and it was made from pure white double-brushed flannel. Ana was sure to love it, and Alex even more! With an evil chuckle, Kali went online and placed the order.

Pleased with her efficiency, she flopped back onto the sofa to look through *The Delights of Tea*—the book that had arrived the day before from Amazon. Kali was a born and bred researcher who still preferred a printed book to online research. This one had gorgeous photos, she saw with pleasure, as she opened it to the chapter headed 'Proper Settings.'

'As long as the setting is gracious and elegant,' she read, *'the tea party can take place anywhere you wish.'* Kali looked over the room with freshly critical tea-hostess eyes, realizing how thrown-together it looked. No designer had had a hand in it. That much was obvious to Kali, and certainly would be to Leighton Durham, and everyone else.

All those decorative objects she'd placed here and there, that were meant to emulate cherished gifts from dear friends, suddenly looked like what they were: dusty clutter. Kali had no dear cherished friends, she realized, a gust of self-pity blowing over her. And those yards of gold damask (not enough for curtains) that she'd picked up on sale and looped over a curtain rod—just looked like a messy mistake. *We can't really afford this house* was the true message conveyed by the Millers' living room décor.

She closed *The Delights of Tea* and studied the cover. A silver tea service and a huge bouquet of flowers were displayed on an antique tea trolley and framed by Liberty print curtains with pleated headings and brass tie-backs. Well, she would have to make do with what she had. A month was not enough time to totally redecorate.

And the gracious setting was the least of her problems. The much bigger headache, that she'd been trying to avoid since the memorial service, was the guest list. Now that she'd bought the expensive invitations and a calligraphy pen, she'd have to deal with it. The invites had to be mailed out that week.

Topping the guest list was Marina. Matt's mother, Beth, lived on the east coast and would never waste the time and money to make a cross-country trip for a tea party, which was good, since she and Marina did not get along, to put it mildly. Then there was Gillian and Jada—Kali's co-conspirators—though they remained adamant that the tea was a problem Kali had brought on herself and so did not feel obliged to help.

Next, was Ana, of course, an unknown quantity except for Kali's concern that she could be unpredictable and potentially explosive. Then there was Gillian's daughter, Isadora, who would be sure to add a touch of the macabre. Gillian had asked if she could bring her, and Kali had felt so badly after that awful scene in the church, she'd agreed. She doubted Isadora would show up, since tea with her mother and her mother's law partners couldn't have much appeal to her. Kali put a mental question mark beside Isadora's name and continued with the list, adding Leighton Durham, then Natalie Krupnik. She and Sandy had been separated for the past year—if they were ever really legally married at all—and Natalie could just decline the invitation if attending would make her uncomfortable, Kali decided.

She also had to invite Helen Sharpe, who liked to be involved in everything that went on in the firm. Politically, inviting Helen was a necessity—she was practically holding the firm together now—and offending her by leaving her out would be a mistake. But it was rumored that Helen had had a long-standing affair with Rick, that Leighton knew or suspected, and that the two women hated each other. What fun to throw them together, Kali thought: the social quagmire of tea. She should write a book herself, at the end of it all. Assuming she survived.

The next nagging question was what to do about the Owen women. Marcia was on the list, of course, and no one at the firm had heard anything further from Grace, though Marcia was sure to know about Ross's other family by now. The box of children's photos and artwork had been delivered right on schedule, and Marcia had been home to sign for it. Kali thought, uneasily, about Grace's sad, puffy face and her comment about being a nobody. But it would be deplorably bad form for Kali to invite her, with Marcia coming. Cruel and unusual punishment for both of them. Wouldn't it?

Then, there was Audrey Owen. She'd made a big fuss over Alex after the memorial service, embracing him and sobbing that he was like a son to her and that Ross had talked so much about him and admired him so much. She'd congratulated Alex, over and over, about his engagement, her eyes full of tears. It seemed Audrey knew Alex (or thought she knew him) well enough to be offended if she were not invited to the tea. Plus, she was English—and tea was a big deal for the English. Audrey might even be of some help with all of it, assuming she would not be too critical.

Her cell phone buzzed just then. It was Gillian. Isadora wanted to bring a friend to the tea—was that okay? "You remember what it's like to be a teenager," she said, "they can't even go to the bathroom without taking a friend."

Kali was pretty sure that Isadora was no longer a teenager, though she was certainly as immature as any. "Okay," she said, "but just tell them, please, no jeans." She was going to add "or any outlandish outfits" before she realized that Gillian was sure to appear in one herself. Gillian thanked her profusely, and Kali added another person to her mental guest list, this one unknown. Feeling confused now, she grabbed a pen and a piece of paper to write all the guests down.

Herself
Marina
Ana
Jada
Gillian
Marcia
Leighton
Helen
Natalie
Audrey
Isadora
Isadora's friend?

Twelve. A satisfying, even number. Twelve was a perfect number, just one shy of unlucky thirteen, and that was good enough for Kali. Alexander's mother had already left for her winter home in Hawaii and would only be coming back for the wedding, and Ana had let Kali know that her own mother was too busy to come in all the way from Burbank.

Should she leave the guest list at a nice (manageable?) twelve, or inflate the list—and the potential for disaster—by adding the most important female clients of Biltmore, Durham & Spears? Would they like each other once they were trapped together in Kali's living room? Did they already know each other? Had they networked? Would they spend the whole time complaining about the firm's fees (for what else, really, would they have in common?) comparing notes and then deciding to dump Biltmore, Durham & Spears altogether? Would they be appalled that Ana was marrying a man twice her age? Was it even proper to ask clients to buy *underwear* for anyone? Maybe, Kali thought, she should invite them for champagne, after the gift opening was over. *The Delights of Tea* had no tips to offer on the etiquette of inviting clients to a lingerie shower for a law student about to marry a senior partner.

Chapter 27

THE NEXT DAY, KALI FOUND ANA IN THE SMALL WINDOWLESS office that was referred to in the firm as "the student ghetto": A grimy, colorless room with nothing on the walls but a spray of picture hooks and some yellow Post-it notes with scribbled messages on them. Ana was reading from a bound volume of law reports, a stack of others at her elbow. "Kali," she said without expression, pushing back her hair to look up from her reading, "what up?"

"I'm surprised to find you here with all the empty offices we've got. Can't we get you one with a window? Have you talked to Helen about it, or Alex?"

"He's kind of busy these days." Ana stuck a Post-it into her book to mark the place, then closed it. She looked tired. "You want to see me about something? I'm sure you didn't come in here to chat about my office."

"I wanted to talk a little more about your shower." Kali was amazed at how easily intimidated she was by Ana.

"What about it? I gave you a list of things I'd like."

"I was writing out the guest list, and I realized that you haven't given me the names of any friends or relatives, except for your mother, who can't come, unfortunately."

"There isn't anyone else."

"What about the associates here at the firm? Are you friends with any of them?"

"You mean the ones who quit already? Or the ones out looking for other jobs?"

Of course, they had all left, or were on their way, Kali thought, except for one or two who were sure to follow. And who could blame them? There was hardly enough work for the partners, let alone associates. "Well," she said, "there are some other women who would probably like to be invited, but it should be your call."

"Invite them all. Invite the world. I'm not having any other showers. Our wedding's going to be at the courthouse. We were planning something bigger, before the plane crash, but now we're just having Dan as the witness."

Was she disappointed? Ana's expression betrayed no emotion. "Big weddings are such a pain," Kali said. "Matt and I had a tiny wedding—and it was wonderful."

"So how do you know big weddings are a pain in the ass if you never had one?"

"My sister, Christine, had one. Super big pain." Kali nodded, feeling a little foolish. Why had she said anything at all? Ana had not asked for her opinion.

"I wish I could yak about this all day, but I've got a memo to do that should have been done yesterday. And to tell you the truth, I'm getting sick of the subject of weddings. But I don't mean to sound ungrateful, so don't think that."

"I'll use my own judgment for the guest list, then."

"I'm sure you'll do an awesome job. It's your house, your party. Do what you want."

"What do you think I should wear?" Jada asked later, as she and Kali were having lunch, "to your stupid lingerie tea? I mean, what is the appropriate outfit for your own execution? No jewelry, right? I remember Marie Antoinette taking off her necklace—or was it Anne Boleyn?—in some movie, before they chopped her head off."

"Oh, come on, Jada. What are you talking about? Marcia and Audrey?"

"Bing! You are so smart! You're totally wasted practicing law! You're a genius!"

"It won't be that bad. They don't even know about you."

"I had *dinner* with Audrey Owen, in her damned portable unit up in Simi Valley!"

"Oh, come on. Nothing awful is going to happen. Audrey's an old lady. I bet she won't even remember you. So much has happened since you went out there. I mean, when was it? Last year?"

"A month ago."

"Oh. Well, she didn't recognize you at the memorial service, did she?"

"That's only because she was so busy reaming out that rector and making a big scene about Ross not getting his full minute of fame."

"Yes, so horrible. But you're worrying too much. She's probably over blaming others for Ross and Marcia's breakup."

"Would a suit of armor be over the top?" Jada raised her eyebrows. "Or is a bulletproof vest enough? Your thoughts, as the tea hostess, and inspiration for this nightmare, are respectfully requested."

'*A Lingerie Tea.*' Kali carefully penned in the words on the inside of one of the invitations.

"What does that say?" Harry asked, climbing up onto his mother's lap.

"A lingerie tea."

"Lin-gurr-ee tea?" Harry frowned, his warm breath on Kali's shoulder. "What's a lin-gurr-ee tea?"

"It's *lingerie*," Kali explained, looking at his adorable, puzzled little face. His eyes, which had been bright blue when he was born, had turned a deep green—the color of the cats-eye marbles Kali remembered from her childhood. His hair, reddish when he was born, was now a lovely blond, with eyelashes and eyebrows to match. Harry was a classic tow-head. "Lingerie is a French word," Kali explained, "meaning ladies underwear. So, a lingerie tea is where a lady is getting married." Harry looked confused. Really, Kali thought, when you tried to explain it to a five-year-old, the absurdity of the idea became so clear. "And all the other ladies—the friends of the lady who is going to get married—have a tea party and give her surprise gifts of underwear."

"Surprise gifts of underwear?" Harry frowned. "Gifts of surprise underwear?" Then he laughed, exposing all of his dear little baby teeth.

"I'm putting out extra plates in case people lose theirs," Molly announced, coming into the kitchen and busily setting six places at the Fisher-Price play table. Kali watched with amusement, noting that her daughter was playing tea party suddenly, when she hadn't asked for her tea set in many months. "They're going to be starving if they don't get some food soon."

"Okay, Honey. I'll cut up some granola bars. Pass me one of those plates."

Molly bustled over to her, with a tiny china plate, then hurried back to the table where she sat down and noisily slurped some water from a teacup. Then she gargled a mouthful.

"That's not how you're supposed to drink tea," Kali said, trying not to laugh. "Why are you slurping like that, Sweetie?"

"Because the animals love it."

"Ah yes, the guests."

Propped up on bright-colored plastic chairs were two stuffed elephants (who were obliged to share a chair, despite their size) a grey plush cat and a yellow lion. They all seemed to be waiting for the fun to begin.

Molly's hair needed cutting—the poor kid could hardly see—and there was a large hole in the toe of one of her pink socks. Feeling like a very neglectful parent, Kali got some granola bars from a cupboard and cut each one into sections, then arranged the pieces on a plate with some chocolate chips and raisins.

"My beautiful pashas," Molly said, looking over the table with approval. "Pasha means plate, in Spanish."

"I didn't know that," Kali said.

"I don't like to say the word 'plates' all the time."

"Me either."

"Know what cups are called in Spanish?"

"Hmm, no. I forget."

"Tashas!"

"Right." Kali had to struggle not to smile. Molly was such an adorable, motherly little muffin, bustling around, setting up the tea party, putting all the animals in their places and feeding everyone.

"Oh no! I forgot to give Nala a plate!" she said. "And the elephants need a cup! They have to share one because they suck the tea with their trunks."

Kali felt sorry for the elephants who seemed to hold a low social position at Molly's tea party: stuffed together onto one chair and forced to share a cup. Molly popped a chocolate chip into her mouth and turned to Kali, peering at her from below her hair. "This food is great. Would you like a seat? I have extra plates."

"I would. Thank you, Molly."

"Just watch out for the cats. There's one pet cat and one jungle cat. They like *to fight.*" She demonstrated with a scratching motion, a fierce expression on her face.

"You are so right," Kali sighed as she squeezed her butt into one of the little chairs. "I do have to remember to watch out for the cats."

When both kids were in bed, later that night, Harry started chuckling again. "Gifts of surprise underwear," he laughed, snuggling under his blankets. "Surprise gifts of underwear!" There was another fit of giggles. Then Molly joined in the giggling, which escalated to howls of uncontrollable laughter, that lasted until midnight.

Chapter 28

WHENEVER GILLIAN FOUND HERSELF IN A STORE AS BIG AS A football field, she was gripped by agoraphobia. She didn't know which way to turn to find whatever it was she wanted; she could never even locate a store directory! She usually avoided monster stores like the Walmart she had just entered since they never sold anything unusual enough to interest her. But today, she was looking for something, well, ordinary. 'Dowdy' might not be too much of a stretch, even 'boring.' And if she couldn't find what she wanted here, there was always Target at the other end of the mall, or even better, Ross Dress for Less.

Surrounded by miles of merchandise in all directions, the beeping of cash registers and the babble and hum of voices, Gillian began to hyperventilate. All the other shoppers seemed to be in a huge hurry to buy what they wanted and knew exactly where to find it.

It was a waste of time shopping for Ana's shower gift in one of the artsy shops Gillian liked in Venice Beach or Silverlake since Ana was not likely to appreciate chain-mail panties or ostrich-feather nipple covers.

Freshly resenting Kali for putting her into such a frustrating, thankless and embarrassing predicament, Gillian adjusted her Himalayan hiking pack on her back and plunged bravely into the store's sea of stuff.

So, what should a woman properly wear to bed with a plagiarist? she thought, thinking of Ana with Alex, and freshly resenting him. Just above eye level, not too far in the distance, she could see a row of truncated torsos modeling brassieres. She headed over and was eventually rewarded by a multitude of bras dangling from plastic-clipped hangers, alongside teddies, slips, camisoles, and tank tops—all jammed together on racks, stacked on shelves, or piled into bins marked down for fast sale.

Where to begin? Ana was Little Miss Perfect. Soon to become Little Mrs. Perfect. If there was one thing Gillian knew intuitively about her, it was that she would be particular about her underwear: using a special soap for delicate fabrics, hanging the stuff up to dry, then folding and aligning everything neatly in her bureau drawers, Marie Kondo style. Or, she might store it in lace-trimmed lingerie bags, with scented sachets tucked into the corners. And Ana was also the type who wouldn't leave her apartment unless all her lingerie *matched*—so unlike Gillian who didn't own a single set of matching anything and whose panties and bras were balled up in one gigantic snarl in the single drawer she had to spare for such annoying stuff.

She stopped at a rack of corset-like things that were supposed to push up and pull in various parts of the female anatomy in attractive and appealing ways. They looked appallingly uncomfortable, rubberized and resistant. She had no idea that girdles were back in style since Madonna's pointy bras and corsets from the nineties. Wouldn't Alex go wild over Ana in one of these iron-maiden jobs? She laughed to herself. She had to be careful not to cross the line into grotesquely bad taste. But what the hell. Nobody said it was *her* job to arouse Alexander Spears!

Moving on, she approached a rack of oversized flannel robes. How hideous! Sober taupe and burgundy flannel. Perfect for a drafty castle in the Hebrides. But, come to think of it, one of these robes might be perfect for Ana. The price was good, and price was definitely a factor. For a kitchen shower, she could have picked up a dozen tea towels for under twenty bucks; for a wine shower, a decent Cabernet would be around the same price. But it was tough to find anything that could be taken seriously as *lingerie* for that kind of money. Three pairs of underpants or a pair of tights, maybe. And she was going to have to buy a gift for Isadora to bring, and for Isadora's friend as well. 'She's no one you know,' Isadora had replied, sullenly, in response to Gillian's question.

Why had Isadora even agreed to go? And why had it seemed like such a great idea to ask her along? Some fantasy about bringing her daughter into the fold, introducing her to the rituals of tea and social conversation, and bonding with other women.

Reluctantly, Gillian turned her back on the plaid robes. Much as the idea of buying one amused her, it wouldn't be fair to Isadora. Ana would open box after bag of shimmering satin and frothy lace to finally open Gillian's large and intrusive box, out of which she would pull yards of ugly flannel. And everyone would conclude, of course, that Gillian had chosen it out of spite: giving Ana the most hideous thing she could find to even that poetry-plagiarism score with Alexander. It would also be wasteful, Gillian's practical side reminded her. Why spend good money on something that would be tossed straight down the trash chute of Ana's apartment building?

No, the challenge was to be subtle: get something attractive and comfortable enough that Ana would actually wear, but that would also make Alexander's dick droop. Gillian would find a perfect willy-wilter: a special gift for Ana, but also for Alex.

Chuckling to herself, she strolled into the more remote regions of 'sleepwear.' There was a rack of pajamas, patterned with pink teacups and made from something called 'blanket fleece.' Guests at Kali's tea might assume Gillian was giving the teacup pajamas to Ana as a souvenir of the shower. No one (except for Jada and Kali) would suspect she bought them because they were so goddamned ugly.

Then, suddenly, a large white mass loomed into view, like the Titanic's iceberg. How gruesome, she thought, moving closer to examine the nightie pinned up on a wall display. It was a sorry, incongruous mix of thick, no-nonsense flannel and cheap fussy lace: two materials that could hardly be less happy bedfellows. It was a mongrel of a nightgown, a nightmare of poor design. It was perfect! Gillian studied it, transfixed by every appalling detail. It had a ridiculous flouncy bottom, three absurd patch pockets (with more lace) and a clown-like floppy bow in the center of a juvenile Peter Pan collar. It was the epitome of Victorian prudery, as interpreted by some cokehead bargain store designer.

She closed her eyes, feeling a rush of nasty pleasure at the thought of Alexander confounded by cotton, flummoxed by flannel. And yet, no one could accuse Gillian of having purchased it out of a desire for revenge. On some level, it might even be considered romantically cozy—a blessed relief from those chilly bits of nothing that Alex would be expecting Ana to parade in every night for his salacious pleasure.

As she waited at the cash desk, the drift of white flannel piled high over her arm, Gillian riffled through a bin of sale stuff. In it, she found a bonus, the perfect token gifts from Isadora and her unnamed friend: two pairs of fluffy orange bed socks with rows of sticky green rubber chevrons on the soles. Feeling a delerious thrill of delicious evil, Gillian stuck her credit card into the chip reader.

Chapter 29

JADA ALWAYS TRIED NOT TO APPEAR INTIMIDATED OR IMPRESSED BY the doorman at Saks. He'd been there since she first started shopping at the Beverly Hills store, two decades earlier. She recalled the first time she'd approached those dazzling doors, and how he'd greeted her with delight: eyebrows raised, arms and doors flung open wide. 'Lovely to see you today!' he'd cried. Flattered at being recognized and welcomed in such an effusive manner, Jada had thought he must have mistaken her for a model, an actress, or one of Beverly Hills' wealthy elite. But after that first time, she'd noticed that this same ebullient welcome was bestowed on every woman who got within twenty feet of Saks' front door. Fat or thin, attractive or homely, in bad taste or beautifully-dressed, black, white or Hispanic, no woman escaped his flattering attention. He would have flung open those doors for a bag lady! Jada had felt two-timed, cheated-on and resentful. No one else seemed bothered by his attitude, however, nor did he seem remorseful or even notice Jada's subsequent snubs.

Usually, when Jada went to Saks, it was because she had a hot date coming up (rare) or (more likely) because she needed to spend a lot of money to lift her out of whatever depression she was in. Since the plane crash, she'd been shopping at Saks a *lot*, which was a concern because her income was diminishing at the same fast clip, all partners having agreed to a thirty percent reduction in draws, until the firm was out of red ink.

Still, since no bankruptcy trustee had yet cut up her Saks card, Jada brushed past the doorman with his hypocritical greeting and strode into her favorite store. She was there for the novel (but never actually sought-after) experience of lingerie-shopping for another woman—to buy something for Ana that would demonstrate Jada's excellent taste and generosity. By such an expansive gesture, she also meant to show that she had forgiven Alex for any unpleasantness between them in the past (and she was still hoping he would throw her some crumb of corporate work) and that she was welcoming Ana into the firm. None of which was—except for wanting that crumb of work—of course, true.

As she glided up the escalator, she looked down over the main floor, admiring the sparkle and gleam of all the cut glass and mirrored surfaces in the cosmetics department. And, as she stepped onto the second floor—and then into the lingerie department—her spirits soared to dizzying heights.

She saw *exactly* what she'd pictured as the ideal gift for Ana: a pair of well-tailored pink silk pajamas. They were elegant, French-seamed and light as air. She imagined, with no small degree of envy, how Ana would slip into that shimmering silk (and out of it) and how she would look in between. One of her long legs would be slung over the arm of a loveseat, the mother-of-pearl buttons of the pajama top undone, except for one, right in the middle, strategically holding it closed. But barely. She would be talking law with Alexander; there would be a pair of reading glasses on her nose, a stack of law books at her side. Her long dark hair would be attractively tousled, her pink lips pouty. Alex would be dazzled by her thorough knowledge of her subject, her keen grasp of the issues, her accurate issue-spotting and the decisive solution she'd come up with to a challenging legal problem. Overwhelmed by Ana's daunting combination of beauty and brains, he would leap onto the loveseat and seize hold of that pajama top. The fragile button would whiz across the room and he and his new wife would slide down, hungrily kissing each other, onto an Oriental carpet that begged for fornication with every plush and sensuous fiber.

Jada cleared her throat, realizing that she'd been panting, took a deep calming breath, and turned over the price tag that hung from a sleeve of the pajama top. Six hundred dollars! Her breathing was suddenly short again.

With an effort, she formed her lips into a snooty smile and strolled over to a rack of silk nighties and matching bed jackets. Perhaps she should buy Ana a simple nightgown. It had to be less expensive than those pajamas.

"So, what did you think of the pajamas?" A salesgirl appeared suddenly, as if Jada removing something from the rack had triggered a store alarm in a back room somewhere.

"Lovely," she said, with no emotion.

"It comes as a set. There's a silk robe to go over it."

"Oh?" Jada said, casually, "how much for the set?"

The salesgirl plucked up the sleeve of a silk robe hanging on the rack. "Well, the robe is eight—"

"Hundred?"

"Of course."

"Okay, I thought it might be thousand. That's my usual price range."

"Oh, good! So, the set would be eighteen hundred."

"Hm. It's not for me. This is for a shower gift, actually."

"Well, aren't *you* the great friend!"

"Not that great."

"It has French seams—"

"I noticed."

"And that collar—that's all hand-work around it." The salesgirl obviously thought the price was quite reasonable—ridiculously low, in fact.

"Well, I hardly know this woman, this bride-to-be chick. And I wanted a shower gift. Not a mortgage—for myself."

"We have some stuff on sale at the back of the department." The salesgirl looked Jada up and down.

"I'll just browse."

"Fine." The salesgirl twitched the sleeves of several bed jackets into place. "My name's Gloria, if you need anything."

And what is it if I don't? Jada thought, turning away from Gloria and the pajamas. She *would* find something in silk for Ana. None of that poly crap. If there was one thing Jada had when it came to underthings, it was class. But these prices! They gave her palpitations. She had never shopped for lingerie at Saks. What could she realistically afford to buy Ana? A lingerie bag and liquid soap? A couple of padded satin hangers? A potpourri-stuffed drawer sachet? All niggling impersonal little gifts that would demonstrate a mean spirit and envy, not at all what she wanted to convey, much as she despised Alex. She needed work from him and was determined to suck up to get it.

She paused at a display of spa slippers. They weren't silk, they were terry cloth, with the SAKS logo embroidered in gold across the toes. There was a headband to go with them: thick terry with a washerwoman knot in center front. It would take someone like Ana to look good in that get-up, Jada thought.

There was plenty of cheap silk to be had in lesser lingerie shops and online and Jada had turned her nose up at it often enough. But cotton was a direction in which she could go. If the thread count were high enough, cotton could be as smooth and luxurious as silk. Terry cloth, though, was out of the question. Ana wouldn't care for being dressed in a towel, unless it was one of those sarong-wrapped jobs twisted around her waist at an exotic Caribbean resort, the kind that dropped to the floor at the slightest touch. With a sigh, Jada replaced the spa slippers and headband on the display.

"Did you have your heart set on silk?" Gloria had materialized again at her side. "I noticed you were turning up your nose at the terry. But what about chenille? We have some luxurious robes I'd love to show you."

"Chenille reminds me of my grandmother's bedspread. But I might consider Egyptian cotton. Or linen."

"Oh! Well. We have a great promotion going on right now. I'm not really supposed to say anything ..."

Jada brightened, though she was skeptical of this statement. How effective could a promotion be if no one was supposed to know about it? Doubtfully, she followed Gloria out of the Designers' section into an adjoining department called *Country Casuals.* "I'm not sure this woman I'm buying for is the country type," she said, thinking of Ana in her pricey, well-tailored work clothes—more upscale than Jada's own.

"Every woman is the country type," Gloria said, "if she gets sick enough." Then they both laughed. When they reached the back of the department, near the change rooms, Gloria turned to Jada and smiled. "These nighties are on sale for eighty-five bucks, this weekend only."

Jada frowned. "When I said cotton, I wasn't really thinking of ... flannel." She studied the row of fuzzy white sleeves and ruffled hems that hung from the tightly packed rack.

"It's imported double-brushed flannel." Gloria pulled one of the nightgowns out and held it up for Jada. "It needs a little steaming," she smoothed her hand over it, "but we can do that for you in two secs. These just came in yesterday. You'd be the first to get one. They're going to move very quickly."

"It's not exactly sexy, though, is it?" Jada ran her fingers along one of the sleeves. "Eighty-five dollars ..."

"An incredible price."

"It certainly is soft."

"Soft *and* romantic. What could be more delicious on a cold winter night?"

"But this is L.A., I mean, I don't know that they've booked their honeymoon in Reykjavik."

"It gets cold in L.A., are you kidding? Or what if they go up to Big Bear? Or Mammoth? Think about it. Your friend, and her new husband, curled up by a roaring fire. Him in some, I don't know, plaid boxers or whatever—who really cares what men wear, right?—but her, your friend, stepping into the glow of the firelight, all demure Victorian whiteness and pretend prudery. Look at the depth of this flounce. Stunning, isn't it?"

"Pretend prudery," Jada breathed, enchanted by the picture Gloria was painting. "I'm loving this, Girlfriend."

"So, he, the guy, the husband," Gloria continued, "undoes this adorable bow here, then all of these great buttons." She had to struggle with a couple of them. "There!" she said at last. "What fun! Men never like anything they can get too easily."

"There must be at least a dozen buttons," Jada murmured.

"He'll have a ball taking all this off your friend."

"I wouldn't have thought a flannel nightie could be about sex."

"*Everything* is about sex. I'm sure I don't have to tell *you* that. Did you notice the lace trim? And pockets? Aren't they *fabulous*? He can slip his condoms in one of these pockets and be all set."

"He's had a vasectomy, apparently," Jada said, marveling at the frankness of the conversation they were having.

"So, he tucks something else in there." Gloria was not one to be easily derailed. "A penile pump, whatever." They both laughed, heartily. "Now let's see if we have a size small. This one's a large." Gloria stuffed the nightie back among the rest and turned over a number of tags. "One small. That's it. Your friend is *so* lucky. Shall I have it gift wrapped?"

"Please."

"We'll throw in a few sachet crystals, do it up in pretty white paper, pale blue ribbon. You'll be so pleased. To say nothing of your friend. *And her new hubby.*"

"Wonderful."

"Why don't you look around for something for yourself while you wait? You deserve to be spoiled too."

"I just might do that. Some little thing…" Jada's thoughts were wandering back to the Designer section and a certain pair of shell-pink pajamas.

"If you hang on a moment, I'll show you another satin robe that will knock your socks off."

"I could use a sexy new robe," Jada said, thinking back to the white terry robe of *some man's* that was in her bedroom closet, and that she had last worn that night after the plane crash. "You know, Gloria, a new robe is definitely what's needed right now."

"Someone special in your life?"

"How can you tell?"

"Something in your eyes."

"And after the robe, perhaps you could show me some sexy little nothings in the men's department?"

"I would *love* to!" Gloria regarded Jada with envy and admiration. "He's a lucky guy, your man."

"I know." Jada smiled. *And maybe someday I'll find the bugger,* she added, to herself.

Chapter 30

"You're not going in that!"

"Why not?"

"It's totally inappropriate."

"*You're* talking to *me* about inappropriate clothes?"

"Yes, I am." Gillian glared at her daughter.

Isadora looked down at herself. "So what part, exactly, don't you like?"

"All of it. The chains, that chastity belt or whatever that is around your waist. That ripcord thing." Actually, Gillian was curious to know where her daughter had found such a sublime specimen of kinky bad taste, but now was not the time to ask. "Please," she begged, "you can't go to my partner's home dressed like that. Promise me you'll wear a dress? I implore you."

"*Implore*? Do you have to be so melodramatic? And I don't even own a dress, which is one slight problem with your plan."

"I'll buy you one. And one for your friend too."

Isadora hesitated. "Do we get to pick them out?"

"Absolutely. But it has to be something reasonable. Nothing too outrageous."

"Fine." Isadora shrugged.

Gillian, who's just returned from work to be confronted by her daughter in an animal-print cat-suit, jangling all over with what looked like medieval torture devices, picked up her leather-laced Korean Yurt bag from where she'd dropped it, a moment before, in the front hall. "I can probably give you cash. But I want to see all the receipts. And no final sale stuff, okay?"

"Cool," Isadora nodded. "I'm not into sales."

Gillian dug down to the bottom of her bag to find her Japanese paper wallet and opened it to see how much cash she had. "That's weird, I thought I had a few more twenties in here." She counted out a series of bills. "I went to the cleaners, bought some wine. Parking was only four dollars..."

"Can't you just give me one of your credit cards?"

Gillian looked at her, still puzzling over the amount of money in her wallet. "Well, I guess so. Let's see ... credit cards. . . . how about this one?"

"You serious?" Isadora's upper lip curled in disgust. "You expect me to find something at *Sears*?"

"They occasionally have nice things, on the second floor. I was there the other day. I could go with you, show you where to look. It might be fun."

"I don't do mother-daughter shopping trips. I'm not five years old, get used to it." She looked with distaste at the credit card. "I thought Sears stores were all closed."

"There's still one, I think, on Crenshaw."

"But you and me are not exactly Sears types, right?"

"Well, true. I don't buy many clothes there."

"The way you dress is a creative expression of yourself. Isn't that what you've always told me?"

"Yes," Gillian admitted, "also true."

"Be an individual, that's what you've pounded into my head, year after year."

"I've hardly pounded it."

"So why can't I just take your Mastercard? Or Visa?"

"Where were you planning to shop?" Gillian's hand remained, protectively, on her wallet.

"I don't know yet. I've got a few ideas."

"But the tea is on Sunday."

"I can shop fast."

Gillian fingered her gold Mastercard, pondering. "I get to see the receipts, okay? And nothing over two hundred bucks."

"Each, right? For me and my friend?"

"Yes," Gillian said. "I suppose so. You should get some shoes, too. And see if someone can do something with your hair. It'll be more than two hundred then, I guess. A lot more. Your friend must have her own shoes, though. I won't have to buy those too, right?" Gillian looked worriedly at her daughter.

"Chill, Mother. I'll keep the costs in line. But can I have some cash too? In case we go somewhere that doesn't take Mastercard?"

"Who doesn't take Mastercard?" But Gillian knew the answer to that: all the weird and creepy places she liked to shop in herself.

"Don't worry so much." Isadora patted her mother's arm. "It'll be someplace cheap."

"Someplace cheap won't take returns."

"Could you please just trust me for once?"

Gillian hesitated, looking again at the chain-link contraption around her daughter's waist. "Just try to look half-normal. That's all I ask. You're an attractive young woman. You have a lovely smile, nice legs."

"Can I go now?" Isadora rolled her eyes as Gillian reluctantly handed over the last few bills from her wallet, along with the Mastercard. "Half-normal. We have a deal, right?"

"I'll do you proud. Little white gloves, a hat with a veil, the whole get-up."

"You'll do no such thing!" Was she serious? Part of Gillian was intrigued; the better part, fearful.

"You just start thinking about your own outfit and don't worry so much about us, okay?"

"Please," Gillian pleaded. "Just don't embarrass me." But Isadora made no sign that she had heard. Her cat-suit-clad backside was already swaying up the stairs, chastity belt clanking.

She wouldn't need Isadora to embarrass her, Gillian thought later as she stood, hands on hips, facing the rat's nest that she called her wardrobe; she could do an excellent job of that herself. She dragged a chair across the floor and climbed up on it to access the back of the top shelf. 'You don't need to bother with a hat,' Kali had said, during their last conversation about the tea, 'just wear whatever's comfortable.' Gillian could tell that Kali was dreading what she might show up wearing, and it gave Gillian a small thrill to think about that.

"If you got it, flaunt it," she muttered to herself, stretching over her head to grab the cloud of dry cleaner's bag that shrouded her amazing black cartwheel hat. If she could find Larry's hot glue gun, she planned to stick three rust-colored roses onto the band to make the hat look more festive, and better coordinate it with her dress. Also, once trimmed with flowers, it was less likely to bring back painful memories of the memorial service to the widows, and Gillian liked to think of herself as sensitive to others' feelings.

The dress she'd bought for the tea was a fantasy of ecru-colored lace, discovered amongst the spandex, the teensy Mary Jane frocks and the 'fifties crinolines in a store called *FIX*. The manager had refused to haggle with Gillian, wouldn't even take ten percent off the dress, though she'd gone in to try her luck several times. *FIX* was an off-the-wall clothing store that didn't belong in the commercial zone where Gillian had stumbled upon it. With its lop-sided wooden sign, jaw-grinding music and change rooms with curtains that didn't quite close, *FIX* was not going to make it there, despite the number of hot young designers represented in its racks.

At the end of the day, Gillian got the lace dress for a quarter of its original price, on the weekend the front window of the shop was papered over with giant red banners that announced: STORE CLOSING! EVERYTHING MUST GO!!! She had smirked about her victory for weeks.

After unbundling the hat from its plastic wrap, she placed it on her bed, then unzipped the garment bag to take out her tea dress. It was a slim silk sheath over which was layered an entire bolt of ecru-colored lace, pleated, gored, gathered and tucked in the most amazing ways. When she wore her boots (leather, high buttoned, laced with satin ribbon) the hem of the dress just tickled her ankles. More lace festooned the deep V collar and the edges of the three-quarter-length sleeves. She worked her way into the dress, then stood back to admire herself in the mirror. With the cartwheel hat topping it off, the outfit would be truly awesome! Her resentment over Kali and the lingerie tea was fading. Without Kali and her silly tea, Gillian might never get the chance to put all these fabulous elements together and make the memorable fashion statement she was about to make.

Chapter 31

"**D**AMNIT ALL TO HELL!" JADA SHUFFLED ACROSS THE CARPETED floor of her bedroom, dressed only in that same man's terry robe. Would she ever get a chance to wear anything but that in her condo? Like those shell-pink pajamas that had cranked her credit card way up over the limit? She hadn't yet bothered to take them out of the Saks bag, as there was no one around to wear them for, and no point in getting them dirty just for herself, since the damned things had to be dry cleaned. Who *dry cleaned* pajamas, for Christ's sake? But they were sure to be considered by Saks as 'intimate apparel' and therefore non-returnable, not even for a store credit.

Jada hadn't had a man since Ross, except for that unsatisfactory skirmish with Dan the evening after the plane crash, and that hardly counted, being no more than a small act of mutual desperation.

She paced, wearing a path through the pile of her plush carpeting, crunching an antacid between her teeth. And even when she'd been seeing Ross, half of the time she was not in alluring lingerie but in some ridiculous get-up to satisfy his masochistic fantasies. And now, thanks to Kali, she was having to confront that whole wretched part of her past by spending an afternoon not only with Ross's widow, but with his tweedy old Stickleback of a mother as well.

'So, tell me,' she imagined herself saying to Marcia as she speared a lemon slice with a delicate silver fork, 'what did *you* get to be for Hallowe'en when you and Ross were still together?' Or, to Mrs. Owen senior: 'Audrey, was it you who'd sewn all those fun little-boy play outfits that naughty Ross used to bring over to my condo? It must have been you. As I recall you expressed a keen interest in zippers.' Then she would politely pass the old witch some gone-off milk for her tea.

Jada had managed to avoid Audrey at the reception after the memorial service, and Audrey must have been so distraught and so busy blaming Marcia for Ross's death, that she hadn't noticed Jada, or remembered her, in the single instant their eyes met. The dinner in Simi was likely forgotten, as was the fact that Ross had had ANOTHER WOMAN (never mind another wife!) before he and Marcia split up. Well, Jada coming eyeball to eyeball with the old Haddock over a tray of sour lemon tarts would refresh her memory PDQ.

She picked nervously at a zit on the side of her nose as she pictured the Owen women wheeling around in formation to tear Jada to bits with sugar tongs and cake knives. It would do them so much cathartic good! They would share a common enemy, be therapeutically drawn together in their united hatred of *her*.

Jada considered again the possibility of not showing up for the wretched tea at all. She could send the gift over to Kali's, or leave it on Ana's desk at the office. Surely, she could come up with some creative (but entirely believable) reason for not going. She could really and truly break her leg, for example—and jumping off her second-floor balcony just might do the trick. But, knowing Kali, she would offer to swing by in her filthy dog hair infested car, or worse, send over Matt (who was sure to remember the blind date he had set up with Jada and a fellow surgeon who'd never called Jada again) to pick her up, crutches and all, so that Jada wouldn't have to miss a single minute of lingerie-tea-fun!

What if she went in disguise? Put on a wig, headscarf, and dark glasses, like she had to do when she went out anywhere with Ross? She could pose as Kali's old friend who was suffering through chemo. But then Kali would have to be in on it, and knowing Kali, she was too much of a goodie-goodie to pull it off.

Get a grip, she told herself. If you're going to be the OTHER WOMAN—a label Jada had never shied away from before—or rather, the OTHER OTHER WOMAN, go down with your head high. Rip some curtains from the windows, grab a few yards of tassels and do it up Scarlett O'Hara style. And then the three Owen women would simply conclude that Ross's *other* other woman was a lunatic who was carrying a concealed weapon, and leave her alone, jabbing their cake forks in some other, less explosive direction. Like at each other.

With a discouraged sigh, Jada took a bottle of Kentucky Bourbon from the top shelf of her closet, then dropped onto her bed to sit, shoulders sagging, in front of the double-mirrored doors of her closet and drink straight from the bottle. Studying her pathetic, terry-clothed figure, she experienced a wave of self-loathing. But that was followed by a tingle of self-respect. Her beaten-down pride began struggling to get up. Then it *was* up! It was looking around, flexing its atrophied muscles, stretching. Yes! She straightened her shoulders, recapped the bottle, re-tied the belt of her robe and looked herself in the eye. Why was *she* suddenly the victim in this hideous melodrama? She was supposed to be the *villain*, the Omarosa, the one who had led Ross by the nose on a merry chase out of the comfort and security of his dual marriages, to practically throw him onto the doomed plane. She was Carmen, for God's sake, not Anna Karenina! She'd never before shrunk from what she was, from holding her head up, no matter what she'd done. Jada had pride, a great wardrobe, and a fantastic figure, whatever other qualities she might lack as a human being. And those essential assets of hers should never go to waste and should always be put to good use.

Pushing back the sleeves of the robe (no longer caring whose it was), she got off her bed and flung open her closet doors. When she was finished putting herself together for this stupid tea party, not one of those squabbling Owen women would ever be able to ask themselves, or each other, what it was that dear old departed Ross had ever seen in *her*.

Chapter 32

"THIS PLACE LOOKS GREAT," MATT ENTHUSED. "YOU'RE GOING to impress the shit out of everyone."

"I'm not out to impress anyone," Kali said.

Not impress anyone? She thought. *Who was she kidding?* The house was so thick with exotic flowers it looked like a tropical rainforest. And there was other evidence, like the heart-shaped soaps and lace-edged hand towels by the bathroom sinks. (Matt had been forbidden to touch those, directed instead to use a rumpled gym towel that Kali pulled from the hamper and pushed into his hand.) And what about the china, the silver, the refrigerator sagging from the weight of cream-filled pastries and dozens of little sandwiches? None of it was meant to *impress?*

"I'm giving a bridal shower for a young woman who won't be having any other showers," Kali said, primly. "Now, isn't there something you should be doing? Like taking the kids out?"

"I'm going to. But first, I want you to know how proud I am of you."

"Yeah, right."

"Really, I think it's great what you've done for this tea thing."

Kali had been vigorously scrubbing the kitchen sink with powdered cleanser and a sponge at the time. "Matt, please. I can't talk now."

"Okay, I guess I'll grab my gear and the kids and hit the road."

"Please don't use that expression, especially when you're going roller-blading. And no letting the kids roller-blade. We agreed."

"Gotcha." Matt slipped behind her to peek inside the fridge. Trays, many trays, everything on them covered by damp tea towels, like so many stiffs laid out in the hospital morgue. He lifted the corner of a towel.

"None of that's for you, Matt!" Kali didn't even turn around—she had eyes in the back of her head.

Wait until the kids got a look at their old dad on his blades, Matt thought. He planned to take them to the parking lot of a 'No Frills' grocery that hadn't yet opened. There, with a half-acre of deserted asphalt laid out before him, he would demonstrate his spins, his dipsy doodles, then shoot a puck around. It would be good to get Harry fired up for the hockey season. The boy was becoming a wimp, hanging around all day with Molly and Emilie.

'Awesome, Dad!' Harry would laugh, as he and Molly sat on the curb, gaping as their (formerly uncool) father whizzed by, swerving and spinning: king of the road, commander of the asphalt. Then, after an all-you-can-eat trip to Burger King, Matt planned to take them to Sports World to get them fitted out with their own roller-blading gear: snazzy pink nylon for Molly, with a Barbie helmet; for Harry, a junior version of his old man's. Matt had mentioned these plans to Kali that morning. "Oh, Matt, are you sure it's safe?" She'd been counting teaspoons in the kitchen, looking worried and distracted, and he was pretty sure she hadn't been listening. He considered sweeping her up in his arms and throwing her over the breakfast table, sending her spoons flying, but decided against the maneuver, unsure of the reception it would get.

From where she now stood in the kitchen, Kali could admire the foyer, and the dining and living rooms in one critical sweep. Her tireless shopping, moving of furniture, scrubbing, polishing and efforts to exact cooperation from Matt and Emilie had paid off. She was actually enjoying this last hour of preparation. The lingerie tea was a necessary event, she realized. It would draw together her partners and friends with the other women who had suffered so much after the plane crash. It was a ritual cleansing, a way to set the law firm back on course, a readjustment of emotional rheostats. What a remarkably astute and prescient idea! How had it ever occurred to her? For one afternoon, twelve women, with little in common besides tragedy and a faltering firm, could talk, laugh, and exclaim over gorgeous lingerie, their heads swirling with champagne bubbles and the aroma of *Lapsang Souchong* and *Darjeeling*. They would forget their squabbles and petty differences, cozily wrapped in the comfort and intimacy of an age-old ceremony. Ah, the delights of tea! Suddenly, Kali noticed the time. She had to get dressed!

Chapter 33

IN HER BEDROOM, KALI TWIRLED IN FRONT OF THE MIRROR, JUST LIKE a little girl. She still couldn't believe her luck, to have found an authentic tea-gown in a vintage clothing boutique. Gillian just might have to kill her in a jealous rage. But Kali's feelings about the gown fluctuated from embarrassment (this wasn't a costume party!) to a sense that she was gloriously upholding (resurrecting?) the fine tradition of wearing the proper gown for a high tea. Long and loose, its skirts swept the ground with an air of quiet authority. But it wasn't as though Kali were done up in stays and corsets and bustles. She had no white gloves, no parasol, no hat—nothing too fussy. She thought she looked glamorous and elegant, once she got the darned thing on and laced up properly.

Music! She'd forgotten to select appropriate background music, since Matt had been so unreasonable about her hiring a string quartet or bringing in a pianist with a baby grand.

But there was already some noise in the house, and it abruptly penetrated Kali's consciousness. Gunfire. Explosions. *"Grimlord has sent his new mutants towards the reality barrier!'* a witchy voice screamed. Kali froze at the top of the stairs. "Matt?" she called, shattering the delicate tea-scented serenity that had, only moments before, enveloped her. "Why are the kids still here?" It was 3:30. He'd promised to have them out by 3:00. What sort of mess were they making down there in the family room? "Matt!" She hurried down the stairs, holding up her tea-gown, terrified of tripping in it and spending the duration of the tea, not playing the gracious hostess, but as a patient in the hospital emerg department, with two broken legs and a fractured collarbone.

Her mother, wiping a teacup with a dish towel, met her at the bottom of the stairs. "He says when he finds his North Face jacket, they'll hit the road. Do you know where it is? The kids are watching some video. They sure are into it, but it seems pretty violent."

"Matt's jacket? I have no idea. But I have to find some music right now." Kali grabbed the skirts of her gown to charge back up the stairs where she hurried from room to room, tweaking bedspreads here, flicking microscopic (or imagined) bits of dust there. Why had she come upstairs? Then, with a surge of panic, she realized that people could be arriving any minute. Music! She'd been on her way to look for some CDs to play, but they were down in the family room, not upstairs.

"Remember, Mom," she said, breathlessly, in the kitchen moments later, "use only filtered water, and pour it over the loose tea as soon as it boils. That's what it says in the book."

"Two college degrees and you need a book to tell you how to make a damned cup of tea?"

"I haven't got a clue about what goes where, or when," Kali said. "Does everyone have tea first? Do we put out sandwiches first and sweet stuff later? Or does everything just get put out at once?"

"The first thing would be to get a tablecloth on that table out there in the dining room." Marina might be a space-cadet, but she could get her act together when needed.

"A tablecloth. Right. I don't know why I'm feeling so helpless, why it all seems so complicated, why none of it makes sense."

"Because it's a regressive anti-feminist trap that nobody bothers with anymore. But you need to get a grip. You agreed to do it, and you'll do it right, okay? And if not," Marina shrugged, "this too shall pass. No need to get bent out of shape."

Kali's father, Boris, was busy amazing Harry and Molly with the trick where he pretended to cut off his finger and glue it back on again. But he was soon dispatched to get the tablecloth—one that had belonged to his Ukrainian mother—from the trunk of the Wolaniuks' car. On his way back in, he paused to study the floral display: the tall pedestal table draped with yards of filmy fabric, topped with a blue and white vase from which heather, thistles and African lilies sprung. "Why do you have a rag over this table out here?" he called to Kali.

"It's not a rag, Dad," Kali called back. "It's an Edwardian wedding veil."

"It looks like those curtains we had in the bedroom on Clark Street, right Marina?"

"It's on loan from my designer. Dad, please leave it alone—I'll have to pay for it if anything happens to it."

"Boris, baby, you need to blow this pop stand." Marina met him in the foyer, took the tablecloth and pushed him back toward the front door. "Go find a bookstore or go to a movie or something for a couple of hours."

Kali's face fell as she opened up the tablecloth and saw that it was resplendent with red, orange and black embroidery. "Oh, Mom," she groaned. "This is the Ukrainian one! I'm having an *English* tea."

"Your grandmother embroidered it herself. I think it's cool."

"I know, but I have all this English stuff out—and this will look weird. I mean, it looks like an Easter egg."

"Your dad will be bummed if you don't use it. He even took it to the cleaners, so it would be nice for your party."

"Okay," Kali sighed, "I guess I'll have to use it."

"You can't break your dad's heart. And you should get over yourself, stop being so pretentious. I mean, really, Kalinka."

"You're right. I'm sorry."

"Everything's copacetic. So, when is everyone supposed to get here?"

"Soon, like any time."

"Mommy!" Molly yelled, running into the dining room. "Can I pick your flowers?"

"No, Sweetie, not right now. But after the party, you can pick all you want. Matt?" she called. "What are you doing? Why haven't you guys gone yet?"

"We're on our way." Matt appeared in his North Face jacket, carrying his roller-blading gear. "Molly wants a flower. Can't she have one? You've got about a thousand."

"Of course, she can." Kali approached the daunting floral display and plucked a daisy from a section near the wall where she didn't think it would show. "There. Okay, Honey?" She kissed her daughter's pink little cheek.

"But I want one of the prickly ones!"

"This one is prickly. See? Ouch, ouch. It's very prickly and pointy."

"No! The *prickly* ones!"

"She means those thistles," Marina said, looking disapprovingly at the arrangement.

"Well, of course, she can't have a thistle," Kali said. She bent down to be eye-level with her daughter. "You can't have a thistle, Sweetie. It might hurt your little fingers."

"What are thistles doing in a bridal bouquet?" Matt asked.

"It's not a bridal bouquet. And if you have any more questions why you don't ask the designer?" She hurried back into the dining room to finish putting the tablecloth on the table and arranging everything on top of it.

Then, there were a lot of scuffling sounds from the foyer, the thunk of Matt's sports bag as it hit the edge of the door, and wails from Molly who'd managed to grab, and prick her finger on, a thistle. Then Harry complained that he was thirsty and wanted some juice. Finally, the front door slammed shut followed, a minute later, by several car doors.

Kali sighed heavily and sank into a chair to try and collect herself. There was an uncomfortable wetness in the chiffon of her gown, under her arms. She wanted a shower. She wanted to run away. She was already a frazzled hostess, and not a single guest had even arrived!

Marina was back in the kitchen where she was slicing her famous lemon loaf. Chop! chop! went her knife on the wooden board. "We should put some parsley on the sandwich plates. Have you got any parsley?" she called.

"No, Mother. Only people who actually cook use parsley."

"Some grapes?"

"No. I'm hopelessly inadequate and unprepared as a hostess." Kali put her head in her hands. How could a tea be so complicated? Why was she so unable to cope? What would she do when it came to really significant life challenges, if she couldn't even pull off a tea party?

Then, the doorbell chimed. Music! Kali had forgotten the music again! As she hurried to the door, the hem of her gown snagged in the hinge of one of the French doors of the dining room. Impatiently, she yanked it free, ripping a large piece out of the lavender silk chiffon.

"Kali! Answer the damn door, will you?" Marina called from the kitchen.

Chapter 34

"GILLIAN! JADA! WOW, YOU BOTH GOT HERE SO EARLY!" Kali stepped back, holding the door open wide, mostly to allow room for Gillian's dress to pass through it.

"We didn't plan this," Jada said, "it just worked out this way."

"But we both thought you could use need some help," Gillian added.

"Come in, come in!" *Before any of the neighbors see you*, Kali thought, then was immediately ashamed of herself. Her partners had obviously gone to a lot of trouble putting themselves together for an afternoon tea—a subject of which, in fairness, they knew next to nothing.

"Nice dress." Gillian gave Kali's gown an envious glance. "And you found shoes to match! They're incredible."

"But look at your dress! There must be six yards of lace there."

"Ten, but who's counting? I brought you a cake." Gillian pushed an enormous white Tupperware tray at Kali. "Take it, please. I've got too much to carry with these presents."

"Oh! It's heavier than it looks. Well, great! You shouldn't have. But thank you so much."

"Life Celebration Cake. It's loaded with fruit and nuts, even granola. Larry's recipe."

"Sounds fabulous," Kali said, wondering what she was going to do with the thing, which had to weigh five pounds.

Jada, dressed in a faux leopard skirt and jacket, with a matching pillbox hat, was inspecting the floral display. "Someone's going to kill herself, tripping over this curtain thing."

"It's not a curtain—it's a veil." Kali was amazed by Jada's shoes. The heels had to be at least four inches high. It hurt just to look at them!

"A veil? Really?" The crown of Gillian's hat grazed the chandelier as she moved in to take a closer look. She fondled the fragile edge of the fabric, then took a step back to admire the whole display. "I'm impressed. Did you do this yourself?"

"Of course not. I didn't do anything. Wrote out the invitations then called a designer and a catering company."

"Don't be so modest. The place looks amazing."

"So, where do you want us to put the presents?" Jada asked.

Then Marina appeared, holding the knife she'd been using on her lemon loaf. She looked menacing.

"Mom," Kali said, "these are two of my partners—Gillian Lawrence and Jada Tyler. This is my mom, Marina."

"That's a groovy outfit," Marina said to Jada. "Is that real leopard?"

"Are you serious? In L.A? Some animal rights nut would have spray-painted me by now if it was. But thanks."

"And you look very nice too," Marina said to Gillian. "I've never seen brown lace."

"It's ecru, actually."

"What?"

"Ecru. Same as my booties." Gillian held up a foot for Marina to admire.

"Far out," Marina said.

"So, where do the gifts go?" Jada repeated. "I need to dump this thing."

"I don't know," Kali confessed. "I guess I didn't think about that."

"For a shower? You serious?" Jada pushed past her. "I'll find a spot."

"Here, Mom. Gillian was nice enough to bring us a homemade cake. It's called Life Celebration. Could you cut it up for the tea table?" They exchanged looks as Kali handed Marina the heavy container.

"Here's our presents!" Gillian said, holding up a box and two little bags. "The box is from me and the little ones are from Isadora and her friend. The black bags were their idea. They're coming, but I was afraid they'd forget the presents, so I brought them."

"Black bags," Kali nodded as she took them, "interesting." *They'll look good on that Ukrainian tablecloth,* she thought. But Marina was right: she needed to let go of her pretentiousness. Wasn't it enough that everyone was coming, and that they were all getting together to heal the wounds inflicted by the plane crash? She didn't need to be a wound-up, crazy-making hostess. She would just kick back, have some champagne and enjoy the event, that's what she should do.

"The place looks bad ass, Kali." Jada, with her gift box, was teetering towards the living room.

"You do too. Those heels are amazing!"

"Jimmy Choo. I can hardly stand, let alone walk. He must really hate women."

"And stockings with seams," Marina marveled.

"There's a garter belt too," Jada said, "but don't ask to see it. Not before I've had something to drink. And I'm not talking Lapsang whatever. I need to sit down."

"Can I do anything?" Gillian asked. "Cut something up? Boil water?"

"Everything's done," Kali said, trying on her role as gracious hostess. "Have a seat in the living room and relax. There's tons to eat, and tea of course."

"When do we crack open the champagne?" Jada eased herself onto the loveseat under the front window. From there, she could get a clear view of the walk, and who was coming up it. "Anyone mind if I smoke?" She dug a cigarette and lighter out of her faux leopard bag.

"I'd prefer you didn't," Kali said, forgetting her gracious hostess role.

"You're going to make me go *outside*? In this get-up? With Audrey and Marcia showing up any minute?"

"Mom?" Kali called. "Could you find something in the kitchen for Jada to use for an ashtray?"

After some clanking of pots and banging of cupboard doors, Marina appeared with a white dinner plate and handed it to Jada. "All I could find." She gave Jada a look that said she disapproved of anyone smoking in her daughter's house.

"Thanks," Jada said, accepting the plate and returning the look.

As Kali arranged the gifts on a small occasional table in the living room, she realized that when she added her own—which was as big as both Jada's and Gillian's—there would be hardly any room for others. She stood her gift on its end, on the floor, to make more room on the table.

"What time did you tell Ana to come?" Gillian asked.

"Four."

Gillian checked her cell. "It's after that now."

"Can't we just forget the tea and crack open the bubbly?" Jada asked.

"I thought we should wait until Ana gets here, and the other guests."

"The bride-to-be is never on time. I'll die of thirst before then."

"We don't you have a glass of water?" Marina asked. "You look like you could use one."

The doorbell rang again. "I'll get it," Gillian said. "It's probably Isadora and her friend."

"Be careful of those flowers in the hall," Kali called as Gillian and her miles of lace and cartwheel hat rustled into the foyer.

"I don't know what to do with that cake she brought," Marina said to

Kali, in a low voice. "No matter how I try to cut it, it just falls apart. It's a big mess."

"Would it be rude not to serve it?"

"She'll be pissed off. We have to put it out."

Kali sighed. *The Social Quagmire of Tea.* It was the book she planned to write one day. Assuming she survived.

Chapter 35

"We came together, for emotional support." Leighton Durham strode into the foyer with the easy authority of a Managing Partner's wife. She flashed her large white teeth and swung her glossy auburn hair—hardly looking like someone who needed emotional support. Natalie Krupnik and Marcia Owen followed, but not as confidently.

The three seemed to have had rolled into the Millers' house like a big cumulus-nimbus cloud. All were in grey as if their grief had faded since the memorial service and their funeral garb along with it. Leighton wore a simple sleeveless A-line with a triple strand of (real, freshwater) pearls. Natalie was in suede: a suit that folded and buckled uncompromisingly as she moved, as though made out of cardboard. And Marcia, who'd lost a lot of weight since the memorial, wore a skinny cotton knit with a matching bolero jacket.

"Welcome everyone!" Kali beamed. "I'm so glad you could all come. We haven't seen you since—well, the service."

"We haven't seen each other since then," Marcia said, looking glum.

"Please, everyone, help yourselves to some goodies," Kali urged. "There's cute little sandwiches, cakes, all sorts of wonderful fattening things." The first hurdle—the mention of the memorial service—had been cleared, Kali thought with relief, with no comment, tears or other reaction from anyone.

"I'll just visit a while first." Leighton went into the living room to sit down on the loveseat beside Jada. "Well, you look amazing, I love fake leopard. And you've even got a matching bag. A hat. And heels!"

"How've you been, Leighton?" Jada said through a ring of cigarette smoke, wondering if Leighton knew that Helen was due to arrive any minute.

"I've been okay, all things considered. Can I bum a cig?"

Obligingly, Jada pulled out her pack and held it open for Leighton. "I really never smoke, so I don't know why I'm doing this now. Stress, I guess," Leighton sighed. "There's been so much to do, tidying up Rick's affairs."

"Right," Jada said, "his affairs." She tapped the cigarette ash onto the china dinner plate.

"Probating the will is a major pain. I told him to get a living revocable trust. But that's lawyers for you—don't expect them to do the right thing when it comes to legalities concerning their families."

"You should see the hell people go through when there isn't a will," Jada said, then realized her reference to 'hell' was inappropriate since Rick was sure to be there by now, and Leighton likely knew it. The firm was still going through the tedious and expensive process of identifying all funds Rick had brought in through his extortion activities—none of which, if and when identified by the State Bar's sniffer-dog accountants, could realistically be repaid by Biltmore, Durham & Spears. The firm could barely keep its head above water these days. The partners had notified the authorities, since they had all benefited financially, without even knowing it, from the criminal activities of their partner. No client had come forward to press charges and for that they were all very grateful, though still nervous that the other shoe would drop sometime soon.

"Where do we put the presents?" Marcia asked, as her eyes swept the room, alighted on Jada, then moved on with no indication of recognition. Jada dragged heavily on her cigarette. Could she safely assume that no photos of her had been dredged up in Ross's box of kiddie stuff, or on any of his devices? And that no one had let anything slip to Marcia about her and Ross—not even Audrey? She looked sideways at Marcia, trying to assess whether she was safely out of the woods. Marcia might be crueler and more cunning than Jada gave her credit for and was going to let her twist in the wind for a while, before publicly outing her in front of all the tea guests, as being the husband-snatcher that she was.

Kali took the gifts from Marcia, relieved to see that they were small: three pretty bags looped with yards of curling ribbon from which pillow-shaped satin drawer sachets dangled.

"Leighton did the shopping for all of us," Marcia murmured, "which was so nice of her. I'm not into fancy underwear these days, now that Ross is . . . not with me."

From her seat on the sofa, Jada pulled on her cigarette, eyes still on Marcia. "Got another butt?" Leighton nudged her, startling Jada out of her trance.

"I thought you didn't smoke," Jada grumbled, taking the pack again out of her faux leopard bag.

"This is a special occasion."

Then the front door opened, after a quick knock, and Helen Sharpe rolled in with her usual air of authority. "Hello everyone," she said. No smile. "Good to see all of you. Where shall I put my gift?"

"Helen, so glad you could make it," Kali said, avoiding the crushing stares from Jada and Gillian, while Helen and Leighton exchanged looks of extreme dislike. It was hard to picture Helen with Rick, Kali thought.

She was a boxy little woman, with short, blunt-cut hair, and those weird eyeglasses without frames. She patrolled the offices of Biltmore, Durham & Spears, striking fear into the hearts of everyone, since everyone, at some point, was "up to something" as far as Helen was concerned (including Helen herself, as it turned out). But, being the head of HR, charged with the duty of making sure that law, order, and decency prevailed at all times, wasn't it hugely hypocritical—even unethical—for her to be carrying on with the (married) Managing Partner? And if she had been—and no one had any tangible evidence of that—why didn't she seem sadder, now that Rick was gone? Kali wondered.

"Ana should be here any minute," Kali said, though no one had asked. She took her phone from a pocket in the side of her chiffon gown. It was 4:30 already. Ana hadn't called or texted. Not a good sign.

"This is so exciting." Leighton swung her hair again. I'm dying to meet the woman who's finally putting a leash and collar on Alexander Spears!"

Jada winced at the mention of dog accessories. *Poor old Ross*, she thought. *And poor old me.* She glanced out the window, dreading the sight of Audrey marching up the walk with a tray of blood pudding or some other horrible thing the English liked to eat.

"Wouldn't I just love to be getting a load of sexy new things?" Leighton sighed.

But your husband is dead, Kali thought, marveling at how well Leighton looked, how happy. She had a right to get over her grief. But so soon? Had she already found someone new?

Marcia and Natalie, on the other hand, looked as subdued as one would expect the recently-widowed to look, and they were the ones whose marriages had already been in trouble, before the crash. Natalie looked especially miserable, slumped in a corner chair, examining her shoes, not making eye contact with anyone. She had managed so well to avoid Sandy's business obligations while he was alive, she had to be wondering what in hell she was doing here with all these women now that he was dead. Especially if it was only a green card marriage that they had. Did she know that Sandy had been investigated for war crimes?

"Audrey and I have patched things up," Marcia said, "as everyone will be relieved to know. But only for the sake of the kids. She *is* their grand-mother. I'll never get away from that fact, will I?"

"Speaking of kids, I'm wondering where *my* daughter is." Gillian glanced, worriedly, out the window.

"What a fabulous hat you have, Gillian! That's the same one that awful minister made you take off at the memorial service, isn't it?" Leighton asked.

Thanks for reminding everyone of the most mortifying event of my life, Gillian thought. "Yes, same one," she smiled. "I added the flowers to make it more festive." She selected a *petit four* from a silver tray on the buffet, desperately hoping someone would change the subject.

"How did you stick them on?" Leighton asked.

"Hot glue gun." Gillian licked her fingers. "It was my husband's. What's a tea for, if not for getting out your great hats?"

"Yo, I'm wearing one," Jada said. "Am I invisible?"

"No, yours is awesome," Gillian said. "I told you already."

"And we'll have to put a hat on the bride-to-be, right?" Natalie said. "A paper plate hat."

"Oh, no," Marcia groaned. "Everyone hates that silly custom."

"I have trouble imagining Ana tolerating a paper plate and bows on her head," Kali said.

"Well, everything just looks lovely," Marcia sighed. "Is Alex coming? Is he bringing Ana?"

"I didn't invite him," Kali said. "So I hope not."

"Men don't understand these things," Leighton said. "Every man I told about this lingerie tea thought we'd all be trying on sexy underwear and modeling it!"

"They wanted to be invited until they found out that no one would be wearing the stuff," Jada said. "Men are such simple brain-stem creatures. As if we were all going to strip down and struggle into split-crotch panties."

"Ooh, did somebody buy Ana those?" Marcia asked.

"What are split-crotch panties?" Natalie murmured. But then the conversation faltered.

Kali wondered if Marcia's affair with her therapist was over. And how she had reacted when she got the FedEx box from the firm. Poor Marcia. For the first time, it struck Kali that the doling out of pretty underthings for a young woman about to get married to a sexy older man might strike a painful chord with the women so recently bereaved. Good thing Pete Johnson's mother was not alive, since she would have discovered by now that her son liked to wear exactly the sort of frilly things that were the whole point of this tea. Really, a lingerie tea was monstrously inappropriate. A kitchen shower would have made more sense. At least it wouldn't have rubbed the widows' noses in the fact that they had no men for whom to wear alluring underwear.

Chapter 36

THE CLOCK ON THE MANTEL TICKED LOUDLY AS JADA EXHALED twin dragon jets of cigarette smoke through her nostrils, her eyes flickering over Marcia, the better to assess how much trouble she was likely to be. "So where the hell's our fabulous bride-to-be?" she finally said.

The doorbell rang again. "That must be her." Kali ran to the door. But it wasn't Ana, it was Audrey Owen. Kali could see her blue-grey hair and faded satin hat with its little half-veil, though the window on the door. "Mrs. Owen! So good to see you again! We could really use your tea expertise today."

"Expertise?" Audrey said, stepping over the threshold. "Not sure what's meant by that remark."

"I mean, since you're English and all that."

"All that?" Sourly, she handed Kali a drab, gift-wrapped package. "I can't stay long as Derek's waiting in the car."

Kali didn't know what to say. There were no men at the tea: this was a woman-only bonding event. But she could hardly let an old man just sit outside in the hot car, could she? On the other hand, with Derek waiting impatiently out there, Audrey wouldn't be inclined to stay very long.

"Please ask him to come in," Kali finally said.

"Oh, he'll be all right. He's got his radio on, and an ice cream. He's not much of a one for these women's get-togethers." She peered around Kali, to see into the living room. "I expect my daughter in law's here already."

"Yes, Marcia's here."

"Well, she would be. Loves to eat, that one does."

"She's getting very thin," Kali said, in Marcia's defense.

"Running around with one's therapist will do that, I expect."

"Well, please, come in, have a cup of tea. And we have wonderful sweet things."

"I prefer savories, for my tea. Derek likes his pudding, of course, but it's too much bloody work at my age."

"We have savories too," Kali smiled, "so come in, come in." But Audrey had already pushed past her, obviously looking forward to showing these silly American women how a real English tea was to be done.

"It was such a surprise to hear that Alexander is getting married," Marcia was saying, as Audrey looked her up and down. "A shock, actually. He'd been seeing a friend of mine, Paula."

"That Paula's a tramp," Audrey said. "She was at our place once."

Jada bit her lip, adjusted her leopard hat, and lit another cigarette. She was pretty sure Audrey had mixed her up with this Paula person—unless Ross had had another affair going on, simultaneously.

"Anyway," Marcia continued, "Paula's super sweet, and she really fell for him. When Ross told me that Alex was getting married, of course, I assumed it was to Paula, not your law firm's summer student."

"Well, of course, in HR, we do our best," Helen jumped in, "but people are people, and the laws of attraction are what they are."

"Just saying, Paula's such a great person."

"I'm surprised to hear you say you like her," Audrey said, scowling at her daughter in law. "My word, what's the world coming to when a married woman goes on about how she likes her husband's mistress?"

"You don't know what you're talking about, Audrey. As usual."

"She was at our house she was, that Paula person. Black as the ace of spades."

"Paula's not black," Marcia sighed and shook her head as Jada shrank lower into her chair, assessing how many exits there were from the living room.

"She is indeed," Audrey exclaimed, "and a right tart she was, in all them zippers and what not."

"Well anyway," Marcia said, "I'm happy for Alex. What's she like, this law student?"

"Very nice," Kali said. "You'll meet her soon."

"Long legs," Gillian added from her grazing station beside the tea table. "Big boobs. Your basic nightmare."

"That comment is inappropriate," Helen frowned. "Ana is a very smart lawyer, and very dedicated to her profession."

"What profession would that be?" Jada asked, snidely.

"Jada, I've warned you about remarks like that."

"Has she made partner yet?" Jada asked, "or does Exec want to wait until she maybe passes the Bar exam?"

"There's been no talk of partnership," Helen replied, "and I won't discuss that issue in this forum. But she'll be a Supreme Court Justice one day—I wouldn't be surprised."

"It's no wonder Alex dumped Paula, then," Marcia said. "She's nothing like that." There was an audible, collective sigh in the room as most thoughts turned, sympathetically, to Paula.

"Shall I pour the tea now?" Audrey grasped the sleeve of Kali's chiffon gown. "It's considered an honor, where I come from, to pour the tea at a gathering of this nature."

"Yes, please, Mrs. Owen, if you think now is the right time. You're the authority."

"Am I the only one who's going to eat anything?" Gillian demanded. "I feel like a pig over here, chowing down by myself."

"Let's just forget the tea and uncork the champagne," Jada said.

"Now you're talking." Leighton slapped Jada on the knee and stood up. "You stay where you are—I'm pouring."

"I'm coming with you," Jada said, glad of a reason to escape the living room.

"Forget the tea?" Audrey gasped. She peered at Jada, her small eyes hard and puzzled. "Now, you look very familiar."

"Oh, all colored folk look the same," Jada said.

"No, that's not it." Audrey frowned. "I'm sure we've met."

Marcia was looking at them, eyebrows raised. "Where would you two have met?"

"We haven't. Poor Mrs. Owen is distraught, which is totally understandable."

"There's a ton of great food," Kali said. "I'm going to put the rest out. We have fresh rolls too—warming up in the oven."

"I've got enough rolls," Natalie said, glumly poking at the waistline of her suit. Then, the doorbell rang again.

"That's probably Isadora," Gillian said. "I'll get it."

"Champagne is on the way," Jada said, following close behind Leighton.

"Shouldn't we wait for Ana?" Kali asked.

"Ana?" Leighton laughed. "Who the hell's Ana?"

As Kali was about to follow them into the kitchen, not at all sure this was the right time to crack open champagne—where was the *Delights of Tea* when she needed it?—she was startled by the sudden appearance of

Isadora, with her 'friend.' "Emilie?" she said, not comprehending for a moment. "*You're* Isadora's friend?"

"That would be me," Emilie smiled wickedly.

"How do you two know each other?"

"We happen to be *besties*," Isadora said, "and business partners too."

"What kind of business partners?" Kali asked, suspiciously. "Does your mother know about this?"

"What's that?" Gillian was suddenly behind Kali, her large hat grazing the chandelier again.

"Me and Izzy have been best buds since the law firm picnic," Emilie said, "which I know you've told Kali *all* about."

"Don't call me Izzy," Isadora jabbed her in the arm.

"I was only concerned about Kali's children," Gillian explained. "You didn't seem to be watching them."

"Sure, I get that," Emilie said. "After all, you're a great mom yourself, right?" Her pale blue eyes took in Gillian's dress, then her hat.

"And your hair," Kali said, in amazement. "What are those? Dreadlocks?"

"Cornrows." Isadora shook her head, making the beads clatter. "Mom paid for us to get our hair done."

"But I didn't mean like that," Gillian said, although, in truth, she was sort of envious.

"Don't you love our fetching little gloves?" Emilie asked. Both girls were wearing fingerless crocheted gloves and matching hats—more like doilies—on their heads. The studs in both girls' noses glittered. Their dresses were loose, sloppy, tie-dyed prints. On Isadora's feet were large, suede high-heeled pumps that were way too big for her.

"Where did you get those shoes?" Gillian asked.

"The Goodwill. They were, like, a dollar, so don't freak out."

"It seems weird to be here without the kids," Emilie said, looking around "especially as your guest, Kali, and not having to do a thing. Did Dr. Matt take the rugrats roller-blading?"

"Of course not. They went to the beach."

Emilie knew how much the whole roller-blading thing frightened her. Why was she here, and trying to provoke a fight? It wouldn't have killed her to have offered to help with the tea. Kali had begged her, even offering double pay, but she'd flatly refused, and now Kali knew why.

"I'm sorry, Kali," Gillian said, as the girls clomped down the hall and into the living room. "They won't stay long. It's their idea of a stupid joke—they're just trying to be funny."

"They're fine. They're actually quite cute," Kali said, still annoyed by Emilie's rudeness, not to mention that she was right—Kali did now have to treat her as a guest. "Why don't we get some champagne? Jada's right. Who needs tea? Nobody likes it anyway."

"What's that?" Audrey said, from the dining room, holding the teapot, in mid-pour.

"Are the clients still coming?" Gillian asked, following Kali towards the kitchen.

"Later."

"Later? What if we're totally in the jar by then?"

"They will be too," Kali said. "I'll make sure."

"There's a man at the door, Kali!" Helen called. "He wants to know where he can change."

In the kitchen, Kali grabbed a champagne flute and held it out for Jada to fill. "I didn't order any man!" she called back.

"Well, why didn't you?" Leighton demanded. "It's not like no one around here could use one, right?"

"Maybe he comes with the sandwiches. He must be from the catering company," Kali said. "I'll go talk to him." She downed her champagne. "In a minute." She held out her flute for a refill.

Her mother turned away from the sink and looked disapprovingly at Kali and her guests. Things were getting out of hand. Women were guzzling champagne, glass after glass, not eating. The bride-to-be hadn't arrived, and it was after five. No one seemed interested in where Ana was, or in drinking tea. She might as well roll a doobie, Marina thought. Nobody was likely to notice, or care.

"Mom, would you go out there and tell the waiter to change in a guest bedroom?" Kali said. She was still puzzling over how the catering company could have missed telling her that they would be providing a waiter. "But make sure he's got the right address." If he was included with the sandwiches and pastries, shouldn't he have arrived earlier, to help set things up? Would there be an extra fee for him? If so, how much? Or was he a tips-only guy? She refilled her glass again, feeling woozy and disorganized.

"Haven't you had enough?" Marina said. "You need to slow down, Kali."

"A good tea hostess always gets drunk."

"Is that what it says in your tea book?"

"No!" Kali hiccupped, then laughed.

Definitely, time to light up, Marina thought, tossing her dishtowel onto the counter and heading out the back door as Jada pulled more champagne bottles out of the fridge.

Chapter 37

"Now's our chance," Emilie said. "We've got to move fast." She and Isadora were alone in the living room, everyone else having drifted back into the kitchen, where it seemed they were going to stay for a while. "You take that fake leopard job and I'll do this one." She grabbed a patent leather bag that was leaning against a chair.

"You expect me to steal from my mother's friends?" Isadora gaped.

"Why not? You steal from your own *mother*. Duh. They're all in there getting shit-faced, and Kali's mom is even outside smoking up. They'll never miss a dime. Get going, Izzy. There's like a dozen bags in here. It's like an Easter egg hunt!"

"I told you, I'm not taking anything from any of these bags."

"What the hell is this? Dope?" Emilie held up something lumpy, wrapped in plastic. "Christ! It's a sandwich. One of those cows brought a sandwich!" She giggled. "Probably the old lady."

"My mother is not a cow."

"Well, okay, I didn't mean your mom, specifically. Though I'm not exactly her biggest fan since she tried to get me fired, ratting me out to Kali, about you and me hanging out at that lame picnic."

"That's a lie. She did not."

"She did so! She told Kali I wasn't watching the kids. So don't get me started on how cool and chill your mom is."

"Well, you should have been watching the kids," Isadora sulked.

"Like *you'd* know something about that. Anyway, forget it. Just get going. There's fat little handbags all over this place."

"I'm *not* stealing from my mother's friends, okay? Or my mom. Not anymore. And neither are you."

"You got any better ideas for quick cash? What do you think we're here for? How else are we going to get our business going?"

"There isn't going to be any business."

"What? Are you losing it?"

"Not with me anyway."

"Don't start on that again, with your lame insecurities." Emilie was clawing at the clasp of Helen's change purse. "You're always saying stupid shit like that. You're a wimp, you know that?"

"You take anything from any of these handbags and I'm going to call Kali. The cops too."

"You'd never do that."

"Oh, yeah? Try me!"

"I don't believe this. After all that I've done for you!"

"You want to step outside and discuss it?"

"You're on, Loser!"

From the kitchen, Kali heard the front door slam, loudly. She hoped it wasn't Matt and the kids back already—everything was already careening out of control. Through the kitchen window, she could see her mother dragging on a joint. That's all she needed, for some neighbor to call the police! Kali hurried out the back door to haul Marina inside.

Leighton and Helen re-entered the living room, filled their plates with sandwiches and tea cakes and sat down to exchange filthy looks and sarcastic comments. "Still battling it out over monitors and mouse pads?" Leighton asked.

"No, too busy with the IRS and outside counsel," Helen said, "going through all our records and files. They might want to pay you a visit, in case Rick kept anything from the firm in his home office, that the authorities might need."

"The firm," Leighton snorted. "There is no firm without Rick."

"Also no extortion."

"These sandwiches look much too rich," Audrey pronounced as she surveyed the buffet. "Loads of butter, I should think." She took one from the tray and pushed it between her teeth.

"Of course, there's butter in them," Marina said. Her pupils were hugely dilated. "They'd be dry as hell if there wasn't butter."

"Derek, my husband, would never take sandwiches for his tea. He likes his pudding or a nice Danish. We get them by the box at Costco. They're quite a bargain when you buy them in the box."

"I thought English people made a great big fuss over tea," Marina giggled. "A gigantic fuss."

"I don't know as I'd say we make a fuss. Derek loves his pudding, but it's too much bloody work for me now. And not good for his condition. Far too rich." She scanned the buffet again, hoping someone would ask for details about Derek's 'condition.' No one did. "Those cinnamon rolls look quite nice," she added, helping herself to two, then gazing around with sharp, expectant eyes. "Now, I'm sure we've met before," she said, as Jada appeared in the doorway, a full champagne flute in each hand.

"I was at the memorial service," Jada said. "I'm bummed you don't remember."

"Well, of course, I remember that—that dreadful service. But there's something about you—I just can't put my finger on it."

"I've just got one of those faces, I guess."

"Did you order donuts?" Helen asked Kali. "There's a truck in your driveway."

"Donuts?"

"I don't think you need any more food," Helen said.

"The truck's likely just turning around. We get a lot of that, on this cul-de-sac."

"I have the feeling Ana's not coming." Helen looked at her phone. "It's going on six. That wouldn't be her in a donut truck."

"I'll go see," Kali said, really feeling the champagne as she opened the front door.

Chapter 38

"EVERYBODY? HELLO? I NEED YOUR ATTENTION," KALI SAID. Grace Owen, in a floral-patterned dress, loomed behind her in the foyer. "I'd like everyone to give a warm Biltmore, Durham & Spears welcome to Grace Owen!"

Grace beamed and waved at everyone. "*Mrs.* Grace Owen."

"Owen?" Audrey repeated, her eyes bright. "That's my name!"

"What a coincidence."

"Are you related to us Owens?" Audrey asked, biting into her second cinnamon roll. "We're from Manchester, but we live in Simi Valley now. My son, Ross, lived in Santa Monica."

"Oh, I know where Ross lived," Grace said, "since I was his wife."

"How's that?" Audrey's mouth, full of half-masticated cinnamon roll, hung open.

"What?" Marcia was looking from Grace to Audrey and back again.

"I said, I was Ross Owen's *wife*."

"*I* was Ross Owen's wife," Marcia said.

"You invited Grace Owen?" Jada hissed, coming up behind Kali. "You shittin' me?"

"Well no, I—Jada, let go! You're hurting me."

"Oh, this is becoming a really bad trip," Marina said. A blob of whipped cream gushed out the side of her cream pastry and plopped onto the carpet. "Peace," she added.

"I got sick of being left out of everything," Grace said. "And Kali? You could have invited me, that day we had lunch. If your secretary hadn't asked me if I was coming, I never would have known about this party, and I would have been left out again." A soft, tissue-wrapped package crinkled under her arm and she toyed, anxiously, with the ribbon on it. "It's rude to crash a party, I know that. I'm not a total slob. But personally, I think I should have been invited. I knew Alex, sort of. I heard enough about him over the years, and I heard all about Ana too. From Ross, my *husband*."

"Ana's not here yet," Gillian said, entering the room and unaware of the drama unfolding. "There seems to be some doubt that she's going to show."

"You think you were *married* to Ross?" Marcia demanded.

"I *was* married to Ross." Grace stood her ground.

"What's this?" Audrey demanded.

Kali and Marina hurried to help her into a chair. "Grace, she's an old lady," Kali pleaded. "Take it easy."

"I don't understand!" Audrey wailed. "How many wives did my son have?"

"Only two," Jada said, "that we know of. So far."

"You!" Audrey cried. "You were at my home! Yes, Ross brought you for supper!"

"And a lovely evening it was, Mrs. Owen," Jada said, avoiding the eyes of Marcia and Grace.

"Ross took you to meet his *parents*?" Grace said.

"*You* were having an affair with Ross?" Marcia gaped.

"Oh, I wouldn't call it that," Jada said, vaguely.

"Well, what would you call it?" Marcia demanded.

"A dalliance, a flirtation, a fling. A couple of damn drinks. I never asked him to leave you and your kids for me. I never even wanted him too! I never even formed that thought, Marcia. Not once! There was no intent. No *mens rea.*"

"I wasn't having *an affair* with Ross," Grace interrupted. "Look at my wedding ring. Even got a diamond." She held out her plump hand. "We were married, me and Ross, Marcia. For over ten years. I've got four of his kids to prove it."

"Children too?" Audrey sank into a chair and put her head in her hands, moaning.

"More grandchildren, Audrey," Leighton said. "You should be thrilled."

Audrey moaned louder. Her satin hat fell off and rolled across the floor, like a loose tire thrown from a truck.

"*You* had an *affair* with *Ross?*" Marcia was advancing on Jada.

"Well, who didn't, right?" Jada said, backing up towards the kitchen.

"You've got to face up to things, Audrey," Grace said. She moved over to her mother-in-law's chair and squatted down beside it, her flower print dress ballooning around her like a parachute. "I'll show you pictures of the kids—that'll cheer you up. They look just like Ross, most of them."

"Most of them?" Audrey was fanning her face with a paper napkin.

"Actually, the two that look most like him aren't his. Isn't that weird? I know all this a shock, but you'll be glad, in the end, that everything's out in the open. And I've been wanting to meet you forever."

"Why are you so pissed at me?" Jada asked Marcia. "At least I wasn't *married* to the guy."

"You were his law partner!"

"Yeah, well, I learned my lesson, okay?"

"But, *you're* the reason he left me alone with five kids!"

Suddenly, there was a loud New York cab whistle. "Ladies? Timeout!

I need your attention please." A well-groomed, muscular young man had appeared in the entrance to the room. He was dressed in black and white satin: a Halloween-type costume of an English butler, but with much less fabric. He held up an old-fashioned boom box and gave them all a thousand-watt smile. "Could one of you gals show me where to plug this thing in?"

"You brought the music?" Kali said. "I was about to go find some." Her head was swimming, nothing was making sense. "And I've already put out the food."

"Nice," the man said. "I'll fill up later. I never eat before a performance."

"What?" Had the catering company included both a butler and music in the price of the tea sandwiches, Kali wondered? That didn't seem likely. "Um, excuse me, but who exactly are you?"

"The entertainment!" he smiled. "A present from your friend, Ana who—sad face emoji—won't be joining us here today."

"Ana's not coming?" Kali repeated.

"Not with us, Hon."

"What?"

"Are you a stripper?" Leighton asked.

"You got that right, Sweet-cheeks."

"You're going to take all your clothes off?" Jada laughed out loud.

"You bet your little fake leopard booties!"

"All *right!*" Leighton clapped her hands. "I saw your show in Vegas. Thunder Down Under!"

"Oh, I *wish*. Do you know how much those little cuties make? I work for tips only—duly noted, please, Ladies?"

"Wait! Hold on!" Kali protested. "No, not in my house, at my tea!"

"Oh no," Audrey cried. "This is too much!"

"Take a chill pill," Marina told her. "Or go upstairs if you this isn't your scene. You don't need to ruin it for everyone else."

"Let's get comfortable," Leighton laughed. "You and Audrey are out-voted, Kali!"

"Wow," Isadora said. "I've never seen a guy strip."

"But I'm English!" Audrey cried.

"In that case, Honey, I've got a special tune, just for you," the man laughed. "You're going to cream your English jeans. And I'll sit on your face, for free."

Audrey fell back in her chair. "Oh, what does he mean? What is happening? Where's my husband? Somebody find Derek!"

Through the ensuing pandemonium, Gillian suddenly remembered where she'd seen those high heeled pumps Isadora had on. They had been in Pete Johnson's desk drawer!

Chapter 39

T HE 'EXOTIC DANCER' AS THE MAN, WHOSE NAME WAS DEVLIN, insisted he be called, struck a seductive pose by Kali's mantle and was about to begin his performance. "Crank it up, Baby," he said. Then, giggling, Leighton hit 'play' on his boom box.

After some static, a single guitar strummed, then a banjo joined in, followed by the sound of someone tap dancing. Soon, a boisterous bump and grind was rolling out of the boom box.

"*I got a souvenir in London!*" the song warbled. "*Got to hide it from my mum! Can't declare it at the customs, but I'll have to take it home!*"

"What a dreadful song!" Audrey wailed from her chair. "What's all this about?" she demanded. "What's going on? I don't understand any of it!"

"*Tried to keep it confidential!*" the tape sang on, "*but the news is leaking out! Got a souvenir in London. There's a lot of it about!*"

"The clap!" Isadora leaned over and shouted in Audrey's ear. "It's about the clap!"

"What?"

"Gonorrhea," Isadora yelled. "Venereal disease!"

"Oh! Oh my!" Audrey cried.

Devlin was peeling off his white gloves, moving his hips in a vulgar way and pouting at the women. Then he tossed the gloves, along with his bow tie, into the arrangement of pompom chrysanthemums on Kali's coffee table. Slithering out of his black satin jacket, then his trousers, he twirled both over his head. His pelvis thrust back and forth, side to side, grinding and bumping to the music.

"Yes. I've found a bit of London! And I'd like to lose it quick!"

Devlin was down to a black waistcoat front, tied around the back, and a white satin, well-stuffed and very tight, G-string. As the women gaped, he mounted one of the upholstered arms of Kali's love seat to make exaggerated humping motions over it.

Boom! Boom! Boom! went the bass drum on the tape. *"Got to show it to my doctor 'cause it isn't going to shrink!"*

"How far is he going to go?" Natalie gaped, eyes wide.

"Pull the plug!" Helen said. "This is a business function."

"So why don't you mind it?" Leighton said.

"What?"

"Your own business."

"Excuse me?"

"If you don't like the show—there's the door."

The fingers of Leighton's hand rhythmically stroked the stem of her champagne flute. Then she gasped and laughed as Devlin, back on his feet, undid the ties of his fake waistcoat, pulled it off and whirled it around, making it flutter over his head. His chest glistened with sweat. Cymbals crashed. Everyone started. The ghetto blaster practically leaped off the floor from the force of the vibrations.

Devlin's G-string swaggered past Audrey, at eye level. She shuddered and drew back. *Stiff upper lip,* Jada smirked, glancing at her. *Close your eyes and think of England.*

'Want to keep it confidential! But the truth is leaking out!

Devlin was down on the floor now, on all fours, making

doggie-humping motions. Then he rolled over and executed a series of energetic kicks in the air.

"The lamp! Watch out for my lamp!" Kali cried, as the floor rolled and tipped in front of her. She was totally drunk, she realized, at her own tea party!

There was sporadic nervous laughter from the women, most of whom sat frozen in their seats, knees tightly together, clutching their teacups or champagne flutes. Then Audrey rose and staggered out of her chair. Marcia rushed to help her towards the stairs, patting her arm and stroking her hair. Grace watched them go, looking piqued. "I'm her daughter in law too," she complained, to no one in particular.

Suddenly, Devlin leaped to his feet, shoved his hands into the front of his G-string, and tossed back his head in a paroxysm of pleasure. He looked around the room as he swayed, pelvis gyrating, taking in the women, one by one, from below half-lowered lids. He seemed to be winding down.

"*Got a souvenir in London! There's a lot of it about!*" Then he was suddenly on the carpet again, this time on his back, simulating an orgasm, pelvis thrusting towards the ceiling. His bare toes dug divots into Kali's carpet.

"He's actually very fit!" Grace shouted to Kali, as the cymbals crashed again and the tap-shoeing rhythm on the tape picked up tempo. "He must play professional sport! Or do you think doing this keeps him so fit?"

"He's going too far!" Helen shouted. "We must stop this man right now!"

The music did, in fact, stop a few seconds later, trickling down to a lone guitar strumming, the same way it had begun. Devlin jumped to his feet and did an exaggerated bow. A couple of the women clapped, there were a few catcalls. Jada put her thumbs in her mouth and gave a loud whistle.

Chapter 40

KALI ATTEMPTED AN EASY, NONCHALANT LAUGH. "WELL! I'M GLAD you didn't go any further with that, Devlin."

"I'm not," Leighton complained. "He was just getting to the good stuff."

"I *am* available for some private time," Devlin smiled at her. "Book early, book often."

"Leave your card," Leighton said.

"We wanted it all off," Jada complained.

"Be quiet you silly person," Helen snapped.

"Ooh, I love where this is going!" Devlin grinned and cantered over to her, fell down on his knees, threw his arms around her legs and wiggled his bum in the air. The sweat rolled off his chin and dripped onto the carpet. The soles of his feet were black. "Nothing like a good cat fight," he added. "Mrreow!" Helen pushed him away, making a horrible face.

"Please, please!" Kali said, trying to act amused by everything. "Thank you, Devlin. That was very well done. But we should be getting back to our tea now."

"Tea?" Devlin laughed at her from the carpet. "You're all dead *drunk!*"

"The man's clairvoyant," Jada said.

"What this man is reduced to, to make a living, is very degrading," Helen said, prying his hands off her. "Not only to him but to anyone who watches his disgraceful performance. I think we all feel a little debased right now."

Grace was wiping her glasses on the hem of her dress and chuckling. "I don't know about debased, but I'm welded to my seat here."

"Ahem!" said Devlin. He jumped to his feet and struck another pose by the mantel. "Attention Ladies. I have a note to read to all of you, so gather 'round." He was panting, dripping more sweat onto Kali's carpet. "It's from Ana. Your absentee guest of honor."

"She's not coming?" Helen asked, "to her own shower?"

"Where is she?" Natalie asked. "Why didn't she come?"

"I'll read the note in a sec," Devlin said. "Can I get a glass of that bubbly all you ladies are enjoying? I believe I've earned it."

"Would you like a bathrobe or something?" Kali asked, handing him a flute and filling it. She was dreading the reading of Ana's note and in no hurry to hear what it said. "Or can I get you your clothes?"

"No, I need to cool down first."

"Here, have some water," Marina handed him a paper cup full of water. "You need to hydrate before you start drinking."

"Thanks, Lovely." Devlin guzzled it noisily, then crumpled the cup and tossed it into the fireplace. It landed in an arrangement of Shasta daisies and cornflowers that had been placed in the grate by Kali's designer. Then, with a sigh, Devlin reached into the front of his G-string and took out a folded paper.

"I wouldn't have thought there'd be much room in there for stationery," Natalie said. Her cheeks were bright pink.

"Correct-o-mundo, Sweetie," Devlin said, "there isn't. Attention, attention!" He put one bare foot up on the edge of the love seat. "I wanted to be an actor once, I'll have everyone know."

"Interesting," Kali said, weakly.

"But now I *loathe* Hollywood. Okay, now you can shut up. I don't care if this is your house. And your sofa, which is *finally* seeing some badly-needed action." He grinned and held up the piece of paper. "This little ditty here was written by your great friend, Ana. The dear departed, you could say."

"Departed?" Natalie echoed.

"Quiet please." Devlin cleared his throat again. "No more interruptions. Here goes." He read, "I'm in the South of France, I've found a new romance." He paused, looking around the room with a provocative grin, then looked down again at the paper. "I hope you loved the dance, and you can keep your underpants."

"Keep your underpants?" Kali repeated.

"The rhyming's a bit forced, but I guess you were all going to give her split-crotch panties or something?"

"We were not!" Helen protested. "I brought some very nice camisoles."

"Whatever." Devlin shrugged. "I don't know—it sounded pretty kinky to me. Oh, there's a P.S. here. It says, I'm sure you will all get, if not what you need, exactly what you deserve." The women all looked at each other, dumbfounded.

"Anyone want to keep the note?" Devlin held out the paper to Kali, eyebrows raised. "Souvenir? Anyone?"

"Throw it out," Kali said, looking around at the remains of her elegant afternoon tea. What were they supposed to so with all the gifts? She had the credit card receipt for that nightgown she had bought. Would she have to pay shipping on the return?

"Okay then." With a shrug, Devlin crumpled the note and sent it through the air to join the paper cup in the Shasta daisies.

"Does this mean she and Alex aren't getting married?" Helen asked.

"That would seem to be the idea," Jada said.

"I wonder if Alex knows," Marcia said.

"I'm sure he'll figure it out," Jada said. "He's a quick read."

"Well, ta-ta, ladies." Evidently bored with his unimaginative and unappreciative audience, Devlin yawned and began collecting the bits of his costume from the various pieces of Kali's furniture.

"Your performance was very good," Grace told him.

"Thanks, Hon." He strutted past her to retrieve his boom box and blew her a kiss over his sweaty shoulder "I'll just pop upstairs and change if that's okay." It was not a question. He gave Kali a long look. "FYI, gratuities *are* the norm for my performance. Whenever you all get your handbags out."

"Well, yes, of course," Kali said. "We'll pass the hat."

"Not mine you're not," Gillian said, grabbing the brim of her cartwheel, which had, miraculously stayed on her head throughout the entire afternoon.

"There's a guest bedroom upstairs," Kali told Devlin. "Please don't use the children's rooms."

"No problem. I'm no perv."

"Well," Kali sighed, looking around the wreckage of her lovely afternoon tea room. "Can I get anyone something else to eat? More to drink?"

"I wonder how much he charged for that performance," Leighton said. "Did you already pay him, Kali?"

"No, I thought he came with the sandwiches."

"Maybe Ana's going to send on his invoice," Gillian said. "As a parting shot."

"I sure am glad I stuck around," Isadora said, happily. All the women looked at her in surprise.

"Oh my God," Gillian said. "I'm so sorry! I forgot you were here, in all the commotion. You shouldn't have seen this!"

"Relax, Mother. I've seen plenty of ass."

"What?"

"In books, mostly."

"Where's Emilie?" Kali asked, suddenly realizing she was not there.

"Gone," Isadora said.

"Gone?"

"She won't be back. Lucky for you."

Chapter 41

"WHEN DO WE OPEN THE PRESENTS?" LEIGHTON ASKED. "If Ana's not coming, and she's not marrying Alex, then we get to keep the things we brought, right?"

"I guess so," Kali said uncertainly. *The Delights of Tea*, she thought, where are you now? She needed to look up 'showers, absence of bride-to-be,' and 'distribution of underwear.'

"Wouldn't it be more fun to mix them up?" Gillian said.

"I agree," Natalie said. "Let's mix them up. No gift tags."

"Who's going to wear the paper plate hat?" Helen asked.

"I'm wondering if we should call Alex and tell him about all of this. Natalie's right. What if he doesn't know?" Kali sat down, abruptly, on the edge of the love seat.

"Don't sit there," Helen cautioned. "That's where that man was doing his business."

"If Ana's taken off for France, and found someone else, I'm sure Alex has figured out that there's not going to be a wedding," Jada said.

From upstairs, came a scream from Audrey, followed by Devlin's angry shout. Then, a vehicle stopped in front of the house, several car doors slammed, and the front door of the house opened, followed by a huge crash in the foyer.

"What the heck?" Matt complained from the foyer. This was followed by a dragging, thumping sound.

Matt!" Kali jumped up. Her chiffon gown hung dispiritedly around her. The rip in the side had doubled in size, as had the arcs of sweat under each arm.

"Am I too late for the whole tea thingy?" Matt filled the entrance to the living room. "I tripped over that curtain on the table out there. I told you it was nuts to put it there, Kali, with all those flowers on it. An accident waiting to happen. I'd clean it up but as you can see," he attempted to wave a crutch, clumsily, "I don't have a free hand."

"Where's Harry and Molly? What happened!?"

"The kids are fine. They're fooling around in the ambulance." With that, the peculiar warbling shriek of an ambulance siren ripped through the room. "The driver's a good guy. But there's a Krispy Kreme truck blocking our driveway. I had to hobble up the lawn."

"But your leg, Matt!" Kali ran over to him. "What happened?"

"Little rollerblading incident, nothing serious." He thunked into the room on his crutches. His right leg was encased in white plaster, from toe to hip. "You girls can all sign my cast if you want." He was wearing a pair of shorts fashioned from surgical scrubs that had been cut off above the knee. "I caught my wheels in a sewer grate—didn't see it coming. My guess is an anterior cruciate ligament tear. I'll get it scoped on Tuesday. The resident didn't have a clue what to do." The ambulance siren warbled again outside.

"I'll go bring the kids in," Marina said, suddenly sober.

"So, how come you girls aren't trying on all the sexy underwear?" Matt asked. "Isn't that the whole point of this do?"

"Matthew, I'd like to know more about this so-called *incident*. I can't believe you're roller-blading, and when you had the kids with you! We discussed this. You promised."

"Partial ligament tear. No big deal."

"But you're in a body cast!"

"Not a body cast. You're incorrect. It's a full-leg cast."

"How long does it have to stay on?"

"Eight weeks."

"Eight weeks?"

Squealing and shouting, Harry and Molly hurled themselves into the room, followed by an out-of-breath Marina. "Guys?" Kali begged. "No running! Indoor voices please!"

Then Cannon barreled into the room, barking loudly, thick tail thrashing wildly, and loped into the kitchen after Harry and Molly, his toenails skittering on the tiled floor.

"Dad's cast is so cool!" Harry yelled, excitedly. "They had to cut off his pants! Can we have some of these cakes?"

"So, where's the bride-to-be?" Matt asked, looking around.

"Apparently, she's not coming," Kali sighed.

"Isn't she supposed to be here?"

"Of course, she's supposed to be here!"

"Take it easy, Kali," Jada said, "the man's been wounded in battle."

"I'll go put a video on for the kids." Matt hobbled towards the kitchen, grunting with exertion. "You girls get on with your tea and underwear."

"I don't believe this," Kali moaned, her face in her hands. "I can't take any more."

Jada patted her arm and passed her a linen napkin.

"It's very difficult, entertaining well," Leighton said. "Some of us never achieve it. We can't all be Martha Stewart."

"Kali? Cheer up. Things are working out well," Marcia said. "Grace and I are actually talking. See?"

Cautiously, Kali looked at them through the cracks between her fingers. The junior Mrs. Owens were sitting companionably, side by side on the sofa.

"We may never be best buddies," Grace said, "but it's not like we've got nothing in common."

"Hey, you two Mrs. Owens?" Jada said to them. "We cool? I mean, you two and me? No hard feelings?"

"Oh, you're fine. We both miss Ross," Marcia said, sadly, "but he wasn't a well man. It's been a real shocker, all this."

"I think he had too much love in him," Grace added. "He just had to spread it around."

"Well, it's great that you three are talking to each other about Ross," Natalie said. "But what about poor Alex? He's been left standing at the altar."

"Ana did him a favor," Jada said.

"A lot of women would kill for a man like him," Helen said. "Ana's much too young anyway. It wouldn't have worked out."

"I can't wait to tell Paula," Marcia said.

"I know someone he might like too," Natalie said. "A super sweet lady."

"I do as well," Helen said.

The small bulk of Audrey Owen, her grey fringe of hair standing out from her head as if she'd been electrocuted, appeared suddenly in the living room entrance. "That man wants to be paid," she said. "That awful man who took off all his clothes! He scared me half to death. There I was, having a quiet little lie-down—all because of him, I might add, and the man barges in, *naked as the day is long*, wanting to know where his bloody clothes have got to. He's in the kitchen now, making a right bloody pig of himself. I'd put a stop to it if I was you, Kali—especially with your children out there. But it's your house, as I say."

"I'll ask him if he takes Visa," Kali said. "Unless everyone wants to chip in?" No one moved. Everyone averted her eyes.

Then Kali's father came into the room, accompanied by Derek Owen.

They were carrying bags of Indian take-out food. "Why aren't you lovely ladies modeling your fancy underpants?" Boris asked.

"Oh, Dad, please," Kali moaned.

"There's a great bloody mess in your foyer," Derek said. "Somebody broke your Chinese vase."

"Oh no! The kids could hurt themselves," Isadora said. "I'll go clean it up for you, Kali." Everyone looked at her, in shock.

"Wow, thanks, Isadora," Kali said.

Gillian beamed at her daughter as Isadora hurried out of the room.

"Let's get on with opening the sexy underwear," Leighton said, excitedly.

"You know your dog?" Isadora popped her head back into the room. "I think he had an accident. I'll clean that up too."

Then the doorbell rang.

"Who could that be?" Kali asked, her head swimming from the champagne.

"Clients!" Jada hissed.

"It's your party, Kali" Gillian said. "You can cry if you want to."

Chapter 42

B Y SEVEN O'CLOCK, THE SEPTEMBER SUN WAS SLANTING IN THROUGH kitchen windows which were still gleaming from Kali's diligent cleaning. She, Gillian and Jada were sitting at the kitchen table. The living room, littered with boxes, tissue, satin sachets, and ribbons only minutes before, now seemed much as it had always been—thanks to Isadora's diligent efforts—though bits of scented sachet crystals would remain embedded in the Millers' carpet for months. Most of the guests had gone. So had Gillian's cartwheel hat. Cannon was thought to be the perpetrator of that particular piece. There had been no trial.

Helen had insisted that she not be forced to trade gifts, snatching back her box of camisoles from the pile of presents, and protesting that it was unreasonable for her to go home with something she didn't want and couldn't wear, when she really liked what she had brought. Marina, too, decided to keep her own gift: a pair of the psychedelic print leggings she'd found in the Hippie Shop Online.

The three double-brushed flannel nightgowns had been reshuffled and somehow managed to find their way back to Kali, Jada, and Gillian. A blizzard of snowy flannel was piled over the back of each of the kitchen chairs the friends now occupied.

Leighton had taken home a red satin garter belt that had been, surprisingly, a gift brought by Audrey; Natalie got a set of five Victoria's Secret thongs in stretch lace contributed by Marcia, and she was as gracious as anyone could be about the polyester sleep shirt that Grace had brought. The two pairs of sticky-soled bed socks went to Audrey who'd pronounced them very practical and exactly what she'd been meaning to get herself before winter set in. And Isadora had expressed delight with the animal print satin nightshirt, bought at Bloomingdale's by Leighton. Grace took home a lingerie bag and three pillow-shaped satin sachets from Helen and said she'd never had anything so pretty and feminine.

The younger Mrs. Owens had eventually moved out onto the Millers' deck where they could smoke, and properly share fond (and not so fond) memories of Ross. So much smoke was rising from the deck it looked as though they were grilling something back there. Apart from Grace, Marcia Gillian and Jada, only Isadora had stayed after the others had gone. She was sitting up on the kitchen counter, picking at the food in easy reach. "Lingerie teas are a blast," she said. "And your cake is so good, Mom."

"It was your dad's favorite."

"Life Celebration Cake."

"I told you we called it that?"

"You might have mentioned it. Like ten thousand times."

Matt had managed to get himself upstairs and was watching a Kings game, his leg elevated on a pile of pillows. Marina and Boris had taken Harry and Molly out to Burger King.

"I'm still trying to picture myself in lily-white flannel," Jada said. "I must have been delirious when I bought it. From Saks too. Flannel is one thing—okay, maybe it has its moments—but this pure-as-the-driven-snow white shit?"

"I'm still stunned that all of us managed to buy exactly the same thing for Ana," Kali said.

"And worse, ended up stuck with them," Gillian added.

"Ana sure would have hated them," Jada said.

"Oh, no question," Kali said.

"They're just so goddamned *ugly*," Gillian said.

"Do you really think so?" Kali said.

"Of course," Jada said. "That's why we all bought them. We were jealous of Ana because she's so young and sexy and smart—not to mention so well-dressed—and we all wanted revenge on Alex for one reason or another."

"Hold on," Kali said, "what if you got the flu? Wouldn't you want to snuggle up in one of these?"

"I'd take my chances with dying, thanks," Jada said.

"Where did Emilie go, Isadora?" Kali asked.

"I fired her."

"You fired our nanny?"

"You *fired Kali's nanny?*" Gillian repeated.

"She's not a person you should have looking after Harry and Molly." Isadora picked at the Life Celebration Cake, averting her eyes.

"Honey, I think you need to explain this," Gillian said.

"If I were Kali, I wouldn't want the sickening details. But she can ask me if she wants, about how she wasn't really looking after the Harry and Molly. And she was stealing stuff from you, like all the time. Makeup, money." She dug into the pocket of her dress and pulled out a crumpled wad of bills. "Here's the cash she took from all you guys' bags. I don't know whose it is, but I didn't want to keep it."

"Unbelievable!" Jada exclaimed.

"Oh gosh. I'll call everyone, see who's missing what," Kali said. "But I still need someone to help with the kids while I'm at work, unless I resign, as Matt wants me to. And he'll be like a giant third child now. He won't be on his feet for eight weeks."

"Take some time off," Jada suggested. "It's not like we're swamped at the office."

"She's got a point," Gillian said. "But don't resign. We need you too much."

"You could hire me, Kali," Isadora said, quietly. "I could be a nanny for Harry and Molly. They're super cute kids."

"You?" Gillian was stunned.

"Why not?" Isadora looked angrily at her mother.

"But Isadora, Honey, you don't like children," Gillian said.

"Who says I don't? And how do you know anyway?" Isadora flushed. "Did you ever bother to ask me?"

"Well, no," Gillian admitted.

"Just because you hate having a kid is no reason to think that I hate kids."

"I don't hate kids. I never hated having you. You were my life. You are my life!"

"You know what, Mom? With your writing, and your mind always somewhere else, until I was thirteen I thought you were deaf."

Gillian stared at her daughter, shocked. "Really?"

"Yeah, really."

"Well," Kali said brightly, "good that all this is being aired out, finally." At the same time, she was worried. Did Harry and Molly also think she was deaf?

"I couldn't look after them for very long, though, Kali," Isadora said. "I signed up for some courses, at Santa Monica College."

"You did?" Gillian said.

"Yup. I'll be working with disaffected teens."

"I'm not sure I could hire my best friend's daughter." Kali was thinking about how often she and Matt bickered, and of how she tore through the house most mornings, half-dressed, and freaking out about everything in her life. "I don't think you'd like working for us much."

"Just 'til you find someone else then?"

"Well," Kali sighed, "I'm sure the kids would love you." They might not even be able to distinguish Isadora from Emilie, she thought. Certainly, with that stud in her nose, and all the tattoos.

"Wait. You think of me as your best friend?" Gillian asked.

"Of course." Kali looked at her, realizing that it was true. "Both you and Jada."

"You do?" Jada said.

"Absolutely."

Jada got up to fling her arms around Kali's neck. "That's so sweet! I'm going to howl!"

"We're all drunk, obviously," Kali said, her words muffled by Jada's jacket.

"Don't I get a hug?" Gillian asked.

"Yes, hugs all around!" Kali cried. "Group hug. Get in here, Isadora."

"I think I'll just get going." Isadora slid off the counter and eased her way towards the back door. "I have some stuff to do. But I can come over early tomorrow, and help you clean up some more. Your living room looks pretty good," she added, shyly. "At least, I think so."

"You cleaned it up already? Oh, Isadora, you didn't have to do that," Kali said. "But thank you so much!"

"Not a problem," Isadora shrugged. "I'm out of here. See you tomorrow, Kali. I'll be here at seven." The screen door banged after her.

As Gillian watched her daughter go, she wiped a tear from her eye. "What a great kid."

"Yeah, you did something right with her," Jada nodded.

"One question," Gillian turned to Kali. "How come you didn't serve my cake, since I'm one of your best friends?"

"Damn right," Jada said. "Why didn't you serve her damn cake?"

"We did serve it. Ask my mother."

"Nobody ate it, then. Is that it?"

"Nobody ate anything. Did you see the tea table?"

"But all the booze is gone," Jada said, "of course."

"I'm sure I can find some more around here somewhere. We could sample Matt's precious single-malt collection, as long as he stays upstairs. We'll be able to hear him coming, though. He can't sneak up on us with those crutches." Poor Matt, Kali thought. Even though his rollerblading was silly and dangerous, she felt very sorry for him.

"There isn't any of Matt's booze left," Jada said. "Our clients drank it."

"What?"

"I had to give them *something*. They were pissed to find out all the champagne was gone."

"Oh, God." Kali put her hand to her mouth. "I can't even remember them coming."

"That's because you passed out," Gillian said.

"Really? Ugh. Who showed up? All four of them?"

"Julia, Deborah, Renee."

"Heather?"

"Heather too. They got here just as your dog—"

"Never mind." Kali sighed. "What will they think of me? Of us? Of the firm?"

"They were cool," Jada said.

"They were?"

"Totally. They just wanted to know why everybody was drunk, and where the bride-to-be was, and we didn't really have an answer to either of those questions, and you were *non compos mentis*. So they drank all of Matt's single malts and left—and they all took their gifts with them.

"Did they already know each other?"

"Absolutely," Jada said. "They network like crazy. Corporate types, you know." She laughed, then sniffed. "They might forgive us. Being women, I'm sure each of them has suffered through some sort of social disaster at some point."

"It's true," Kali said. "You can call it what it was, and I don't even mind you saying so."

"Yes, well, we can thank our dear departed Richard for the idea of inviting clients in the first place," Jada said.

"So, let's move on. It's not your fault, Kali. Let's drink to Richard and the other dead guys," Gillian said.

"We're out of booze, remember?" said Kali.

"I've got a better idea," Gillian said. "Why don't we have a pajama party? We can wear our flannel nighties and eat my Life Celebration Cake!"

"Oh, sure," Jada said, "and do each other's hair and write on Matt's cast. Give me a break."

"Come on, it would be fun!" Gillian said.

"I'm not putting on that ridiculous mess of flouncy polyester. N'uh uh. Not me."

"It's one hundred percent virgin cotton," Gillian said.

"I'm not nearly looped enough to wear anything with the word 'virgin' in it."

As if on cue, Gillian and Kali each grabbed a double-brushed flannel nightgown from a chair back and, smiling wickedly, advanced on Jada. "Get your cell, Kali," Gillian said, "this will be one for the Biltmore, Durham & Spears intranet."

"There isn't one anymore," Jada said, nervously backing away from them. "Our computers all got repossessed. We only got to keep the mousepads."

Chapter 43

TOTALLY CONFUSED, AND HOPELESSLY LOST, KALI DROVE PASSED A thrift shop, a row of blue city dumpsters, then a block of neglected yellow brick warehouses—many of them covered in graffiti and all of them missing windows. This couldn't be where Gillian wanted to meet, she thought. Here, in the middle of nowhere. It was scary L.A. territory, *Bonfire of the Vanities* territory. In her freshly-cleaned and waxed BMW, Kali was a plump little pigeon of a slow-moving target. She held her cell phone up on the steering wheel, squinting to see the Google map. Though it was dangerous and illegal to drive that way, it was less dangerous than pulling over to put in the address and reset the GPS. "Speak!" she ordered her cell phone. "Say something!"

"Okay. What would you like me to say?" her phone answered, politely.

"Directions!" Kali said.

"I'm sorry. I do not understand."

"Get directions!"

"Please let me know what you would like me to do."

"Give me the directions!"

"Okay, directions to where?"

"To the address I just put in!"

"I'm sorry. I still do not understand."

"Home then!" Kali commanded, "take me home! HOME!"

"I do not know where home is. I do not know you. In fact, I don't know anything about you," the phone replied, miffed.

"Oh, why don't you just shove it up your ass?" Kali cried.

"There is no call for that language," her cell replied, then fell into a sulky silence.

Frustrated, Kali shut it off, then pulled over to park in front of an abandoned auto glass place. She took some deep breaths, looking around and realizing she had no clue where she was. *Calm down,* she told herself—*just turn the phone back on and type in the address Gillian gave you.* The GPS had gotten snarled up, that was all—it was confused by the one-way streets, the construction detours, the U-turns and illegal turns that Kali, in desperation, had recently executed. No wonder the phone was in a snit.

She was an hour late for the scheduled meeting when she finally found the place, with its weather-beaten sign and dim yellow lamp glimmering dully above it. It was the exact same place where she had pulled up over a half-hour before. "Sorry, sorry," she apologized to Gillian and Jada as she got out of her car. "I went the wrong way on Sepulveda. I was sure you said this place was east of the freeway." Her partners looked at her, unimpressed. It was a very hot day; they were perspiring visibly, standing on the sidewalk in front of the Speedy Auto Glass.

"We're waiting for the real estate agent," Gillian said. "He's even later than you."

"Why are we waiting for a real estate agent?" Kali had not questioned why Gillian wanted this meeting, just accepted that she wanted to talk about the future of the firm.

"Because this piece of shit building on this shitty street here, is where Gillian thinks we should open our new women-only firm," Jada said.

"I happen to live on this the street, Jada," Gillian said. "Number seven."

"Well, it's not *that* bad, this street," Kali said.

"Are you kidding? I was afraid to get out of my car," Jada said. "And I'm black!"

"I love what you've done with the front of your house, Gilly," Kali said, supportively.

"You don't need to flatter me. I'm not insulted. I know who I am, and I love the house," Gillian said. "You two are newbies at real estate. You've got no vision, but I get that. My mom didn't either—she cried when we bought the house. But this neighborhood is being gentrified as we speak. Real estate is going to go through the roof. Larry was right— he predicted it would happen. And this old auto glass place, which used to be a shoe factory, is so cheap right now the three of us could buy it tomorrow. It just needs some love. Five years from now, nobody's is going to be able to afford Sidney Street. We could sell the building and retire." She checked her phone. "Where is that idiot?"

"Idiot?" Jada said. "We three are standing here, baking in the blazing heat waiting for an idiot?"

"Figure of speech. He's a friend of mine. Oh, here he comes now!"

B.M. Bradly was bounding down the street towards them, smiling and waving.

"Your real estate agent is that loser who was at the funeral taking notes?" Jada demanded.

"What does he know about real estate?" Kali asked.

"Well, he got his real agent's license first try," Gillian said, feebly.

"I thought he was a writer," Jada said.

"His last book had a saggy middle," Gillian said. "It didn't do well. It hit the remainder table before the ink was dry on the pages.

"That's a reason we should trust him with our money and investment in real estate?" Kali asked.

"He's been watching *Homes Plus* forever," Gillian said.

"That's his curriculum vitae?" Jada asked. "Homes Plus?"

"He's agreed to take a big cut on his commission," Gillian said.

"Cut? How big?" Jada asked.

"Like, fifty percent."

"Nice to see you again," Jada smiled, as B.M. finally reached them, out of breath, his hair awry.

"Ladies?" he said, with a little bow. "Please, take my card." He handed them each a business card. "And allow me to escort you on a guided tour of this glorious 1928 art deco edifice, former shoe factory, later warehouse, after that auto glass cum wreckers, but soon be the new offices of the cutting edge, all women law firm of Lawrence, Tyler and Miller."

"I believe that would be Miller, Lawrence and Tyler," Kali said.

"Tyler, Miller and Lawrence," Jada said.

"Let's just take a look at it," Gillian said. "We can draw straws over lunch."

"You know, I do see some real possibilities here," Kali said, a while later, as they walked through the vast open space inside the old warehouse. Admittedly, it was a mess: bare concrete floor, oily parts of machines, rusted chains, paint cans, beer bottles, and garbage. On the exposed beams across the ceiling, pigeons cooed and fluttered. "And I love all the stained glass."

"Right?' Gillian said, excitedly, "and the casements. Floor-to-ceiling, can you believe it? They don't build them like this anymore."

"I'm liking this idea," Jada nodded, "I mean, it needs a ton of work, but I'm coming around to seeing your vision, Gilly."

"With our own shop, I could have flex hours," Kali mused aloud. "I could spend more time with the kids, even come in late, after they're in bed, assuming Matt's home."

"Oh, totally," Jada said.

"We could all have flex hours—make our own schedules that suit us, not to please an Executive Committee, or Helen Sharpe," Gillian said. "I could take a day off to write without somebody on my back wanting to know where I was."

"As long as our clients stick with us, and we keep them happy, and we meet our bottom line," Kali said, "we can do anything we want. We can define our own work terms for once."

B.M.'s face lit up. "I know a really good architect who could throw together some drawings real fast, so we can move on to cost estimates for the renovation. You don't have to use the entire space for offices, if you don't need all the room. That area downstairs would make a great Starbucks, for example."

"Please, no," Jada moaned.

"Just one idea," B.M. said. "It could be anything. And when your firm gets really successful and you need a bunch of new lawyers, you've got the room for them. There's even a parking lot in the back, that comes with the building. I don't need to tell you what a huge plus that is in L.A."

"You talk a good game," Jada said, cocking her head and looking him up and down, "for somebody who doesn't know what he's talking about. I admire that in a man."

Chapter 44

AN HOUR LATER, KALI, GILLIAN, AND JADA WERE SEATED AT A table in Rodney's Oyster Bar, back in Santa Monica, perusing the impressive list of California oysters that was chalked on a giant board on one wall. A waiter filled their wine glasses with a crisp, chilled *pinot gris*.

"Before we talk about the firm anymore," Gillian said, "I have some exciting news for you guys. My novel's going to be published!"

"The one about the dentist?" Kali asked.

"*At Whit's End*," Gillian nodded, happily.

"Wow. Who's publishing it?" Jada asked.

"A small press. Teeny tiny. They're just getting started—only one other title so far."

"Would we have heard of them?" Kali asked.

"I doubt it. They don't have a great name." Gillian avoided her friends' eyes.

"How bad can it be?" Jada leaned in. "Come on, out with it."

"It's called Guttersnipe Press."

"What the hell's a guttersnipe?"

"Who cares?" Kali said. "You're being *published*."

"It's a great accomplishment," Jada said, "and I mean that. Can't wait to read it."

"Thank you," Gillian blushed with pleasure. "It wasn't the deal I'd been hoping for, to be honest. I always fantasized about some New York publisher flying me out for a big book launch, with giant cardboard cut-outs of me in every bookstore window—that kind of thing."

"You're too good a writer," Kali said. "You don't do that shlocky stuff. Plus, there are hardly any bookstores anywhere anymore."

"True enough," Gillian conceded.

Kali raised her glass. "To Whit's End!"

"Whit's End!" The three clinked glasses.

"And, I have other news," Gillian said. "Even bigger news. Are you ready for this?"

Kali and Jada looked at her, then at each other, not sure whether to be happy and excited or deeply concerned. "So?" Jada said, uneasily.

"I saw Sandy Krupnik!"

"What?" Kali and Jada reacted together.

"I did! In the Last Bookstore. Yesterday! I know it was him. And he saw me too. We locked eyes, then he turned and ran out of there. I followed him, but he must have ducked down an alley or jumped into his car or something. He gave me the slip, but it was him for sure."

"Whoa, Gilly," Kali said. "A lot of men could be mistaken for Sandy. He wasn't all that distinctive-looking. I mean, a shlubby, middle-aged attorney with white socks and sandals?"

"My point exactly. Who else would dare to go out like that in L.A? I know it was him!"

"The inquest was pretty conclusive," Kali said. "No one could have survived."

"But all four guys had good reason to disappear, right? They were all up to something. Okay, cross-dressing is maybe not a good enough reason to fake your death, but still. What if Pete just wanted to get away from it all, or had some terrible secret we don't know about yet?"

"You mean like a desire to put on his wig and his mama's clothes and go fishing every day for the rest of his life?" Jada said.

"Exactly." Gillian's cheeks were bright pink.

"I guess we've all had similar thoughts," Jada conceded. "I mean about the four of them having good reasons to disappear—be presumed dead."

"I just don't know where this type of thinking is going to get us, though," Kali said. "I, for one, am not going to spend the rest of my life searching every face in the crowd for those four guys."

"I agree," Jada nodded. "That wasn't Sandy. So put that thought right out of your head, Gilly. If he was still alive, he wouldn't be shopping in bookstores in downtown L.A. Hell no. He'd be lying low in some remote, fish-friendly place, waiting out the seven years to be presumed dead. Same with the others. Marcia and Grace have got seven years to wait before they can battle it out over whatever insurance their man had."

"I didn't expect you to believe me," Gillian shrugged, "but I have a really strong feeling that those four guys live and walk among us. Plus, my eyesight is excellent. I know who I saw."

"This topic is a downer," Kali said, "so can we change it, please? Let's talk about our new offices. I'm really liking the idea of that building on your street, Gillian. I can see the exposed ducts, concrete floors, stainless steel lights. It would be very cutting edge. And we'd get to make our own rules about coffee and cookies—and no Helen Sharpe to tell us what to do, and boss us around."

"Hold on," Jada said, "I've got news too. A new man in my life."

"Oh, Nice! Is he a lawyer?" Kali asked.

"Of course not."

"What does he do?"

"He's in transportation," Jada said, vaguely.

"A pilot? That's sexy," Gillian said.

"You think I'd go for a pilot after what happened?"

"Then what?" Kali said. "Shipping magnate?"

"Is he a trucker? That's so romantic," Gillian said. "Does he own his own rig?"

"I don't see that what Darius does for a living should matter, but he's in the courier business, if you must know."

"Sounds great," Kali said. "They're so busy these days. Does he have his own company?"

"He *is* a courier, actually." Jada lifted her chin. "Bicycle, for your information."

"One of those guys who ride around in Spandex?" Kali asked. "With the dreadlocks and walkie-talkies?"

"It's a whole creepy underground culture," Gillian said.

"You know what? You two are occupation-snobs."

"Hey!" Gillian looked hurt. "I was being complimentary. Bicycle couriers are totally cool."

"Darius happens to have his Masters' in mechanical engineering. He's young, sexy, smart, and best of all, black. For the moment, he's chosen to be a bicycle courier. And I respect that choice."

"He sounds totally awesome," Gillian said.

"He also happens to be in incredible shape."

"Can't wait to meet him," Kali said.

"So how's Isadora doing?" Gillian asked, looking apprehensively at Kali.

"Oh, she's just amazing. The kids adore her. I only wish she could stay with us longer. We're so organized with her there. I know where everything is, for a change."

"That's because Emilie was stealing from you all the time," Gillian said. "You weren't losing your mind. She counted on you being too busy to notice what she was up to. That was her M.O. She was gas-lighting you the whole time. She stole stuff from Isadora too, and me. She was really bad news."

"Well, thanks to your wonderful daughter, she's gone," Kali said. "Why don't we order some food?"

"Hog Island, Bodega Bay, Kumamoto, Grassy Bar," Gillian read aloud from the list of the day's fresh oysters.

"I already know what I want." Jada tapped her nails, on the table as she gazed at the waiters—so cute, with those snappy white towels around their waists. "Oysters all taste the same anyway, like slimy wet toilet paper."

Just then, Kali's cellphone pinged. She took it out of her bag to read the text on it. "Uh oh. Alexander."

"What does *he* want?" Jada demanded.

"He's here, over at the bar." Kali, Jada and Gillian looked over to see Alexander smiling at them and waving from a seat at the bar.

"This can't be good," Jada said.

"He wants to know if he can join us." Kali looked up from her phone.

"Tell him no," Gillian urged. "No way. We're going to be an all women firm, we agreed."

"Join us for lunch, I think he means."

"Screw that," Jada said. "We're here to celebrate our liberation."

"But we can't say no. He's right there, staring at us. Maybe we should just be nice? I mean, he was our partner, and he was left standing at the altar. He likely just wants to have to a drink with us. For old time's sake."

"We're not staying with him and Dan in the old firm. Let's be real clear on that," Jada said.

"He already knows that. We're not negotiating."

"For a drink, okay," Gillian said. "But that's it. This was supposed to be a happiness freedom lunch."

"Just a drink," Jada repeated. "I'm not going to get put off my entire lunch here."

Kali texted Alex, and a moment later he was bounding over, then pulling up a chair at their table.

"How's everyone doing?" he grinned, looking from Kali to Gillian to Jada. As if he cared. Gillian and Jada exchanged looks.

"All good with us," Kali said, thinking that Alex looked like a wreck. It had to be painful, getting dumped by Ana, then having the partnership dissolved and being left with Dan to try and build Spears & Chatwell from the wreckage of Biltmore, Durham & Spears. "How are you holding out?" Kali was still playing nice, while Jada and Gillian looked disdainfully at Alex, annoyed at having their woman-power lunch intruded upon by a file-stealing plagiarist.

"Good, good. As well as can be expected." Alexander signaled a waiter over. "Bring me a Manhattan," he said, "and a platter of Bodega Bays for the table."

The women looked at him, shocked. As if they weren't able to order for themselves! And who said they all wanted Bodega Bays? He hadn't even bothered to ask.

"I'm actually pretty busted up," Alex sighed.

"You and Dan will do fine," Kali said. "I'm sure of it."

"Not about work," Alex said. "Of course we'll do fine. We've already got in a ton of new business."

"I guess you're pretty upset about Ana then," Kali said. "Must be rough."

"It's hideous getting dumped," Jada said. "Not that I ever was, I'm just saying."

The waiter appeared with Alex's drink. He took a big gulp as he suddenly teared up. He sniffed, grabbed a napkin, then blew his nose, loudly. "Sorry, Ladies. I apologize for interrupting your lunch."

"It's okay," Kali touched his sleeve.

"You'll be fine." Gillian rolled her eyes.

Alex blew his nose again, nodded and sighed.

"You must miss her," Kali said.

"I don't, actually," Alex said. "Not at all, not one bit."

"So what are you crying about?" Jada asked.

"The dog," Alex said, overcome with emotion. "She left the damned dog. I never wanted a dog. *She* wanted a dog. She went out and got the dog, and now I'm stuck with it! What am I supposed to do with the dog? I can't just take her to a shelter! And she won't even return my calls, that bitch."

"You talkin' about the dog or Ana?" Jada asked.

"I can't believe this is all you care about, Alexander," Gillian said. "That you're now inconvenienced by having a dog. You had your fun with Ana, you knew she was getting a dog and you went along with it. And now you don't want to take responsibility for it. Ana probably lives in an apartment with roommates, and you've got a giant house. This truly sucks, Alex."

"Why would I expect a dingbat like you to understand?" Alex downed the rest of his Manhattan. "A poetry-hack writing dingbat."

"Hey!" Jada said. "Her book happens to be getting published, and she didn't rip off anyone to write it, unlike a certain person at this table. You need to leave. Nobody asked you to settle in here. You're an intruder."

"She's right, Alex," Kali said, as the waiter arrived with the platter of oysters. "This is our lunch."

"Here's your Bodega Bays!" the waiter beamed. "Let's clear some space on the table."

"Hold on. Those are going to be take-out," Jada said. "You'll have to get him a *doggie* bag." She indicated Alex.

"We didn't order them," Gillian explained. "This person did, and he won't be joining us for lunch."

"Oh," the waiter said, taken aback. "Sir? Would you like me to set up a table for you? Or would you like to enjoy these at the bar?"

"Forget it." Alex pulled out his wallet, then tossed some bills onto the table. "Enjoy your lunch, losers." He threw down his napkin and walked angrily out of the restaurant. The waiter looked after him, blinking.

"I guess we should eat these," Kali said to the others. "I mean since they're paid for."

"They're very good," the waiter said. "Fresh in today."

"Put them down, thanks," Jada said. "It's a free lunch, right, Girls? Alex owes us that much. And we've got to be economizing now that we're going to be owning our own law firm."

After the waiter had gone, Kali filled her glass and those of her two best friends. "To moving on," she said, "and to our own, totally cool, all woman law firm!" They clinked glasses and drank.

"And to absent friends," Gillian said, raising her glass again.

"Absent friends," Kali echoed.

"And may they stay absent!" Jada was thinking the last thing she needed was Ross back in her life, wanting to hole up in her condo to wait out the seven years until he could be legally presumed dead. She quickly tossed back some wine and knocked on the wooden underside of the table, for luck.

The three friends then drank, laughed and talked excitedly about their plans for their law firm, until the waiter came by to say that Rodney's would be closing until dinner time, and asked them, politely, to leave.

THE END

About the Author

Sylvia Mulholland was born in Hamilton, Ontario, Canada, and has lived in many cities including Toronto, Ottawa and Vancouver, Canada, and Los Angeles. She attended Ontario College of Art & Design, then the University of Toronto and the University of Ottawa, where she obtained her law degree. In 2001, she moved to Los Angeles and obtained her MFA from American Film Institute, where she also won the prestigious Sloan Foundation Scholarship for excellence in screenwriting for her screenplay about Einstein's first wife, the physicist, Mileva Maric.

Sylvia's debut novel, *Woman's Work* was published in the UK (Hodder & Stoughton), Canada (General) and Germany (Goldmann) followed by her second novel, *Lingerie Tea*, by the same publishers. Her novel, *A Nanny for Harry*, is now available on Amazon and on Sylvia's website at sylviamulholland.com.

Sylvia is licensed to practice law in both the US and Canada and has her own law practice in the field of intellectual property. As a woman working in the highly competitive field of law, raising two children and pursuing a writing career, Sylvia knows well the challenges of trying to do it all. In her novels and shorter pieces, she writes with humor and empathy about women, work, the legal profession, marriage and family life. She currently lives in Long Beach, California, with her husband, an aerospace engineer.